Appalachian Undead

A Zombie Anthology

EDITED BY
Eugene Johnson & Jason Sizemore

An Apex Publications Book
Lexington, Kentucky

ISBN: 978-1-937009-18-2

Cover art by Cortney Skinner

Cover design by Justin Stewart

APEX PUBLICATIONS

www.apexbookcompany.com

PO BOX 24323 LEXINGTON, KY 40524

For the legions of undead fanatics

CONTENTS

PREFACE

EUGENE JOHNSON

I grew up on horror movies. Not just horror movies but everything horror and everything of the fantastic. My grandmother used to let me watch them when I stayed at my grandparents' house, which was pretty often. So I watched horror movies a lot. I mean, *a lot*.

I remember watching *Creature from the Black Lagoon*, *King Kong* (in black and white with 3D glasses), the old Hammer films, and other B-horror movies on the Saturday double feature. As well as TV shows like *Amazing Stories*, *Monsters*, and endless *Twilight Zone*s (both the black-and-white original and the 1980s redoes), just to name the few. During the day, I would read all types of comics, from Marvel's *Spider-Man* to horror comics.

It did not stop there. Grandma took me to the theater as well, where I saw classics like *Poltergeist* and *Gremlins*, and not-so-classics like *Critters* and *Time Bandits*. I was raised on everything horror, science fiction, and fantasy, and I loved it. There was something about the monsters that made me both want to run in fright and stay to care for them at the same time. I remember sleeping on my grandparents' couch (which was my bed, 'cause I was too afraid to sleep upstairs by myself) and staring off in the darkness, afraid that something would get me.

Then I saw a movie that changed the way I looked at monsters: *Night of the Living Dead*. It was Halloween, and my brothers and I were staying at my father's house for the night. We were lying on one of those old sofa beds, looking for something to watch. We ended up watching this old black-and-white movie about a group of people holed up in a house, trying to survive as they were attacked by reanimated corpses that had returned from the dead—with a hunger for human flesh. The whole experience was strange and transported me to another place, a place of possibility. I remember wondering what we would do if this really happened. Anyone could get bit or die, only to return as one of the living dead.

I wasn't sure if I didn't want to be one, or if I did.

I remember seeing more zombie movies after that: The *Evil Dead* movies, *Zombie,* and many more. In 1985 came *The Return of the Living*

Dead. My mother and a friend of hers took me and my brothers to the drive-in to see it. I sat in the back, terrified, as I watched the dead return to life. They came out of their graves. They were smart and they were fast. These zombies were a far cry from the stumbling, mindless monsters in *Night of the Living Dead*. I remember being freaked out, hunched down so far I had to peak over the seat to watch the movie. To make it more interesting, it started to rain at the drive-in. Those of you who have seen the movie know that rain plays an important part. I was horrified.

Throughout my life, I stayed a fan of horror movies of all types, but it was the zombie movies that I had a soft spot for. I started looking for them where I could find them, from *Dawn of the Dead* (1978), *Day of the Dead, Dead Alive, The Video Dead, Resident Evil, Shaun of the Dead,* and many more. There was just something about the undead.

It was not until later that I started to understand what it was about these movies that I liked so much. Most other horror was supposed to be scary, but didn't bother me too much. Zombie movies got to me. What scared me so much was that *they were us*. The horrible part was that we had no control over whether we became monsters. Zombie movies strike at the heart of society and human behavior. Not to mention the other thing that was appealing: Zombie movies deal with apocalypse and survival, two things that catch a lot of people's attention.

When I was sixteen I moved to West Virginia, the heart of Appalachia, from a city in Michigan. I came to live with my grandparents. Though I had visited them in West Virginia before, it was always a culture shock. My grandparents lived in a small town called Fort Gay in the middle of nowhere. They had a small, one-story, two-bedroom house on eighty-two acres of land. It was ten miles to the nearest town, and there wasn't much around besides a Burger King, a McDonald's, Foodland, and a few other little stores. There were no movie theaters, no Blockbuster Video, no malls. The nearest of any of these was an hour away, either in Huntington, West Virginia, or Ashland, Kentucky. A very different world than I was used to.

Where I came from, I could ride my bike straight to the nearest theatre or store. In West Virginia, people had it a little bit harder than us city folk. The land was not flat and smooth like the city. There were hills, mountains, and old dirt roads that curved every which way; traveling by car was a roller-coaster ride. It was hard to find a job, because there were not a lot of them nearby, and the ones that were there rarely came open. In West Virginia it was harder to make a living. But even though things were tough, the people still thrived. They remained in good spirits.

Back then I believed I wanted to be a filmmaker, and I thought about doing a zombie movie in West Virginia. In 2009, I got the chance to help on a short zombie movie with my friend, director Paul Moore. Paul had directed movies for Lionsgate and Syfy, and wanted to create a short zombie film that he had written, titled "Homecooking." He later changed the title to "Leftovers." I loved it and was brought on to help make the movie as the executive producer. Shooting the film was great, and it went on to show at Screamfest in Los Angeles and at Dragon*Con.

Afterwards, I had the idea to edit an anthology of zombie stories set in Appalachia. When I was a kid I loved anthologies. I liked flipping around and finding new writers and new stories. Around that time, I started working as an editor on The Zombie Feed website, an imprint of Apex Publications. I told Jason Sizemore, CEO and grand poobah of Apex, about my idea, which I titled *Appalachian Undead*. I wanted to have some of the best writers in horror, both new and old, write some great new zombie stories set in the Appalachian region and culture. We also wanted it to look at the beauty and magic of the region as well. But above all we wanted really great stories.

Jason liked the idea and agreed to publish it—if I could manage to get the good stories, the good authors. We got so many submissions it was hard going through them. In the end, we got some great stories covering all different parts of the region and culture. We have stories dealing with moonshine that has the ability to bring the dead back to life. A mine with a deadly secret. A zombie game preserve. And many more.

We got great people to do an introduction, a foreword, an afterword. Not to mention the cover art, which was done by my friend Cortney Skinner—just awesome! We have a terrific book to present to you.

But we could not have done it alone. I want to thank Jason for giving me a chance to publish this work, as well as my mentors and friends Elizabeth Massie, Cortney Skinner, Geoff Fuller, and Karin Fuller. I also want to thank my family: my fiancée Angela; my three children; Angela's parents, Fred and Debbie; my brother Jeff and his family; my grandparents; and Angela's family—Aunt Bea and Joe, their daughter, Amanda, her husband, Jeremy, and Chris, their son. I do not have the words to express how much their support means to me. Not to mention God; I would not be here without Him.

Everyone was just terrific in supporting me and helping in any way they could. I owe them so much. I want to thank my friends Lia Staley, Niki McDonaldly, Eliot, Chris, Michael, Mary, Parker, and John and Jaimie Stroud for their support and belief in me. And, of course, the awesome writers: S.G., Elizabeth, Bev, Ronald, Lucy, Paul, Karin, Jonathon, John Skipp, Dori, Eliot, Simon, Geoff, K. Allen, Tim Waggoner and Tim Libbon, John Everson, Steve, Maurice, S. Clayton, Gary, and Rebekah, all of whom wrote some amazing stories for the book. I could not have done it without any of them. So I hope you enjoy the book as much as I enjoy presenting it to you.

Eugene Johnson
Summer, 2012

INTRODUCTION

S.G. BROWNE

Let's talk zombies.

I like them. You like them. We all like them. They're kind of like ice cream that way. Except for the chunks of decomposing flesh.

I always thought Ben & Jerry's should come up with a zombie-themed ice cream. Vanilla and chocolate ice cream with veins of raspberry goo and chunks of dark chocolate and walnuts. Maybe throw in some cherry pieces to add some additional color. Call it something like Reanimation Ripple.

But back to zombies.

It used to be zombies were slow, mindless, and predictable. No running. No thinking. No being domesticated and kept as a family pet. They just shambled along, moaning and groaning, hungry for human flesh. Occasionally, they would lose an appendage, maybe even be good for a laugh or two, but they more or less came in a single flavor: vanilla.

Today's zombies, however, come in an assortment of flavors. Just like ice cream. And here, in this collection, you'll find that variety well represented. Fast zombies. Slow zombies. Zombies in a coal mine. A zombie game preserve. Zombies with a collective consciousness. You'll even find a story with a zombie chicken.

But what ties all of these tales together is the setting.

Admittedly, I've never been to Appalachia. I've never experienced firsthand the terrain or the culture or the people who live there. The closest I've come to visiting the area was watching *Winter's Bone* and *Deliverance*—neither of which exactly gave me the warm fuzzies.

So if any region seemed like a good fit for a collection of zombie stories, then Appalachia is the place.

Running through 420 counties and 13 states from southern New York to northern Alabama, Mississippi, and Georgia, Appalachia has been a source of enduring myth since the late 1800s. For more than a century, a sense of mystery has shrouded the region because of its isolation, inhabitants, and history.

This is the home of Daniel Boone, the Whiskey Rebellion, and the famous feud between the Hatfields and the McCoys.

And now, appropriately, it's the home of the living dead.

Early 20th century writers helped to perpetuate the stereotype of the region as poor and desolate and culturally backward, filled with uneducated people who spent most of their time coal mining and moonshining and feuding. And in spite of attempts over the past several decades to dispel these myths, the past has clung to Appalachia like a diseased shadow and followed it into the 21st century.

Which brings us to the twenty-one tales you'll find in this collection by twenty-one modern-day writers, all of whom have spun their own tales about a region where people have thrived under the worst of conditions. And what could be worse than having to deal with the living dead?

So lace up your hiking shoes, grab your gun, and pack up only what you need. If you get in the way or get hurt or fall behind, don't expect any special treatment, because if you're not from here, then you're an outsider. And outsiders aren't looked upon kindly.

In Appalachia, people take care of their own.

S.G. Browne,
Author of *Breathers: A Zombie's Lament*

WHEN GRANNY COMES MARCHIN' HOME AGAIN

ELIZABETH MASSIE

Elizabeth Massie is a Bram Stoker Award- and Scribe Award-winning author of horror novels, short horror fiction, media tie-ins, mainstream fiction, and historical novels for teens. Recent works include Homegrown *(a mainstream novel from Crossroad Press),* Playback: Light and Shadow *(an e-novella from Random House, prequel to the 2012 horror film,* Playback*), and* Sundown *(a collection of horror shorts from Necon E-Books).* Desper Hollow, *her upcoming zombie novel from Apex Publications, is based on the story you are about to read. "Abed," a short film based on her graphic, controversial zombie story of the same name, has been completed (Familiar Productions) and is awaiting release. Massie lives in the Shenandoah Valley with the talented illustrator Cortney Skinner. She is the founder of Hand to Hand Vision, a project that raises funds for those in need by auctioning quality handmade arts and crafts, and Circle of Caring, an anti-bullying bracelet campaign. Both can be found on Facebook.*

Granny Mustard was the matriarch of our family, older than anyone of us knew, skinny as a pole bean, dry as a husk, and gray as wash water. Lived in the same mountain-top cabin since her birth, watched her six sons and three daughters grow up around her and build their own cabins on nearby Allegheny slopes, watched a couple of them die. Never shed a tear, never skipped a beat. Watched grandkids and great-grands be born. Then watched a few of them die, too. Rabid fox bites. Falls from trees. Never wept, never slowed down.

We stayed out of her way except when she called for us. Me, her great-granddaughter Suze, my sister, Jenkie, all the rest of us. We tended our own vegetable patches and chickens, walked down to the school in the mining town of Beaver Dam when we wanted to and stayed home when we didn't, picked crabapples, fought with each other, killed snakes and spiders. Wondered about the world beyond the mountains, but not enough to make us want to go there.

And so it was, when Jenkie and I got called over to Granny Mustard's cabin on the first day of July, we went. A little nervous, but used enough to her cold-water stare and the way she snapped her twig-thin fingers in your face to get your attention. We figured she wanted us to run some kind of errand down in Beaver Dam. She'd run out of sugar or buttons or yeast. None of us had much money, but Jenkie and I each had ten dollars in our pockets from my Mama, who said we could use it for whatever we wanted next time we went down to town—candy, make up, Mt. Dew. (I had no idea how Mama got that money, though I know sometimes she'd go into Beaver Dam and stay all night, then come back smelling like cigar smoke and leather polish.) I hoped Granny Mustard didn't want my ten dollars, but if she asked me to buy her something with it, no way on earth or in hell I would say no. Granny was never denied.

She sat on her porch, creaking back and forth on the oak sapling rocker. In her hands was her paring knife, and on her lap was a bowl of damsons. She liked to peel 'em and make jelly. It was good jelly, too. The only sweet thing ever come from Granny Mustard.

We reached the bottom of her porch step, stopped, and looked at her, waiting. You never spoke first 'round Granny Mustard or you chanced getting a slap across the mouth. She finished with the damson in her hand, dropped it into the bowl, then lifted her gaze toward us, squinted though there wasn't hardly any sun at all, and said in her slow, crackling voice, "I need you girls to help me a bit."

There were three rooms in Granny Mustard's cabin. The front room where she had a ratty, over stuffed chair, a chifferobe with one of the drawers missing, a small table and lantern, her cot, and a tin bedpan. Through the door to the kitchen, and off the kitchen, the bedroom.

She took us to the kitchen and pointed into the big, metal bowl on the table that she used for washing dishes and cleaning catfish.

"See that there?"

We looked.

In the bowl was a chicken. Well, it had been a chicken. Now it was freshly chopped chicken parts. A head. Feet. Wings. Torso. Not plucked for cooking but just chopped up pieces with feathers poking out. I looked at Jenkie, and she looked at me. I made the mistake of shrugging, and Granny Mustard whacked me between the shoulders with her bony hand.

Then she sniffed, pinched her nose, and said, "Dyin' ain't on my agenda."

I hesitated, and said, "Yes'um."

"Got too much to do."

"Yes'um."

"So I aim not to do it."

"Yes'um."

I thought of my daddy, who'd died four years earlier from the black lung, and my cousins Rickie and Cecil and Pansy, who were dead from stupidity and buried with the rest of them in the family plot at the corner of Granny's weedy yard. Then I thought about Granny Mustard and figured if anyone could live forever, it would be her.

Jenkie and I stood silently, shuffling about in our well-worn sneakers, as Granny Mustard went into the pantry and came out with a jar. We knew those jars. Moonshine jars. Granny made moonshine out of crabapples. Only one we ever knew to make it out of those tiny little marble-hard fruits.

"Ain't what you think," she said, shaking the jar lightly and letting the brown liquid slosh around inside the glass. "Ain't shine. Not normal shine, anyway. It's special shine."

Jenkie bit her lip, nodded.

"I need you to help me catch pieces," said Granny.

I started to say, "Pieces of what?" but didn't want another whack, so I just nodded.

"Get ready now," she said, her milky blue eyes glinting.

Jenkie and I said together, "Okay."

"Lean in!" she ordered.

We leaned in toward the bowl. We glanced at each other uncertainly.

Then Granny Mustard unscrewed the lid of the jar and poured the contents over the chicken parts, like she was making one of her marinades.

We watched, we stared. Granny put the jar down and looked into the bowl, one hand on her angular hip, her brows drawn.

The head twitched.

I flinched.

The head twitched again, and the beak started opening and closing, slowly at first, then picking up speed until it looked like a castanet I saw a Spanish lady use once on TV, back when we had a TV and it worked.

"Lord a-mercy!" whispered Jenkie.

Then the legs began to tremble, the claws clutching and unclutching.

"Get ready, I said," said Granny Mustard.

I swallowed and heard my throat click.

The dismembered wings started flapping futilely. The torso started turning on its axis.

Then all the parts, in one explosive shudder of feather and flesh, scrambled, flopped, and skittered around the base of the bowl and then up and over the sides. The sluggish torso tried to roll up and out but couldn't quite make it. Granny grabbed for one leg, but I instinctively jumped back until she barked at me, and then I grappled for the other leg, which slipped past me and plopped onto the floor.

Jenkie snatched up a wing as it scooted to the edge of the table. It flapped feebly in her hand. I dove for the escaped leg, which was now hopping around drunkenly on the worn linoleum. I spied one of Granny's empty moonshine jars on the nearest shelf; I snatched it up and dropped to my knees, then, with a quick move, brought it down over the leg, trapping it against the floor.

"Head!" said Granny. I glanced up to see her leaning over, holding one leg and the second wing, with her elbow pinning the roly-poly torso to the tabletop. It had made it up out of the bowl, after all. "Get it, Suze!"

I looked around, keeping the jar pressed to the floor so the leg wouldn't be able to scratch its way underneath. "I don't see it! Where is it?"

Granny Mustard jerked her head in the direction of the back door, which was cracked open a couple inches. I leaned back so I could see around the table legs, to spy the chicken head dragging itself toward the door, the beak opening and closing, opening and closing, snap, snap, snap.

"Jenkie, you get it!" I said, but Jenkie was still holding the wing, whimpering like a baby as it fluttered in her fingers.

"Head! Don't you dare let it get outta this house!" said Granny.

I scooped up the jar, with one hand underneath, and stumbled toward the door just in time to slam my foot down on the head and hear it crunch beneath my shoe.

"Damn that, Suze!" said Granny. "Ain't supposed to kill it! S'posed to see how long it lives!"

"I…." I began. I wasn't really sure what someone was supposed to do with chicken parts that weren't dead.

We stood, Jenkie and me staring at each other, Granny staring at us, the leg in the jar clawing at my hand, tickling something fierce. Then the leg went still. The torso under Granny's elbow stopped trying to buck itself away. The wings ceased flapping.

Granny's cheeks puffed for a moment. Then she said, "That's it. Toss all this garbage out back in the slop pile."

We did as we were told, stomping through the poison ivy and chicory, past the still shed to the slop pile, a low, lumpy hillock at the tree line where all Granny's dead pets had been buried and where she tossed kitchen scraps. We were afraid to look straight at each other.

"Maybe we can go on home," Jenkie whispered as we wiped our hands on our shorts, the chicken parts flung onto the pile with a couple handfuls of dirt tossed on top for good measure.

I shook my head. "You crazy? She didn't tell us we could go."

"Well, we could say we heard Mama callin'." Her eyes were tiny and bright in the afternoon sun. They looked like the eyes of a hog that knew an axe was hovering over its head.

"She got better hearin' than you and me put together. She'd hear Mama callin', or not callin'. She'd know we was lyin'."

"I don't want to go in there no more, Suze."

"Me, neither. But we ain't got no choice."

Jenkie grabbed my elbow. "What's Granny doin' in there? What's with that shine?"

I yanked my arm away. "Shut up, she's probably watchin' us from the door."

We clenched our fists and our jaws and headed back to Granny Mustard's cabin. Inside, we found her plucking another chicken—a whole one this time—her arms covered in feathers and tiny spots of blood. Without looking up she said, "Now, nothin' you seen today is anyone's business but mine and yours. You hear me?"

"Yes'um."

"Yes'um."

We waited.

Granny Mustard turned her head toward us. It was like watching a hawk turning to consider a chipmunk. "Ya'll go on now. Come back tomorrow 'round noon. Don't make me come lookin' for you."

"No'um."

"No'um."

We walked out of the cabin, across her scrabby yard, and then ran the rest of the way home.

The special shine wasn't made of just crabapple mash, we found out as the summer slogged on, but had other stuff boiled up in it. Bloodroot. Sassafras. Pig liver and cow brain. Not sure how Granny Mustard came up with her recipe, but we eventually learned that she'd been working on her concoction for years, knowing someday she'd be really, really old and facing the Grim Reaper. She said some people believed in a fountain of youth, but that was just nonsense.

We kept her secret, helped her gather additional ingredients from the forest – mosses, lichen, pine pollen, scrapings of barks from different trees - to try in new combinations, then found dead bugs and dismembered foxes or pieces of crows in the forest to test it all on. Sometimes the new recipes were worse. Well, worse in Granny Mustard's eyes, since they didn't make the dead critters or critter parts move at all. Sometimes they were better (again, in Granny's eyes) in that they made the dead critters or the critter parts move faster, stronger, or for a longer time before conking out.

When we were done, we hauled buckets or sacks full of the critters out to the slop pile and buried them.

We didn't sleep well at night. My teeth felt soured, and my chest was tight. Sometimes I dreamed there were chicken heads under my pillow, creeping up to my face to chew it off. Sometimes I dreamed there were smashed bugs, long dead, wriggling around in my cereal bowl. I awoke in the middle of the night, screaming, thinking dead groundhogs were eating my feet.

Mama brushed it off as me going through adolescence. "Every girl your age gets them bad dreams and worries. By the time you're sixteen, you'll be all done with it." Jenkie told me she woke up in the night, too, but was too scared to yell. She just lay there sweating and shaking.

Now, Granny Mustard's had a long and busy life, I think I told you already. Raised her kids while her husband, our long-dead Grampy

Mustard, worked in the Beaver Dam coal mines. Granny raised and slaughtered stock, grew and harvested vegetables, cured hams, baked breads, built and fixed broken chairs and tables, cleaned, churned, pumped, chopped, and stitched. But her most profitable venture was moonshine. Now, moonshine ain't a bother to the law so much now like it was in Granny's younger days, but it's still a dangerous business. That's 'cause there's rival shiners in the mountains, shiners who sell to the locals and who don't want competition. Granny sent her sons and grandsons to smash others' stills and beat them into compliance. And they've tried to do the same to her, though never were successful. Granny's got too much muscle-heavy family in the cabins around and below her for them to get through.

Granny's moonshine sells up and down the mountain, in Beaver Dam and some of those other mining towns scattered along the ridges and in the hollers. She makes enough from it to buy the food she can't raise and the supplies she can't make herself. She gives some to her family at Christmas, tells them they best use it wisely (no gift from Granny is ever given with a smile or without restriction), but the rest she hides somewhere, I don't know where. Or I didn't know where.

'Til I found it.

Hiding in a metal box in her closet under the floorboard. What looked like thousands of dollars all tied up in strings. I'd been chasing a mouse to try out a new batch of special shine on, found the little pinchy-hole, and pulled up the board and there it was.

I told Jenkie.

We swore on our mother's life and our own that we would never tell anyone where it was. We would leave it alone.

Damn Jenkie.

It was August by then. August 15th, my birthday. Mama gave me twenty dollars and let me and Jenkie go down to Beaver Dam to get me a present. I wanted a CD player with a cord so I wouldn't have to keep buying batteries. (Yes, some of our family's cabins are close enough to the grid, though the electricity gets turned off every couple months for late-pay.) Anyway, my brother Rex used to have a player, but it busted. I could get one for less than twenty dollars at the Dollar General, have some left over for a couple Snickers.

So we went down there, hiked the two and a quarter miles from our home into town, then along dusty Main Street to the store. Mama went with us, not to watch over us since I was fourteen, for crying out loud, but she wanted to stop by the Beaver Dam Motel to check on her job application. She said she needed about an hour and not to come get her, she'd come get us. We said, "'kay." That gave us more time to look around.

The Dollar General was next door to the Waffle House. On the east side of the street with them was Harmon's Hardware, the Beaver Dam Baptist Church, and the Cut-n-Curl. Across the street on the west side was Angie's Antiques, the Exxon station, the motel, the Mountainside Diner, and CJ's Car Repair. That was pretty much all the business in town, 'cept at the south end where you'd find the gated entrance to the Beaver Dam mines. Off Main Street, lots of little houses, trailers, shacks where most of the miners lived, dotting the slopes up among soot-covered trees.

Mama veered off to the motel, and Jenkie and I went for the Dollar General, tugging open the front door and getting blasted by air conditioning. Painful cold. Good.

Joe, the old dude who ran the place, was at the check-out, digging in his nose, pretending to be scratching it when he saw he had customers. Norman Butterman, the 22-year-old assistant manager, was sucking on a Tootsie-Pop and staring through the cold case where the bottles of soft drinks and milk sit. Norman glanced over at Jenkie and winked. It set my teeth on edge. Jenkie's just a year older than me.

"Jenkie, hey," said Norman.

Joe wiped his hand on his hip and sniffed.

"Hey, Norman," said Jenkie.

I just puffed my cheeks and went back to the part of the store where they sold the players and other electronic stuff like alarm clocks and digital kitchen timers. I found a CD player that was round, silver, had a cord, and cost $14.98. That would leave some Snickers cash. I snatched it up and headed toward the front, to catch Jenkie and Norman talking.

Norman: "You had a nice dress. I could take you to the Miners' Ball next weekend."

Jenkie: "You ain't a miner. You can't invite me."

Norman: "Hell I can't. My daddy and brothers are miners. Family's welcome."

Jenkie: "I got a dress."

Norman: "I mean a nice dress. I seen that yellow piece of rag you wear on Sundays."

Jenkie: "Ain't a rag. But I could buy me a nice one, if you were aimin' to take me to the dance. I got money."

Norman: "You ain't got shit. Your family's 'bout the poorest one on the mountain. Everybody knows that."

Jenkie: "You're wrong there, mister. I got money, lots of it. Found it up in my…."

Me: "Whoa, hey, Jenkie, what're you talking about?"

Jenkie flinched and looked at me, wide-eyed. "Um, nothing."

"Yeah, what're you talking about, Jenkie?" asked Norman. "You got money? Where'd you find it?"

"She's pulling your leg, Norman," I said, slapping the CD player on the check-out counter, hoping I didn't bang it so hard I broke it. Joe sniffed again, scanned the tag. "She's always making up stuff. Can't believe half what she says."

"Am not," said Jenkie. She was pissed.

"Enough," I said.

"You're not the boss of me, you're younger than me, so shut up!"

"Here." I shoved the twenty-dollar bill across to Joe.

"I'll tell you in secret, Norman," said Jenkie, glaring at me. "And you'll keep it secret, right?"

Norman grinned. "Right."

"Don't open your big-ass mouth anymore," I said. I crammed my change into my jeans pocket and scooped the CD player under my arm. "Come on, Mom's waiting."

"No, she's not," said Jenkie. "She's at the motel, checking on her job application."

Joe chuckled.

"What's so funny?" I asked him, but he just sniffed.

"Jenkie, come on!"

"No, you go on, Suze. Norman's gonna take his break now, ain't you, Norman?"

"Sure am. Ain't I, Joe?"

Joe shrugged. "Whatever."

I grabbed Jenkie's sleeve with my free hand; she shook me off. "Get out of here, Suze!"

I grabbed her again; again she pushed me off, hard enough this time that I stumbled back over a stack of "fridge mate" Pepsis on the floor and crashed on my butt. As I flopped back and forth then staggered up, Jenkie leaned into Norman and whispered something.

"No shit?" he said, brows up.

"No shit."

"Damn it, Jenkie!" I wailed. "You are so in trouble now, you won't believe it!"

"I can trust Norman, can't I, Norman?" said Jenkie.

"You bet." He winked at her, then at me, and I knew he couldn't be trusted any more than a hungry hog could be trusted in a corn bin. I stormed out of the store, CD player cord slapping my thigh, and went to sit on the curb on my bruised butt in front of the Waffle House. How dare Jenkie tell Norman about Granny Mustard's money? And I was sure that's what she'd done. I'd just have to get up there when Jenkie wasn't around and hide it all over again.

But the thought of going to Granny's cabin alone made my stomach turn sour.

Jenkie came outside and stood with her hands on her hips in the middle of the road, moving back and forth as traffic sputtered past, until, almost a half-hour later, Mama appeared from the motel, straightening her skirt and frowning like someone just stole her dog.

"What you doin' here, child, I ain't called for you today."

Granny Mustard stood just outside her cabin door on the porch in the dimming light of the setting sun, one hand on her hip, the other holding the big tin ladle she used to stir the special brew. Her eyes were narrow. Blue shadows streaked her cheeks. Her cobweb hair stood up straight like it was trying to fly out of her scalp and up to heaven ahead of her.

"I...." I began. "I wanted to bring you this bread I made." I held out a loaf of bread I'd baked that morning, knowing I'd need some excuse. I'd made three loaves and left two for the family, telling Mama, who hadn't been paying attention to what was going on in the kitchen 'cause she was deep into reading catalogs, that I'd only made two. Don't need any suspicion, no, ma'am.

"Bread? I got plenty bread," she said.

"Well."

"Well, don't just stand there, bring it on in the house. Since you're here, you can help me with something."

I went in with her, back to the kitchen. She'd been cooking more special shine, I could see. New plants I didn't know the names of and peculiar-smelling mushrooms littered her counter top. The pot on the stove was boiling. Two lit lanterns hung from nails in the ceiling beams (unlike us, Granny was not on or anywhere near the grid), filling the room with wavy, yellowed light.

I handed the bread to Granny Mustard, then glanced over at the closed door of her bedroom. What excuse could I use to get in there, dig out the box of money, and hide it again? The back of my arms were cold.

Granny tossed it in the tin breadbox. Then she stirred the liquid in the pot and slid it off the stove eye. "Think I got it right this time," she said without looking at me. I almost asked her why this time since it wasn't right last time or the time before that or the time before that, but bit my tongue.

"Get that ring neck." She jerked her head in the direction of a bucket by the door. There was a big rock on top of the bucket. I removed the rock and gingerly pulled the foot-long snake out by the tail. It coiled slowly, gently, lifting its head in an attempt to reach the warmth of my hand.

"Here!" Granny snapped her fingers, and I passed the snake to her. She picked up her wooden meat mallet and whacked it once on the skull. It stopped squirming.

"I think I found just the right ingredients this go 'round," she said. "Was missing the amble-weed. My mama always said stay away from the amble-weed, like she was a-scared of it. But I figured it was worth a try. You'll see what I mean."

"Yes'um," I said.

Granny stretched the little snake out on the table, dipped out a ladle-full of the newest brew, blew on it a bit to cool it down (would a dead snake really care if it was hot, I wondered, but no way in hell would ask) then poured it over the body. She leaned over it, her white brows drawn together. I leaned, too.

The snake lay still, its scales reflecting the lantern light. Granny licked her lips, and that creeped me out. Like she was so excited she could eat it all up with a spoon.

Then it moved. Not so much like the first dead stuff I saw come alive, all spazzy and fast, but slower, like it was waking up. The tail began to flick sluggishly back and forth.

"Watch," she said.

The head began to move then, tucking, lifting, waving. The eyes were no longer black, but had taken on a strange red hue. I thought it was the lantern light at first, but then Granny Mustard must of read my mind, and she said, "They all get like that with this new shine. Red eyes, like blood gets pooled in there somehow. Nothin' to worry about. Okay, now."

The snake shivered as if coming out of a deep sleep, then began to crawl across the table toward the edge. I put my hand on the table, leaning in closer to have a better look. The snake immediately veered from the edge toward my hand, its tiny mouth open, its needle fangs ready.

I jerked my hand back several inches. The snake kept coming.

Granny Mustard grabbed it by the tail, and it fought her with a strength that took my breath away. Granny swung it back into the bucket. She put the rock on top. I could hear it thrashing about, whacking the side of the bucket.

"How long'll it live?" I asked, realizing too late I'd spoken without being spoken to. But Granny didn't seem to notice this time. She was all caught up in her shine and her snake.

She pulled a jar off the top shelf over her icebox. In it were several June bugs, little red eyes, scrambling around on top of each other. They looked to be trying to get at Granny's hand, like they wanted to bite it. It even looked like they'd been able to crack the glass a little. "These been back alive three days. No sign o' dying."

"Oh."

"I'm close, then, ain't I?" she said almost wistfully. "If only I could get rid them red eyes and get 'em to pep up a bit like some of them earlier critters."

"Yeah."

Granny Mustard ladled some of the shine out of the pan and into some empty jars, screwed on the lids. I glanced back over my shoulder at the bedroom door. Maybe when Granny Mustard needed to use the outhouse I could....

"What's up with you?" she snapped at me, and I looked back. "You worryin' 'bout something in there?"

"No'um." My breath caught. My heart picked up a painful thud, thud, thud....

"You sure?"

"Yes'um."

She didn't look convinced, but she wiped her hands on her dress front and said, "I need you to get me more of this amble-weed, this here." She held up one of the plants I'd never seen before. Tiny leaves, nearly black, with a thorny stem. "Take the lantern, now. I don't want to wait 'til mornin', I want to get this done. You go up past the High Nob, over to the pine copse on the side of Dinny Ridge. They grow…."

There was a thump on the front porch. We both turned.

"What's that?" Granny Mustard snarled.

"I don't know."

Another thump. And a loud, deep laugh.

"Sounds like…." I began, and then the front door blew in and three men fell in after it.

"Hoo hoo, Granny Mustard!" hooted one.

"We come for a lil' visit!" shouted another.

The third didn't say anything but just laughed again. I knew their voices immediately, even in the deep shadows of the front room. Mark Via, one of the area moonshiners. Jerrod Butterman, and his son, Norman.

Granny grappled for her butcher knife; I threw myself back in the black corner behind the icebox, pulling myself up as small as I could be. I heard them stride into the kitchen, stomping and kicking boxes and Granny's churn out of the way.

"We just here for a short spell," said Jerrod. "Heard you got something to share with us."

"Ain't got shit, you devil boys!" said Granny. I could imagine her waving her butcher knife at the men, not backing up or backing down.

"Oh, I think so." This was Norman. "Heard you got some cash in a box in your bedroom closet. Don't say it ain't so. Got it on the best authority."

"Who said anything 'bout that!" screeched Granny, and I could tell by the tone of her voice, how it got all high and squeaky, that she knew exactly who had said something about that.

"Don't matter none, just give it to us, and we be gone," said Mark.

"Pfft!" spit Granny.

"Don't wanna hurt you, old lady," said Norman.

"But I do wanna hurt you! Now out!"

Then there was a crash, and a grunt, more grunts, and a snarl that sounded more dog than human. Panting, a yelp, and a chair going over.

I put my fingers in my ears, but it didn't do any good.

Another grunt, and growl, then a shotgun blast.

Thud.

And silence.

Silence.

A chuckle, not so full of humor this time.

"Shit-damn," said Norman.

"She shouldn't-a fought us," said Mark. "Stupid old witch."

"Shit-damn."

"Well."

"Well," said Norman. "Jenkie said the money's in there."

I heard someone yank open the bedroom door, then clomp across the room and tug open the closet door.

Thumping, scraping, then: "Oh, yeah. We got it, buddies. We done got it!"

There was laughing then, and then clomped back into the kitchen.

"How much you think's in there?"

"I dunno. We can count it later. Got to do something about Granny Mustard."

"Leave her here, why do you care?"

Jerrod snorted. "We don't need nothin' that seems suspicious. She's an old lady, prone to wandering, right?"

"She is?" asked Norman.

"Shut up, Norman, she is, okay? So we bury her and let her family think she's gone loony and walked off a cliff somewhere."

"Oh. Okay."

There was more thumping, grunting, the back door of the kitchen opened. From behind the icebox I could see a little bit of them as they pass out the door, dragging Granny Mustard. One of them—Jarrod, looked like—had picked up a jar and was tucking it in the pocket of his overalls. The special shine. The newest batch.

Once the door clapped shut, I listened and counted to fifty. I had to start over a couple times because the hammering of my heart threw my count off. Then I sneaked out into the kitchen and peer out the door across the backyard.

I could see them in the faint light of cloud-shrouded moon, Jerrod holding Granny by the heels, her head bonking on the stones that protruded from the weedy ground. Mark had picked up Granny's shovel from beside the still shed and carried it in his arms like a baby. All three had their shotguns slung over their shoulders. I slipped out of the cabin and tiptoed to the corner of the still shed so I could see and hear better. I watched, squinting, wanting to scream at them but swallowing back each urge as it tried to force its way out onto the gnat-filled air.

They stopped at the far side of the yard, kicked around, looking.

"Let's take her on out into the woods," said Mark.

"Shit on that," said Jarrod. "Too much work. Here's a hillock, lots of good soft soil. I say we just bury her good and deep in there. The family knows the hillock's here, see the scraps? Won't raise no suspicion if we do a good job, put her in deep."

Mark and Norman shifted beneath their shotguns and finally said, "Okay."

They dug a while, chuckling as they unearthed pieces of Granny Mustard's old pets and turned them back down into the earth. Then Mark dragged Granny to the hole and rolled her in. They covered her back up and tamped the dirt down.

"Ha! We done it. We safe now," said Norman.

Mark pulled the jar of the new special shine out of his overalls pocket. I thought he was going to drink it and wondered what it would do to his insides. But instead, he upended the jar and poured it onto the dirt under which Granny Mustard and her dead pets lay.

"Here ya go, you old woman!" Mark laughed. "Here's your stinkin' shine. Won't be makin' anymore of this stuff. Won't be takin' our business away from us!"

"And we'll be spendin' your money for you, so you don't have to worry it goin' to waste!" said Norman.

They sauntered back across the yard, and I withdrew behind the still shed as the shovel was replaced against its wall. I heard them going around the cabin. Their voices faded.

I waited.

And waited.

The moon appeared, nearly full, from behind the clouds. The yard was bright now, silvered, the craggy weeds casting razor-sharp shadows across each other.

I stepped out from behind the still shed and then stopped.

The hillock was moving.

I took a step back, watching.

The soil at the top began rippling, crumbling, chuncks rolling down the side. I caught my chest. I caught my breath.

Then she came out of the hillock. Granny Mustard, a big shotgun wound to her face so that she only had one eye and a chin remaining. The eye showed red in the moonlight. It was looking at me.

The hillock continued to bubble and rumble. Several of Granny's old cats clambered out of the dirt, slowly, two of them mostly bones but the one that died just last week still wearing clumps of fur and flesh. The skeleton cats foundered quickly and fell back dead. The other cat, its red eyes blinking, followed after Granny Mustard. Behind it, several half-pigs, dog pieces, and chicken parts dragged themselves from the hillock and into the yard.

I turned and ran.

I thought I heard Granny's mouthless face call after me, "Suze! You best get back here or you'll be sorry!"

I'm at the Beaver Dam Motel now. Folks who run it thought I was looking for Mama, but I said, "No, I just need a room please, now please!" They said it would be $20 for the night, and I said Mama would be good for it, just please give me a room.

They rolled their eyes and said okay.

I'm in Room 4. Room 4 of 10. All on the first floor, of course. Damn it all. But maybe she won't find me. Though she always had a powerful sense of smell.

But can she smell with her nose blown off? And can she pull a door off its hinges?

If she does, then what?

Then what?

Through the walls of the motel room I hear commotion up at the office. Yelling. Crashing. Someone…something…angrily screaming my name.

Shit.

Oh, shit.

SITTING UP WITH THE DEAD

BEV VINCENT

Bev Vincent is the author of The Stephen King Illustrated Companion, *which was nominated for both the Bram Stoker Award and the Edgar Award, and* The Road to the Dark Tower, *nominated for a Stoker. He is a contributing editor with* Cemetery Dance *magazine and is the author of nearly seventy short stories, including appearances in* Tesseracts Thirteen; Shivers II, IV, *and* VI; When the Night Comes Down; Evolve *and* Evolve 2; Legends of the Mountain State; Specters in Coal Dust; Thin Ice; Ellery Queen's Mystery Magazine; *and* The Blue Religion. *He is a regular contributor to the Storytellers Unplugged blogging community and writes reviews for Onyx Reviews. His next book will appear in April 2013. Visit him online at bevvincent.com.*

Clayton heard a crack in the distance. Gunshots had been echoing across the mountainside for the better part of a week now. Besides the public cemetery, there were a lot of family plots around here. Nasty business. At least it was daylight. He and his partner didn't have to worry about what lurked in the shadows beyond the range of the lights that ran off the portable generator. He didn't envy the men who would take over from them when the sun dropped behind the mountains.

Several of the granite slabs that covered certain graves—meant to keep animals from getting at the bodies—were shattered ruins, smashed from beneath. Decayed corpses, their heads destroyed by shotgun blasts, lay half in and half out of craters near the headstones. Reminded Clayton of minefields he'd seen, in another life.

He'd helped dig most of these graves. By hand. Took pride in his work. Considered it the last act of respect you could show a person. He always made sure the sides were as smooth and straight as possible. If a stone fell from one of the walls, he used a trowel to mend the gap with mud. Then people started using backhoes, digging graves that looked ready to collapse before the coffins were lowered into them.

People used to know how to mourn properly, too, Clayton thought. The deceased's family stopped all the clocks in the house and covered the mirrors with black cloth. The church bell rang once for each year of the person's life. The women baked while the men prepared the body, the coffin, and the grave. The family stayed with the deceased all night. Sitting up with the dead, they called it. Another sign of respect, but it had a practical side, too, as did most traditions: to make sure nothing got at the body—including the family pet. No embalming back then, so if the body didn't go in the ground the next day things got unpleasant.

Clayton had never held a public job. Earned his living farming and logging, so he was usually available to gather his tools and pitch in when somebody died. Didn't expect anything in return, either, except a drink of cold water and maybe a sandwich for lunch if the work was hard. Community service, some called it, but to Clayton it was just doing what was right. Even now, he believed the dead deserved his best effort.

He was too old to dig graves any more. Too old for most things. His vision was failing, his back hurt, his knees ached, and there was gravel in his left hip joint. Some days it even seemed like his hair hurt, what little he had. Not too old to take his turn watching over the cemetery with his shotgun, though. Still, it would have been nice if he could've brought the vibrating chair his son had given him a few years back. He'd thought it a foolish gift at first, but danged if it didn't do the trick.

Brogan, the other guy's name was. Old name for a young man. A few decades ago he probably would have worked in a coal mine, but those jobs were mostly gone now. Outsider technology stole the food from hardworking men's mouths. Then it stole their lives. Video games and satellite TV 24 hours a day and the internet. Everyone got busy doing nothing.

When the epidemic broke out, folks thought they were safe here, isolated in the mountains, but Clayton had known it would only be a matter of time. Everything from the outside, good, bad, or indifferent, ended up here eventually. The world was smaller than it once was. Before the power went out for good, he used to watch his granddaughter three thousand miles away, waving and blowing kisses at him.

After the insanity started, he discovered he could track the plague's progress on the computer his son had insisted on setting up for him. He became another internet addict, sitting in his vibrating chair and clicking from site to site for hours on end. Stayed in touch with his son until Tacoma went dark. Figured out when the outbreak was headed this way and helped the community prepare for the worst.

Clayton had seen many strange things in his eighty-three years, but this disease beat all. The dead were going insane, rising from their graves craving human flesh. How was that even possible? Made no sense. People said it was a sign of the end of times, but those fellas in the Bible never wrote about anything like this—not even crazy John and his revelations.

They stockpiled food, water, weapons and ammunition, gathered everyone into the church, the school and the town hall, and sent teams to watch over any place where people were buried. Which was how Clayton ended up spending the past week in the public cemetery. It was located on a patch of high ground overlooking the town. Red bud trees and dogwoods had been planted throughout to provide color in the summertime. Spear grass—what the locals called "spar grass"—grew on many of the graves. A few bore wilted flowers, the evidence of visits from loved ones. No one would be coming to visit any more.

As a boy he had played among these tombstones. One of his friends had fallen into a collapsed grave during a game of tag. They'd laughed about it, and teased their friend mercilessly, but it had scared them all. Clayton was no longer afraid of falling into a grave. He was afraid of what was falling out of them. The things he and Brogan had seen over the past seven days would drive any man to drink. They'd treated the dead so well, given them a view of the countryside and oriented the graves so that the first rays of the morning sun would fall on them, and how had the dead repaid them? Not with gratitude, that's for sure.

He got to his feet, thinking about eating one of the granola bars in his backpack. Brogan leaped from his perch on a stone bench, a look of alarm distorting his face, his shotgun at the ready.

"Relax," Clayton said. "Just stretching my legs." He also had a crick in his back, but he saw no need to mention that. Brogan would probably never find out what it was like to get old. They were fighting a losing battle, just like when he was in the jungles on the other side of the world. The opposing army was growing vaster every day.

Near as they could tell, anyone who'd died within the past five years stood a good chance of being infected by the virus or bacteria or whatever it was. The first thing they'd done was to mark all the recent graves with yellow ribbons. It wasn't a hard and fast rule, though. Cynthia Farmer had been resting peacefully for a good seven years before she burst from the ground, as mad as a rabid dog. Clayton had fond memories of her. Died of appendicitis at forty-six. Left Otis to look after their three children. He'd tried not to think about that when he pulled the trigger. Now she resembled a creature from one of those old movies he used to watch late at night after Melinda died.

He'd known all these people. That's what made their job so hard. Bad enough to have to kill an unknown enemy—he'd done his share of that overseas. But to shoot the woman who once lived down the street, or the man who used to cut your hair, or the little girl from church who'd been struck by a car while riding her bike.... It gave him nightmares.

What must it be like for them, he sometimes wondered. To be suddenly yanked back into the world of the living. Not alive, but no longer dead, either. Trapped underground, too. The deceased couldn't want this curse any more than they had wanted death in the first place. No wonder they went crazy. Clayton wasn't philosophical, but it made him wonder what kind of god would allow this to happen. It was an abomination.

"Oh, no," Brogan said. "No, no, no."

Clayton looked over to see what had the young man so agitated. Brogan stood slack-jawed, staring. Clayton followed his gaze. Took him a few seconds to see the problem. The grass over one of the graves rippled and bulged. Clayton recognized the signs. Something was burrowing to the surface, and it wasn't a woodchuck.

"Daddy," Brogan said. The young man's fingers went white as he clenched the barrel of his shotgun.

"Take a walk," Clayton said. "I got this." He put a hand on Brogan's shoulder and pushed. When the young man didn't move, Clayton moved his hand to the middle of his back and shoved harder. Propelled him away from the grave that was about to erupt like a boil, spewing forth Brogan's father, who had died of a heart attack the previous winter. Not his father, though, not really. Something animating his father's bones and wearing what remained of his skin. Probably covered in mold. Nothing anyone should have to see. Brogan took a few steps and then stopped. Shoulders drooped. Head sagged. Sniffled. Clayton didn't blame him.

Clayton checked his shotgun. Fully loaded: seven rounds in the magazine and an eighth in the chamber, plus more in his pocket. Made sure the safety was off. Approached the grave and waited. He wished there was a way to shoot the creature before it broke through the ground. Brogan would have to find a way to deal with his father's mutilated body littering the battlefield with all the others. Clayton uttered a silent prayer of thanks to a god he was no longer sure he believed in that Melinda had died long enough ago that her sleep wouldn't be disturbed.

A patch of grass near Clayton's feet rose and fell, rose and fell. Then a hand burst through, grasping at the air as if it might provide leverage. Then another hand appeared. Finally the head emerged, pallid and skeletal, lidless yellow eyes wide open, lipless mouth agape. This wasn't a man—it was a monster. It wanted to tear the flesh from his bones in huge bites. Wanted to infect him with the disease so that he too would stalk the earth for eternity. Clayton took a breath, aimed and squeezed the trigger. The shotgun blast was loud and final. All movement at his feet stopped. Clayton pumped another round into the chamber and topped off the magazine with a shell from his pocket.

He heard a cry behind him and turned, prepared to comfort Brogan. Instead he saw the young man struggling with two creatures that had escaped from their confines while Clayton was dealing with Brogan's father. It had been a mistake to send Brogan away, he realized. He had gotten soft and lost sight of their mission. One of the monsters sank its teeth into Brogan's shoulder. The other was feasting on his calf. Brogan tried to fend them off, but he lost his balance and toppled over.

The creature chewing on Brogan's neck turned with a snarl when Clayton approached. Lurched toward him, arms extended. Clayton fired. Pumped and fired again. And again. Finally the creature collapsed.

The other one came at him on hands and knees. He pivoted and fired twice more in rapid succession. The creature rolled onto its back like a possum playing dead.

He reloaded before approaching Brogan. The young man was writhing in agony. Blood gushed from his wounds. He put up his hands to ward Clayton off, but Clayton knew what had to be done. Brogan was now the enemy. He'd gone over to the other side.

Clayton pulled the trigger. Looked away. Suddenly weak, he leaned on his shotgun for support. Breathed through his mouth. His heart thudded. For a moment he forgot all about his aches and pains.

He didn't want to look at the other bodies, but something compelled him. Respect? One belonged to Phoebe Baker, a schoolteacher who had died from a stroke a couple of years ago. In life she had been frail and bent, but the disease had made her strong enough to get the better of Brogan. The other had been John Tolby, a farmer who'd been crushed under his tractor this past summer. Probably why he'd been reduced to crawling.

Clayton took a deep breath. Took stock of his situation. Something was wrong. It was too quiet. How long had it been since he'd seen a car go past, or heard a gunshot to let him know the battle was still being waged? Too long, he decided. The sun was almost all the way down, casting deep shadows over the town below. He thought he saw figures lurching and shambling through the streets. Was it his imagination? Maybe. Maybe not.

The other team should have been here to relieve them by now. He glanced at the generator. He knew how to run it, but he couldn't imagine sitting up with the dead by himself. He was tired and hungry and sore. And terrified. When there'd been two of them, they could cover each other's backs. Now it was all up to him.

His hip felt like it was filled with broken glass instead of gravel. He limped over to the plot where Melinda was buried. His name was on the headstone, too, along with his date of birth. He didn't think he was up to another trip around the cemetery. Wasn't up to shooting any more old friends. He was weary to the very core of his soul—if such a thing existed. He had his doubts. *Just as well,* he thought. *Made the rest easier.*

He lowered himself to the ground. Leaned back against the headstone that bore his name. Laid the shotgun on the ground. It was too cumbersome for what he had to do next. Fumbled in his pack for the Colt .45 he'd brought back from overseas. Two wars were too many for any man. Even one was too many. Time to sign off.

He rested a hand on the patch of sod beside him. Remembered what it was like to reach out for Melinda's hand when they were in bed. Let the grass run between his arthritic fingers. Closed his eyes. Pressed the tip of the pistol barrel under his chin. Paid no attention to the growling and gnashing he heard approaching from the other side of the tombstone. Ignored the fetid smell that reached his nostrils, and the grasping talon that touched his shoulder as his finger tightened on the trigger.

COMPANY'S COMING

RONALD KELLY

Ronald Kelly is the author of numerous Southern-fried horror novels and story collections, including Undertaker's Moon, Fear, Hell Hollow, Midnight Grinding, The Sick Stuff, *and* After the Burn. *He lives in a backwoods hollow in Brush Creek, Tennessee, with his wife and three young'uns. "Company's Coming" is his first published zombie story.*

Auntie Rose sat on the front porch of her cabin and looked down off the mountain, into the darkness.

Not that she could see much more than that. Once, she had cherished the stars in the velvety sky of night or the blue-gray mist that clung below the pinnacles of the lofty pines that grew plentiful along her end of the Tennessee Smokies. She had relished every fine blade of summer grass or fire-hued autumn leaf. But two cataracts as thick and opaque as her yellowed thumbnail had robbed her of such wonders. Now there was only shadow and light and fleeting movement.

And sound. Sitting there in the heat of August, she snapped beans from her garden and listened. The night had brought a steady stream of sounds and noises, all bad. The baying of hounds, the distant voices of drunken men, and gunshots. Sounds that had made old Auntie's labored heart pound in her chest in a painful symphony of dread.

Then the sounds had faded, and the night had grown quiet again. Auntie pouched a chaw of tobacco and leaned back in her rocking chair. For a while she bided her time, rocking and chewing and snapping and humming one old-time gospel song after another. She was halfway through the Free-Will Baptist hymnal, when other sounds echoed in the darkness. She stopped dead still—her rocking, her chewing, her snapping, and her humming—to prime shriveled old ears for listening. A moment later, it came again, the sound of movement in the thicket several yards down the hillside, past the smokehouse, past the dilapidated henhouse and the privy she still used (except for the coldest of nights, when she made do with the chamber pot beneath her bed). It came again…the sound of branches being pushed aside, the crunch of footsteps on shale and loose limestone, the swish of legs parting dry weeds.

Company's coming.

The thought of unexpected company once excited and pleased her. *Who could it be this time?* she would ask herself. The mailman, the preacher, her friend, Sadie Watkins, from the other side of Pea Ridge? But, now, she feared the secret visitor. The TV had made that so…and the radio…and the gunshots and the screams of folks being eaten alive down in the valley. And the stench of bloated decay and death on the move.

Auntie Rose set down her bean bowl and reached for the old Winchester leaning against the wall behind her. She stood, trembling and unsteady, and with some effort, worked the lever, jacking a fresh shell into the breech.

She licked her dark lips and peered into the night, knowing that the yellow bug-bulb of the porch light could reveal only so much.

"Who be there?" she demanded. "Show yourself or I'll shoot 'ya. Shoot ya where you stand!"

The sound of slow, shuffling footsteps across the rocky earth centered her attention on a spot scarcely thirty feet away. Through the veil of her cataracts, she could make out two forms, or rather the pale flesh of their faces. They were of their kind. The ones who had turned God's green earth into a living graveyard, teaming with the unruly dead… searching…searching for what? Food? Companionship with their own putrid fraternity? The Pearly Gates, slammed shut and locked, denied them by a tiny, twisting bacteria?

Auntie's nostrils flared as the stench of them reached her. "What do ya want? A meager meal of ol' Auntie? Well, you'd best forget that thought! You'll not be gnawing on my brittle, old bones!"

Still holding the rifle, she reached down and felt for the wire cage sitting on the edge of the porch. She found it, opened the crude door, and felt around inside. The occupants of the makeshift pen clucked and flapped, trying to dodge her probing black fingers. But Auntie Rose had nabbed chickens for suppertime countless times during her 83 years, and she was no slouch at the art. Her nimble fingers closed around the throat of a speckled hen, yanked her from the cage, and tossed her toward the approaching zombies.

Once, she'd tried doing the decent thing. She'd taken to snapping the poor birds' necks before offering them up for sacrifice. But those rotten bastards refused to go for the bait. They ignored the dying chickens and kept right on coming, the smell of vibrant flesh and flowing blood triggering something irreversible in their putrefied brains. Then only a bullet in their upper skulls would stop them and, unfortunately, she'd be one round shy in her ammunition bag.

The hen squawked as it floundered in the open air and landed at the feet of the visitors. The larger of the two—a man she reckoned—reached out, quicker than she would have expected, and grabbed the chicken before it could escape. There was a frantic struggle, the sound of ripping flesh and gristle, and then the wet, chewing sounds of devourment. Auntie was surprised when the man gave half of the murdered hen to his companion. The other was female, a city woman more than likely. Mingled with the stench of decomposition was the fancy scent of a store-bought perfume...like lilacs blooming over an open cesspool.

"Right nice for you to share," Auntie said with a chuckle. "Now y'all go on and eat your fill, and I'll sit on back in my chair. These feeble legs aren't as sturdy as they once were."

The old woman sat down heavily in her rocker, feeling a bit dizzy in the head. She still clung tightly to the .44-40, though. Its muzzle was aimed unerringly at the two walking dead. As they grew nearer—not menacingly so, but oddly curious—she squinted into the gloom, detecting a smaller patch of paleness held close to the woman's chest.

"What is that you've got there?" she asked. "Is that...heaven forbid.... That's not a baby now, is it?"

She knew that it was true when she heard the noisy sound of suckling and smelled the odor of clabbered milk in the air. The female zombie was feeding her young.

"So y'all has a little family, is that so?" The thought of the three continuing such an intimate union after death both touched and broke the old lady's heart. "Lordy mercy! What's this sorry ol' world come to?"

The man and woman simply stood there. It was as though Auntie's voice somehow pacified them, maybe made them feel human and alive again. The baby pulled away from its mother's bloodless nipple and cooed in a moist gurgle.

"Was that y'all they were shooting at earlier? Who was it after ya? Ol' Lonnie Pendergast and his nasty redneck buddies?"

The man moaned with a hoarse sound that was half frustration and half anger. He moved closer to his wife and young'un and would've probably put his arm around them…if he had been able to. From what little Auntie Rose could see, a good portion of the zombie's left arm was missing below the ragged stump of the elbow.

"Yeah…that's the way I feel about him, too." A secret rage of her own flared in Auntie's soul. Lonnie Pendergast who had tormented her and her kind in grade school, filled her locker with pig shit in high school, and raped her beside the lonesome stretch of Plunkett's Creek when she was scarcely seventeen, just because—as he put it—he had wanted to "see how a piece of black ass felt." She had said nothing about the violent attack; to do so would have meant death for her and endless grief for her family.

As he had grown older, Lonnie had taken over his father's position as the head of the local Ku Klux Klan…burning crosses, bull-whipping, lynching from time to time. When the Klan had become "unfashionable," and the virus had conjured the dead from their state of silent immobility, Lonnie had found a new enemy to hate and harass. An old man himself, Pendergast still roamed the mountains, sipping his precious moonshine as he and his sons and grandsons hunted the undead with the same sick passion they had once reserved for defiant young blacks.

"You may think you've escaped them, but not for long," Auntie assured them. "They'll come after you, and they'll track you down with those dogs of theirs. And they'll stop at nothing until you're shot in the head and burnt to ashes." Auntie Rose knew that she should have wished a similar fate on them as well, but strangely enough, she didn't. There was something about the couple and their baby that pulled at the old woman's heartstrings and made her feel compassion, rather than horror and disgust.

"I'll hide you folks, if'n you want," she finally told them. "Y'all can hide yonder in the smokehouse. Just be quiet and quell your ungodly hunger, and maybe they'll pass you on by."

At first, she was certain that they didn't understand a word she was saying. Then the woman stepped forward and extended a pale hand.

Don't do it! Auntie's mind hollered at her. *She'll grab hold of you and yank you plumb off the porch! Then they'll light into you like buzzards on a dead possum!* But she ignored the voice and, against her better judgment, reached down and took the hand offered her. It was cold and stiff, but grateful.

"You're welcome," Auntie told her.

She listened as they retreated into the darkness. A minute later, she heard the creak of the smokehouse door as it was opened and closed. Then all was silent except for the singing of crickets and toads in the night.

Auntie Rose turned to go back into the cabin. As an afterthought, she turned and yelled, "Now don't y'all get no hankering in the early hours and come aiming to eat me. You do, and I've got a bullet or two for yo' asses."

There came a soft, snuffling sound from the direction of the smokehouse—could it have been laughter? Then the noise faded, and the night grew quiet again.

As it turned out, her company stayed much longer than she would have imagined.

For the next three days, Auntie Rose would arise to find the two zombies and their undead infant waiting in the yard, a few yards away. In broad daylight, the elderly woman could make them out a little better. The man was tall and dark haired, wearing a gray suit and a red necktie.... Either that or he had blood running down the front of his shirt, she couldn't rightly tell which. The woman wore a pretty pink dress that was stained by dirt and the leaking of bodily fluids. Her hair was blonde and all messed up, bearing what appeared to be dead leaves and twigs, and the left side of her scalp was laid open, exposing the yellowed bone underneath. The baby was still something of a mystery; small and pale, held in the crook of its mother's arm, either suckling or sleeping.

For the most part they simply stood there and listened to her talk. And Auntie Rose could surely talk! She ended up telling her whole life's story before it was over and done with. Auntie reckoned she had been awful lonesome and hungry for company for so long, that she found herself rambling on and on. But the zombies didn't seem to mind. They just stood and listened.

Toward evening, she would feed them, either from the chicken cage or a trap she'd set out back of the cabin. Usually, there was a plump jackrabbit or woodchuck to appease the hungry couple. She'd toss the frantic animal to them and then walk back inside for awhile until they were finished. The squeals of the frightened critter along with the ugly sounds of rending flesh and splintering bone tended to drive Auntie's blood pressure up a notch or two. But she knew that it was their way now, and she didn't begrudge them of their appetite or their bad manners.

At bedtime, they would leave. She would call out "Goodnight!' to them as they ambled back toward the empty shed of the smokehouse and closed the door behind them. Strangely, during their nocturnal departures, Auntie couldn't help but feel a bit sad and lost. She had grown strangely fond of the little family that came visiting every day. It was like having kin of her own again, even though she knew in the back of her mind that she was only fooling herself into believing such crazy notions.

Then on the fourth day, shortly after midnight, they finally came.

Auntie Rose was startled into wakefulness by the roar of engines and the brittle crack of gunshots fired skyward.

Company's coming!

Rebel yells and loud laughter assaulted her ears, but one man—and one man only—came immediately to mind.

Lonnie Pendergast.

Auntie pried herself from the comforting embrace of her feather bed and, taking the Winchester in hand, made her way across the cabin's single room to the front door. As she stepped out into the muggy warmth of the summer night, her faulty eyesight was assaulted by the haloed glare of fiery torches. She barely made out what looked to be several four-wheelers and a good-sized pickup truck, and then her attention was drawn by those who stood in the yard before the porch. Men—maybe a dozen or more—reeking of sour sweat and liquor. They joked and laughed amongst themselves, until she approached the edge of the porch and showed herself. Then they lapsed into silence. All except the head of them all.

"I know they're here, Auntie Rose," said Lonnie. "You'd best go on and tell me now, a'fore I climb that porch and put a hurting upon you."

In the firelight, she could make him out, still tall and brawny at such an advanced age, but sporting an unwashed mane of stringy white hair and a beard that hung clear to his breastbone. She couldn't see his face clearly, but then she didn't have to. She could imagine it as it had been that evening at Plunkett's Creek, full of piss and vinegar, his tobacco-stained teeth leering cruelly, the eyes as dark and dangerous as those of a timber rattler.

Auntie lifted the rifle and pressed the stock against her scrawny shoulder. Several of the men stepped back, but Lonnie Pendergast held his ground.

"You sorry trash, get on outta here!" she demanded, her coarse voice wavering with emotion. "You just leave them poor folks be! They haven't done nothing to you!'

"They exist…that's all the reason I'll ever need, you damned ol' bitch," Lonnie told her. "Now, tell me…where are they? The henhouse, the tool shed? Maybe in that smokehouse yonder?"

The nervous shifting of her eyes provided the answer. "They're in that smokehouse, boys. Douse 'er with gasoline! We're gonna have ourselves a bonfire!"

Auntie Rose's heart leapt in her chest. "You take one step toward that there shed, and I'll put you down like the diseased dog you are, Lonnie Pendergast!" She shifted the barrel of the rifle, centering the sights on the pale blob of his face, where she believed the junction between his eyes was located.

At the same time, she heard a distinct metallic ca-click. "You're not too blind to see this hogleg gun I've got in my hand, are you, Rose? It's a big'un. Forty-five caliber. Large enough to blow a hole in you that I could heave a hedge-apple through…and I ain't lying."

And she knew that he wasn't, either. But she refused to back down. She thought of the unfortunate family that huddled in the smokehouse. "Like I said before, Pendergast…cut outta here or you're a dead man."

Auntie saw the dark outline of the pistol sag a bit and, for a second, thought that she had succeeded in making her point. Then it was back up in a flash.

They pulled their triggers at the same instant. Lonnie Pendergast's face grew dark beneath a veil of coursing blood, while a blow like a sledgehammer struck her full in the stomach, followed by a skewer of white-hot agony that ran her through, from belly button to backbone.

Auntie stumbled backward and dropped her gun. Almost afraid to, she felt at the wound in her guts. A puckered hole the size of a nickel throbbed just below her left ribs. The wound in the small of her back was much worse, twice as large and ragged with bits of hanging meat and slivers of sharp rib bone stuck in the pulp.

"Dear God, deliver me!" she wailed. Blood and bile boiled up her throat and into her mouth.

Then the men abandoned her and their fallen leader. With torches held high, they converged on the structure of rusted tin and weathered gray wood, the air filled with their cussing and laughter. Unable to stand there and watch, she turned feebly and, supporting herself with the doorframe, made her way back into the cabin.

Somehow, she made it to her feather bed at the far side of the room. She lost her footing and dropped heavily onto the mattress. The impact brought a scream tearing from her ancient throat and a geyser of hot blood jetting from the hole in her belly.

She lay there for what seemed an eternity, listening to what was taking place; the crackling of flames as the smokehouse went up like dry tender, the garbled cries of the two zombies, and the terrified wailing of the dead baby. Then there was the sound of the shed door bursting beneath heavy boots and a dozen guns fired in unison.

"No!" muttered Auntie Rose. Her voice was scarcely a whisper as she felt her consciousness slowly fade. "Not my friends. Don't take... my...."

Then her protests were swallowed by merciful, painless oblivion.

I'm dead, she thought to herself upon wakening.

But, then, no...she couldn't be. Auntie was icy cold, but that was more from loss of blood than anything else. Her abdomen still pained her immensely, as though someone had taken a bean stob and impaled her from belly to back. Weakly, she laid her hand on the mattress beneath her spine. The linens were wet and tacky with congealing blood.

She breathed in a shuddering gasp and smelled the acrid odor of wood smoke. Then she remembered, and she cried out. "Damn you, white devils!" she moaned feebly. "Damn you for what you've done!"

Auntie Rose lay there, feeling the strength drain from her arms and legs until she could feel little at all, except the hellacious hurting in the pit of her belly. She prayed for the good Lord to take her, and she was sure that He would, in His own good time. She just wished that He would put her at the top of His list of things to do and get it over and done with.

In the darkness, she heard something. The sound of the cabin door being pushed open and the gritty shuffle of something crawling slowly across the hardwood floor. The stench of burnt flesh stung her nostrils.

Company's coming....

Auntie turned her head and, at first, saw nothing in the gloom. Then a tiny hand appeared over the edge of her blood-soaked bed, partly charred flesh, partly stark white bone. Her breath hitched in her chest when a small, round head rose above the twisted plain of the patchwork quilt, more skull than face, except for the upper right-hand side. One eye remained intact...a stark blue pupil amid a glistening sea of bloodshot yellow.

The baby giggled softly and came for her.

But she did not refrain. Instead, Auntie reached out with a frail black hand. "Come, child," she whispered. "Partake of me."

Soon it was there, beside her, nuzzling her, working its way beneath the bloody folds of her night gown. She felt it take the nipple of one of her flaccid breasts into its mouth, a breast that had not let down milk for nearly half a century. The fire had burnt the rotten gums away. Toothless bone latched on...gnawing, tearing, burrowing.

Auntie Rose shuddered and closed her eyes. She did not cry, nor scream. Instead, she felt the dark tide of death approaching...quietly, soothingly. All sensation faded as her systems shut down, one by one: kidneys, lungs, heart, brain.

As her soul departed, she sensed something else ready to take its place. Due to the baby's bite, the virus was within her now. Ready to reactivate dead nerve endings and bring bloodless muscle and tissue back into service.

It waited on the threshold, ready to barge in and visit for a spell.

Company's coming.

REPENT, JESSIE SHIMMER!

LUCY A. SNYDER

Lucy Snyder is the Bram Stoker Award-winning author of the novels Spellbent, Shotgun Sorceress, Switchblade Goddess, *and the collections* Sparks and Shadows, Chimeric Machines, *and* Installing Linux on a Dead Badger. *This story takes place directly after the events in* Switchblade Goddess. *Her writing has appeared in* Strange Horizons, Dark Faith, Weird Tales, Hellbound Hearts, Chiaroscuro, *and* GUD. *You can learn more about her at www.lucysnyder.com.*

My familiar, Palimpsest, kept insisting we go back to Madame Devereaux's house in the heart of the swamp to properly thank her for curing him of lycanthropy. And I kept telling him it wouldn't work; he was stuck in the form of a bear, and it would be awfully hard to explain to the townsfolk if we stopped to get a cake and flowers down at the Piggly Wiggly. Not to mention the difficulty of finding a rental car with a seat that could hold 800 pounds of grizzly.

Fate smiled on his determination a couple of weeks later. Well. Smiled is the wrong word. It was more a fately smirk. A newly hired guard—one who apparently dozed off during his orientation on the strange creatures living in my father's castle—stumbled onto Pal after my familiar's morning swim in the moat. The guard, a kid barely out of school, freaked the heck out. And lit Pal up with his taser. Which would have been an act of epic, life-ending stupidity on the guard's part had Pal been a normal grizzly bear. But instead of sending Pal on a man-slaying rampage, the powerful shock triggered his polymorphic enchantment, and he began rapidly (and painfully) cycling through his past familiar bodies until the guard stopped zapping him.

When the smoke of burnt fur cleared, Pal was in his ferret form. Small. Cute. Nonthreatening. Portable. Clearly it was time for a trip down south.

So just a few days later, I pulled my rented Dodge Ram truck up in front of Madame Devereaux's sprawling, blue ranch house. The old witch was bent over the engine of her 1968 Volkswagen Beetle in the shade of the huge magnolia in her front yard. Her African mudcloth sundress and orange Crocs were smudged with black oil and red transmission fluid. Her granddaughter, Shanique, sat close by on a metal folding chair, holding a red toolbox at the ready, clearly trying to keep her brand new purple sneakers from getting greased.

"Hey there!" I waved to them as I got out of the truck with Pal perched on my shoulder.

Madame Devereaux straightened up, squinting at us from behind her thick, old-fashioned bifocals. "Jessie Shimmer, is that you?"

"Yes, ma'am."

"Ain't you got that paw of yours fixed yet?" She pointed at the gray satin opera glove covering my left hand and forearm.

"Oh, it's fixed. No more hellfire." I pulled down the cuff of the burn-proof glove to show her my pale, luminous flesh. I was glad it was closer to normal. Having a hand made out of flame is great if you're trying to barbecue things, but it's lousy for pretty much anything else. It's especially hard to hold onto anything when your hand doesn't have any bones; I'd had to rely on my natural talent for spiritual extension, a type of parakinesis, and even that failed if I wasn't paying attention. My Frisbee game sucked hard.

"It still looks weird, so I still keep it covered up," I finished.

"What you doing here? Your daddy need something?"

"No, ma'am.... Pal here wanted to come back to see if there was anything we could do to thank you for curing him."

The old lady seemed simultaneously flustered and annoyed. "I done told you I don't need no payment for that!"

"It's not about payment, ma'am.... He just wants to do something to thank you."

We went back and forth for a couple of minutes in gentle argument until Shanique finally said, "What about your healing stone, Grandma?"

"Hm," Madame Devereaux rubbed her chin. "I reckon gettin' that back would be a fine thing."

"Healing stone?" I asked. "Where is it?"

"Boudreaux Metier borrowed my best crystal to cure some of his coon hounds what came down with distemper last year. It's a relic your daddy gave me, a dark purple amethyst carved in the shape of the goddess Hygieia. 'Bout four inches high. Boudreaux said he'd just be a couple days with it, but he ain't brung it back yet. I tried to call him on his cell, but I reckon he dropped it down the sump again.

"He lives a ways back in the swamp, and I just ain't been up for going out there on my own."

She paused, wincing. "Boudreaux always wants you to set a spell, see, and try whatever vile rotgut he's brewed up from his still. I think that boy's done burned out his taste buds. Anyway. If y'all were to go get that stone back for me, I'd surely appreciate it."

"Consider it done," I replied.

It was almost evening before Madame Devereaux's directions got me on the road to Boudreaux's place out in the swamp. She'd warned me that my truck's GPS wouldn't be much good, and sure enough, the device was telling me I'd reached a dead end even though I could see a straight path of mud-reddened gravel parting the thick forest of pine trees and cypresses. I could have cast a spell to track him, but that required a bit of Boudreaux's hair or a toenail clipping or a personal item, and Madame Devereaux didn't have so much as a mason jar of his moonshine.

We followed the road down into a darkening hollow, then up onto a small hill where we encountered the real dead end. A couple hundred yards away, I could see an Army-green house lurking in a clearing. The two-story plantation style house had seen better days; the double wraparound porches were warped, and Spanish moss dripped from the upper railings. A couple of rusty cars on blocks and cords of firewood were piled in the yard around the building.

"I can't say I like the look of the place," Pal told me telepathically, craning his neck out the window and sniffing the piney air. "I smell carrion."

"Boudreaux's got coon hounds," I replied. "He's a hunter. Of course you smell dead things. He's probably got a critter pit or something to dispose of carcasses."

Despite my words, far more sinister possibilities were already crowding into my mind. So after I killed the engine, I went to the trunk to get out my Mossberg shotgun and a sheathed knife I could slip inside my boot. A girl can't be too careful. My defensive magic is pretty decent, but sometimes there's just no substitute for a firearm or a blade.

I slung the Mossberg over my left shoulder, and Pal perched on my right, his whiskers twitching with anxiety. Still, he didn't complain. I began to make my way through the litter of leaves, small branches, and scattered car parts toward the house. Halfway there I stepped over the crumbling remains of a low stone wall that, once I'd crossed it, we both realized contained some kind of warding magic.

"Oh dear," said Pal.

I reached down, picked up a couple of tinder-dry pine needles, and spoke a couple of old words for flame. The charm seemed to stick in my throat. Nothing happened. Not so much as a spark or wisp of smoke. Crap. I'd run into a magic-dampening field before; it had been powered by captive witches and wizards trapped in a thrall circle. Not an easy piece of spell work. The stones behind my feet didn't feel strong enough to be the source.

Pal was staring at the unlit needles in my hand. "This does not bode well."

"No, it doesn't," I thought back to him. "But Boudreaux's a friend of Madame D.... If he's in trouble she'd want to know. Especially if the trouble could spill over to her and Shanique."

Still, it was time to do a couple of quick tests before we went any further. My left eye was an enchanted stone; I blinked through a couple of views to confirm that the suppression field wasn't affecting items imbued with permanent magic.

"My ocularis is good, so whoever's casting this isn't that powerful." I reached into my pocket, found a lighter, flicked it with my thumb. A sturdy little flame flashed to life. "And we've got fire. So my shotgun will still work. It'll be fine."

We continued on to the house. I kept the shotgun slung at what I hoped looked like a casual angle, but I could bring it up in a hurry if I needed to. If we were being watched, I didn't want to seem threatening. We got to the front of the house and went up the creaky, mossy steps onto the worn porch. I knocked on the brown steel front door. Waited. No answer.

"Hello, Mr. Metier, are you there?" I called. "Anybody home?"

I was about to knock again when I heard the deadbolt slide back, and the door swung open to reveal a tall man dressed in a tattered black dress shirt and muddy black tactical pants. His hair was a filthy, gray-streaked blond mane, and his long beard was turning into dreadlocks. He didn't look or smell like he'd showered in months. And it was more than just dirt, old sweat, and crusty underwear; he wore an unmistakable stench of meaty rot.

"Whatchu want, girl?" He had the voice of a man who'd smoked a million cigarettes and glared down at me with eyes the color of an algae-sheened cesspool.

"Madame Devereaux sent me." I couldn't keep my voice steady. "Are you Boudreaux Metier?"

He shook his head, and as his beard moved, I saw that his black shirt was topped with a stained clerical collar. "I'm Brother Hiram. Boudreaux is busy with the Lord's work."

"Jessie." Pal's voice was tight with fear. "This fellow doesn't have a heartbeat. We should go. Now."

"The Lord's work?" The magic suppression spell, no doubt. If this guy had enslaved Boudreaux, he probably wasn't working alone. I had the horrible feeling I didn't have nearly enough ammo. Time to call for help. I fixed a smile on my face and carefully backed away. If I got past the first car on blocks I could sprint for the stone fence and be past the wards in maybe five seconds. "He must be real busy. I'll just come back later, okay?"

Brother Hiram opened the door wide and strode toward me, his frown deepening. "You say Madame Devereaux sent you?"

"Yes." I half-stumbled off the porch and down the stairs. Maybe I should drop the neighborly pretense and just shoot him. But that might not stop him. I didn't know what he was. He seemed too smart and self-aware to be a zombie. A headshot would just annoy a vampire. I couldn't remember what to do with a ghoul or a revenant. Heart? Stomach? Decapitation?

"That Madame Devereaux is a hoodoo witch, ain't she? That must mean you're some kinda witch, too." Brother Hiram was staring at my gloved hand as if it still glowed with hellfire.

I raised the shotgun to my shoulder, aiming at his throat. If I got him with a good solid blast under the jaw, maybe I could pop his skull off. "Don't come any closer."

"I reckon the Bible's pretty clear on the subject of witches." He stopped coming toward me, but didn't raise his hands or avert his stare. "The good Lord said in Exodus 22:18, 'Thou shalt not suffer a witch to live.' "

Then there came a rustling all around, the sound of cold bodies unfolding themselves from leaf-covered shallow graves and straightening up on dead legs. I turned to see how many creeps were coming toward me; a quick glance around showed at least thirty undead men in ragged clothes shambling toward me. Crap.

I only looked away from Brother Hiram for maybe a second, but that was enough. Before I knew it he'd rushed forward and grabbed the barrel of my shotgun with a strength I didn't imagine he possessed. Before he jerked it out of my hands I managed to pull the trigger, hoping to get him in the face, but the blast went wide. My ears rang.

Hiram held the Mossberg high, swung it around and slammed the butt into my sternum. Right over my heart. The blow woofed the air out of my lungs and hurt like hell. I stumbled backward, bright stars sparking in my vision, but managed to stay on my feet. Pal's little claws dug into my shoulder as he scrambled for purchase.

"I ain't in a mood to suffer the likes of you." Hiram glowered at me, gripping my shotgun in his dirt-streaked fists.

His ragged mob was nearly on me. I had time to do exactly one thing, so I grabbed Pal with both hands and tossed him up into what I hoped would be safety in the branches of the nearest cypress.

"Go get help!" I thought to him as I turned to face the men surrounding me.

"What am I, Lassie?" His voice teetered on the edge of hysteria. "We're out in the middle of nowhere—how am I supposed to get any help?"

I kicked a man dressed in a rotting flannel shirt and camouflage pants; his lips had been mostly eaten away from his face by maggots. "Call Madame Devereaux! She's in my contact list.... If she doesn't answer, try my brother!"

"And your cell phone is where?"

"Glove box!" I punched a guy who had pus-filled holes where his eyes should have been.

"Is the truck locked?"

It was. I swore, kicking away a guy who had a spiked billy club strapped to the decaying stump of his right arm.

"Jeepers creepers, Pal, go find a car battery and lick it or something! Embiggen yourself and break in!" I thought back.

"Y'all stop foolin' around and git'er down, already!" Brother Hiram barked.

The zombies dog piled me, pressing me down into the leaves and slimy mud. I thought I would pass out from their weight and stench. A moment later, one of them had looped a rope around my neck, and they were dragging me through the yard as I gagged and fought for breath.

They pulled me up onto my knees beside a huge woodpile and held me there, my arms outstretched. I didn't fight them, taking a moment to try to get my bearings and breath back. I was completely surrounded. I'd have a chance if I could just get my shotgun back, but without it, I was pretty much screwed.

The hidden boot knife's sheath was jammed painfully into my calf. No way to reach it.

I heard the sound of heavy footsteps in the leaves, and the mob parted to let Brother Hiram through. He stood in front of me, still holding my shotgun. His face was grim. "You are a witch and an abomination unto the eyes of the Lord. But ye shall repent, and before this day is over you will be calling the Lord's name with all your heart, and He will welcome you with open arms into His kingdom. Eternal salvation will be my gift to you."

I dearly wanted to tell him in graphic anatomical detail exactly where he could stick his salvation. But I had a rare moment of prudence and realized that anything I had to say would just make things worse. So I held my tongue, watching to see what their next move would be.

Hiram nodded at his rotting crew. "Git 'er ready."

Two of them carried over a 6"x6" square wooden post beam. A pair of iron D rings had been securely screwed into the middle of the rough-hewn beam, as if it was supposed to be hung someplace. Someone had routed a series of well-worn grooves a few inches from each end. The wood was mildewed; it looked like it had been spending a lot of time near the water, and it was stained with something dark and rusty. Old blood. The beam was a bit longer than the width of my outstretched arms; I guessed it was probably six feet even. Six by six by six. What the hell were they going to do?

Dead hands pulled me up, turned me over, and threw me down on the beam, binding me tightly by my wrists to the wood with coarse sisal rope that fit neatly into the grooves. My stomach churned as I realized what they had planned.

"We used nails for the first couple of crucifixions," Brother Hiram said. His expression had changed now that I was seemingly helpless; he was looking down at me with something that almost seemed like kindness in his dead eyes. "But nails make the wood too weak after a while, and I seen a couple of people pull off the nails entirely, and then the whole thing's over too quick. Rope's better all the way around."

Hiram paused. "I reckon God wants us all to suffer so we'll appreciate Heaven when it comes along. So I ain't doing my bit for the good Lord if you die too fast. You need time to really reflect on the pain you'll be feeling and accept Him into your heart, and I aim to give that to you."

They hauled me up to my feet and kicked me forward onto a muddy path that wound down through the trees. The guy in front of me was shirtless, and a huge swath of flesh was missing from his side. I could see nearly all his ribs. In my light-headed terror, his bones reminded me of a xylophone or marimba, and suddenly the Violent Femmes' "Gone Daddy Gone" was playing inside my head.

The wooden crosspiece was a hell of a thing to carry. It weighed probably fifty or sixty pounds, which normally wouldn't have been much of a problem if I just had decent grip on it, or even if they'd put it up on my shoulders. But the damn thing was dragging halfway down my back, twisting my arm joints out of their sockets. They'd bound the scratchy ropes so tightly that my flesh hand was turning puffy and purple; I didn't know what my eerie hand looked like beneath the glove. I couldn't pull the crosspiece up, I couldn't put it down; I was constantly off balance. When I fell, they'd haul me up and shove me down the path again.

By the time we got to the edge of the swamp, I was half blind from exhaustion and perspiration, gasping for air like I'd just run a marathon. My jeans and T-shirt were covered in red mud and dead leaves and pine needles. My arms and shoulders ached horribly, and my hands had gone completely numb.

"Git'er on out there," Brother Hiram said.

The dead men pushed me out into the chest-deep water, and my vision cleared enough to see the tall wooden post set out in the middle of the swamp; it looked like a stolen telephone pole that they'd stripped of its original hardware. A pair of newer steel hooks was bolted to it about three feet from the top. On each side of the tall post were short steps made of cypress logs.

They pushed me out to the post, and the tallest of the men grabbed each end of the crosspiece and hauled it and me up out of the water. After a couple of shoulder-wracking tries they got the crosspiece hung from the hook. They splashed back to shore, leaving me hanging out there in the damp heat and eerie quiet.

My booted feet dangled about two feet from the deep-green water; I tried to grip the pole with my legs to take the weight off my arms, but the wood was too slippery. It smelled like they'd smeared it with axle grease. The sun beat down on me, merciless as Brother Hiram, and mosquitoes whined in my ears. My arms were screaming, and I could already feel the hang-strained muscles in my chest beginning to spasm.

I closed my eyes, concentrating.

Pal, are you there? I thought. *I could use some help over here. Pal?*

No response. Either he was too far away for telepathy, or.... I didn't want to think about the alternatives.

I'm so screwed, I thought.

A low roar rolled across the water. It sounded like a huge crypt slab being dragged across the hollow marble floor of a mausoleum. I was suddenly aware that, beneath the stench of the dead men, I could smell the sharp rankness of reptile offal.

My skin broke out in goosebumps despite the heat. I scanned the water, spotted what I first thought was the fat trunk of a downed tree. And then realized it was moving. Toward me.

The swimming gator was nearly as big as a dragon. It was easily twenty feet long and had a maw of sharp, jagged teeth the size of steak knives. And, as it came closer, I saw that it had milky white eyes, and patches of its thick hide were missing from its back, revealing grey, leathery muscle beneath.

Somebody started spewing profanity and shrieking about zombie gators. It took me a couple of seconds to realize I was the one making all the noise.

"Taking the Lord's name in vain won't help you none," Brother Hiram called. "You best start repentin'. I gave ol' Rufus there a sacrament of my own blood, and he's an instrument of God now."

I squeezed my eyes shut and took a deep, painful breath. *Stop panicking. Panic won't help.*

What could I do? For the first time, I wished my left hand were still a torch of cursed hellfire; at least then I'd have a shot at burning the ropes and freeing myself. The knife in my boot was plenty sharp enough, but even if I had the circus freak flexibility to swing my foot up to my hand, my fingers were too numb to grip anything.

What about the anti-magic field? Those took a fair bit of juice to maintain, and I didn't see any ward stones along the banks. I tried speaking a couple of simple charms for lights in the air, but I got that same sticking-in-my-throat sensation, and the words failed. Crap.

I was running out of options. My stone eye worked, but it was only good for different sight; I couldn't shoot laser beams with it or anything. I made a mental note to ask my father about getting an upgrade.

"Rufus ain't had no food for a while, so he can't jump real high," Brother Hiram said. "Probably he'll only take your feet at first. It'll take him a while to chew those fancy boots of yours, I 'spect, but once he's got your meat in him, he'll get friskier. He'll get your knees on his next jump, and after that it's a mite hard to predict. I seen him get hold of one feller's innards on the third jump and start windin' 'em out of his body like he was unspooling a hose. You shoulda heard that feller start prayin'! It warmed my heart to see him find God like that."

I swore in frustration and slammed my head back against the wood.

"But don't you worry none," Brother Hiram added. "If he takes a mite too much of your giblets, I can give you a sacrament so you'll stay awake. Even at his friskiest Rufus is a little too big to get more'n chest high. As long as your head's still on your shoulders, you'll be able to keep repentin' all night."

Christ on a crutch. Well, at least he'd confirmed how I could kill these creeps. If I ever figured out a way off this damn pole. I wondered briefly if Brother Hiram meant to come out to where I was hanging to give his "sacrament," but then I saw one of the zombies hand him a case that contained a black Spyder air rifle, a tub of bright orange paintballs, and an embalming syringe. Hiram took out the syringe and plunged the thick needle into his own neck. Once he'd filled the barrel with his tarry blood, he began injecting it into the paintballs.

Well. That would do it. He'd just have to get some of his blood in my mouth or on an open wound to turn me. An easy shot from where he was. I was screwed a hundred ways to Sunday.

The monstrous gator was still cruising toward me; it was maybe fifty feet away now. The rotten-fish stench of him was starting to make my eyes water. I wracked my brain, trying to figure out what I could do. If I could just get to the knife in my boot, I could get myself untied and climb the top of the pole—it didn't look like they'd greased the wood above my head—but that would take magic.

I stared resentfully at my left hand, wishing I could get the damn thing to flame up one last time. Before it had been cursed fire, it had been gone completely, courtesy of having been bitten off by a demon. At least when I was nothing more than an amputee, I could still grip things, courtesy of my parakinesis, and nobody could tie my missing arm up—

Wait a minute, I thought, my heart beating faster. *Who's to say that couldn't work now?*

Parakinesis was a kind of magic, sure, but it was a natural talent I'd improved with practice. It wasn't a spell. If my eye still worked, my parakinesis should, too. The trouble was, I'd never tried to disconnect my spiritual extension from my flesh.

Rufus was less than twenty feet away. I didn't have a choice—I had to make this work.

Okay. I closed my eyes and took a deep breath. I concentrated on my left arm, the feel of the ropes biting into my gloved wrist, the hard wood against my elbow, the sun burning my bared skin. I lifted my knees, imagining that I was kneeling on solid ground, imagining that the ropes just weren't there. I pictured myself dropping my freed left arm down to my boot. And then I could feel my fingers sliding down into the leather shaft, grasping the handle of the knife, and pulling it out.

The huge gator let loose a tooth-rattling roar right below me, and I don't think I've been so startle-scared in my whole life. It literally spooked me out of my skin. I scrambled up to the top of the pole, clinging for dear life with the knife clenched in my fist, and it took me a long second to realize that my consciousness had entirely left my flesh. My real body hung there limply, unconscious, not breathing. I saw myself in spiritual form as a faint, translucent glow. A glance at the dead men on the shore told me they couldn't see me like this.

White-eyed Rufus heaved himself out of the water and made a snap for my swaying feet, missing by a couple of inches. Crap. I had to hurry if I didn't want to become a permanent ghost haunting this swamp. But while I was a ghost, I was freed from not just flesh but most physics. I knelt on the crosspiece and began to saw at the ropes binding my flesh wrist to the wood. The last strand abruptly snapped, and my body swung down, perilously close to Rufus' jaws. Almost as bad, the torsion on my still-bound arm was bending my elbow the wrong way, and I worried it was about to snap. I grabbed myself by the back of my T-shirt and hauled my body up onto the crosspiece with one hand while I slashed the remaining ropes with my left.

A sudden dizziness washed over me; I realized my unconscious body's face was turning blue. I pitched forward, back into my flesh, and awoke coughing and gagging, strained lungs burning, desperately grabbing at the pole to keep myself from tumbling off the wobbly crosspiece to the waiting teeth below. My arms were trembling, my hands barely able to grip the wood. The knife, meanwhile, had splashed down into the swamp.

A bloody paintball whizzed past my right ear.

"I gotta say, I seen a whole bunch o' witches, but I ain't never seen 'em pull a trick like that. I guess I need to have a talk with ol' Boudreaux about the importance of the Lord's work. You might be feelin' right clever right now, but I got a flame-thrower back at the house. We'll see how you pray when I set your pretty little face on fire."

I felt exhausted and light-headed; I didn't think I could spiritually project myself again for a while. I scooted around so the bulk of the post was between me and Brother Hiram. Hopefully, it would block most of his shots. I didn't think he could really hurt me unless he got blood in my mouth or eyes, but it was better to not take the risk. For all I knew, he had laced his paintballs with shards of glass or something else to cut skin.

I closed my eyes again and concentrated on reaching out to my familiar. *Pal, are you out there? Pal?*

Jessie, I couldn't get through to anyone on your phone. His voice was distorted in my mind. I hoped that meant he'd been able to change his form. *But I have another idea. Where are you?*

Down at the swamp, I replied. *Hurry*!

Rufus bellowed again and began to slam the post with the side of his enormous head, trying to shake me off my perch. Brother Hiram fired a couple more paintballs at me that went wide. Undead mostly don't have very good daytime vision, and that was a small mercy.

Suddenly, I heard an even louder, bearish roar from the trees above us. My heart jumped with surprise and hope. Pal must have found a battery with a really good charge and had managed to get himself into his form that blended all his past bodies: He was a gigantic shaggy spider with a four-eyed head that looked like a saber-toothed tiger's by way of a mescaline hallucination. In his forelegs, he gripped a pair of rusty machetes.

"Yeah, Pal!" I hollered. "Kick their asses!"

Pal galloped down on Brother Hiram's crew, swinging the blades right and left. I saw arms and heads fly along with sprays of black blood. But then the ghoulish preacher grabbed my shotgun and started blasting away at my familiar. Pal shrieked as buckshot bit into his side, but he grabbed one of the zombies and threw him on top of Hiram, knocking him down. The weapon flew out of the preacher's hands and landed in a thatch of swamp azalea partly overgrown with kudzu vines.

I swore. Adrenaline flooded my bloodstream, giving me energy I thought I'd lost for the day. I had to help Pal: I had to get to shore, somehow.

Rufus was leaping at me again, his claws scrabbling at the pole as if he hoped to be able to climb the wood. His mouth was open wide, gaping like a baby bird's.

I climbed higher on the pole, held on for dear life, gritted my teeth, and used my legs to lift the wooden crosspiece off the hooks. And at that moment, Brother Hiram finally got his wish: I started praying.

"Please, God, let this work," I said to the sky, my whole body shaking with fear and exertion. "Please, please, please."

Then I dropped one knee, letting the wooden bar tumble down. Bulls-eye! Rufus gave a strangled roar as the wood rammed right down his gullet, and he fell backward, furiously shaking his head to try to dislodge the crosspiece.

It wouldn't distract him long. I jumped down into the water and swam as hard as I could toward Pal, who was hacking up another zombie. Brother Hiram had almost pulled my shotgun free of the kudzu.

Cursing, I surged out of the water and kicked Hiram in the small of his back. He stumbled but didn't fall, and swung the shotgun toward me. I was ready for him this time; I grabbed the barrel and slammed my knee into his groin. There was the sound of old bone cracking, and his grip loosened enough for me to wrestle the weapon away from him.

And then I did what I meant to do in the first place: I jammed the shotgun under his chin, closed my mouth, and pulled the trigger. His head came apart like a rotten watermelon, and his body collapsed like a sack of garbage straight down to the mud.

The zombies fighting Pal abruptly dropped their fists and weapons, seeming confused and unfocused. Most of their cunning and motivation had apparently come from Brother Hiram. I looked out at the swamp; Rufus had stopped struggling against the wood stuck in his throat and once again resembled nothing more than a half-submerged log.

"Are you okay?" I called to Pal.

"For now." Pal lopped off a couple more heads, then tossed me his second blade. "I'm sure my blood's been tainted, but I should be able to keep my mind about me for a few more hours. And I know Madame Devereaux can cure what my own powers cannot. Let's finish these fellows off before they get hungry and decide to wander into town."

I helped Pal decapitate the rest of the gang, and then we went back up to the trail to the old house.

Brother Hiram had left a couple of sentries behind, but they were just as dumb and befuddled as the others now that he was dead. Once we'd put them out of their misery, Pal stuck his tongue in a handy electrical outlet and shocked himself back down to his ferret form. We searched the house and found both Boudreaux Metier and Miz Deveraux's healing crystal up in the attic.

Boudreax wasn't undead, exactly, but he was agonizingly thin and sick-looking. Hiram had chained him to the floor and drugged him into a trance with whatever the old-fashioned glass IV was dripping into his arm. He was reciting the same spell over and over through his chapped, blistered lips: this was the source of the anti-magic field.

The carved healing crystal sat discarded on a nearby set of dresser drawers, surrounded by ceramic knickknacks and sundry other junk. The image of Hygeia looked enough like the Virgin Mary at first glance that Brother Hiram probably never realized what it was. I grabbed the crystal and spoke the magic word Madame Devereaux had given me to activate it. It glowed blue in my hand.

I knelt beside Boudreaux, gently pulled the needle from his arm, and pressed the statuette against the suppurating ulcer it had made. It glowed brighter, and his deathly pallor flushed to an almost-healthy pink. He stopped chanting, his jaw falling slack. A snore rattled in his throat.

"Hey, Boudreaux." I patted his cheek. "Wake up."

His eyes popped open. After a moment of unfocused, chain-fighting panic, he seemed to see me, realized I wasn't a zombie, and relaxed.

"Where's Hiram?" he croaked.

"Dead," I replied.

"Good." He coughed. "That's the last time I invite my damn in-laws over for Thanksgiving! You wouldn't have a Dr. Pepper, would ya?"

"I saw some in the kitchen." I began to undo his chains. "Let's get you downstairs, and then we'll all go over to Madame Devereaux's."

Boudreaux stared at the crystal in my hand. "Aw, crap, I was s'posed to get that back to her!"

"Don't worry about it. I'm pretty sure she'll understand that you've been a little tied up over here…."

SPOILED

PAUL MOORE

Paul Moore is a filmmaker who has written and directed four feature films, most recently Keepsake *and* Unbroken. *In 2009, he wrote and directed the short film,* Leftovers. *The film is a tale of a woman's struggles in the wake of a zombie apocalypse and her efforts to rationalize life in the world of the dead.* Leftovers *premiered later that year at Screamfest in Los Angeles, and Paul is excited at the opportunity to revisit the characters in the world of* Leftovers *with the short story "Spoiled."*

Claire sighed.

The clouds overhead were swollen and distorted and the sky was a sheet of unvaried grey. Rain was imminent. Claire's body ached. Every muscle felt like a rusted spring and her head throbbed with exhaustion. She lifted her face from the scope and wiped the back of her hand across her eyes.

She blinked away the strain and surveyed the strip mall again.

Nothing moved. Although in Claire's experience, anything still or quiet elicited immediate distrust in the world of the dead.

The strip mall sat atop a gentle slope that rolled upwards from a seldom used state highway. It was the kind of place that had served as a community center for people that found themselves trapped by an accident of birth. Born in between. Dead before they could walk. Trapped somewhere between sea and shining sea.

Claire slung the rifle over her shoulder as she stood. Experience told her the grocery store and the fast food chains would have been looted long ago, but they were still buildings and the storm on the horizon looked as though it had more than a few days of fury to unleash. She'd marked a nail salon nestled in the bend of the mall as the most likely candidate for shelter and least likely for an encounter, human or otherwise. Claire drew a mental map as she cautiously navigated the crumbling embankment.

***

Claire felt the damp weight of the air as she crept along the rear of the strip mall. The clouds would open soon, and she needed to find cover. She shrugged the thought off. Her boots crunched loose pebbles as she crept along the fractured blacktop

Something wasn't right.

Claire's hand slipped to the butt of the pistol holstered at her side. Her finger curled around the trigger as she drew the firearm.

To Claire's right, the burned-out hulk of a box truck sat on rusted rims, a scorched monument to the panic and chaos of the initial days of the Spread. Ahead, empty boxes and overturned dumpsters flanked the loading docks lining the rear of the mall. Her footsteps echoed off the pavement as she advanced.

Claire cocked her head as she pinpointed the source of her anxiety. Something was rustling through the garbage on the far side of the dumpster. She had encountered plenty of scavenging animals since the Spread began. Most times it was something as harmless as a raccoon. Once she had to face down a starving coyote. That had been a bad day for Claire, but in the end, it had been a worse day for the coyote.

This sound was different. It was deliberate, methodical. Two things distinctly human. In the days since the Spread, Claire had learned two things about human beings. One was that there was nothing that they wouldn't do to one another to insure their own survival.

The other was that she preferred the company of coyotes.

Claire raised the pistol to firing position as she stepped around the dumpster. Her thumb drew back the hammer with a click that echoed along the concrete walls. The figure crouching before her froze.

"Stand and turn around slowly," Claire said. "No sudden moves."

The scavenger's grimy hand released a crumpled juice box. It dropped to the pavement next to tattered sneakers. The figure splayed its hands as it rose and turned toward Claire.

Beneath the hooded sweatshirt and surplus military jacket, a young woman stared back at Claire, brown eyes quivering and growing wet. Dark hair hung in mats around her filthy face, and her cracked lips were trembling.

Claire glanced down at the girl's swollen belly, estimating that she was about seven months along.

The girl's eyes were like a doe's, wide and full of panic.

"I doubt there's anything to eat in that garbage."

The young woman lowered her hands.

Claire's hands tightened around the pistol's grip.

"Easy," she warned.

The girl held Claire's gaze as her hand slipped beneath her jacket. A moment later, she withdrew her hand. She held two dead rats by their tails.

Claire slowly exhaled.

"I guess I was wrong."

The girl's wrist flicked as she tossed the rats onto the ground between them. The carcasses hit the pavement with a wet splat. Claire's pistol remained trained on the girl.

"Open your jacket. Slowly."

The young woman's hands curled around the jacket's worn edges as she pulled it open. Beneath the jacket, a thin, stained T-shirt clung to her pregnant belly.

"Turn around and lift the back."

The tears welling in the girl's eyes finally gave way, tracking through the dirt on her face as she turned her back to Claire. She lifted the back of her jacket to reveal an empty belt. Claire lowered the pistol.

"You're not going to try and kill me, are you?"

The back of the young woman's head shook from side to side.

"Fair enough," Claire said as she slid the pistol back into its holster. "You can turn around."

The young woman turned around, lowering the jacket.

"And you can keep the rats."

The young woman's eyes flicked suspiciously from Claire to the rats and back.

"Really. It's okay."

The young woman knelt, and her hand curled around the rats' tails as she snatched them from the pavement and fastened them to her belt.

"What's your name?"

The young woman looked up from the rats and regarded Claire. Claire watched as she reached beneath her hood and peeled the matted hair away from her neck. A puckered scar marred the skin on the right of the girl's throat. Claire recognized it immediately.

It was a bullet wound.

"Of course," Claire sighed.

The young woman's eyes widened as Claire's hand slipped into the pocket of her jacket.

"The other night I asked God for a traveling companion."

The young woman trembled as Claire pulled a plastic-wrapped strip of beef jerky from her pocket and offered it to the frightened girl. The girl darted forward and snatched the jerky. Her fingers ripped through the plastic.

Claire watched as the young woman bit into the dried beef.

"Good to know his sense of humor is still intact."

Claire shot upright, the lump in her throat blocking her scream. She blinked madly as she listened to the rain hammer the roof. Sweat dripped from her brow as she looked around the storeroom. The girl slept soundly next to her, distended belly rising and falling with each breath. The floor around them was littered with empty candy wrappers.

Claire lay back against her folded jacket and wondered just how hard the rain was; what it could wash away.

The Spread: Day 222

"What do you think?"

The sun was setting behind the rolling hills of Appalachia and the amber light cast long shadows across the trailer park. Dilapidated mobile homes sat derelict, discarded lawn furniture and abandoned cars spread out before them.

Claire wondered if the neglect had started before or after the Spread. She shrugged the thought off and looked over at Carrie.

In their days of traveling, they had come across a a small café. The food inside was rancid, but there had been something of use, the whiteboard leaning against the register. Once used to advertise lattes and soups, it was now the bridge between the two women.

Carrie's fingers flexed as she drew the dry-erase marker across the whiteboard and flipped it in her hands. It read: *Howlers?*

Claire looked back at the darkened windows of the mobile homes.

"Maybe. But there's nothing for them to eat out here."

Carrie's brow furrowed as she wiped the board with her sleeve. Her fingers clenched around the marker as she wrote and flipped the board again. Two letters.

Us.

Claire smiled despite herself.

"Point taken."

She shaded her eyes with one hand as she scanned the uneven horizon.

"If not here, where?" she asked, "We're running out of daylight."

Carrie tapped Claire's shoulder. Claire's gaze followed her outstretched hand.

A lone cabin sat nestled amongst the trees on the lowest ridge of the nearest mountain. Claire unsnapped the binocular case on her belt. She raised the binoculars to her eyes and adjusted the center dial.

The cabin swam into focus. Nothing moved. The windows showed only shadow inside.

Claire sighed as she dropped the binoculars back into their holster.

"It's a hike. A few miles at least."

She once again shielded her eyes as she stared at the setting sun. It was just beginning to slip below the mountains.

"I think we can make it."

The door to the cabin crashed inward as Claire stepped inside. The barrel of her shotgun glinted as she swept it through the fading afternoon light. Dust floated in the air. The room reeked of mold and neglect. Floorboards creaked under her boots as she stepped inside.

The cabin looked typical for a weekend lodge. Fireplace, cheap furniture, breakfast bar, kitchen. A short hallway led to the rear of the cabin.

As Carrie stepped into the doorway, Claire trained the shotgun on the hallway.

"Wait here."

Carrie nodded.

The second bedroom was almost identical to the first. Simple furniture, cheap blankets, family photos on the wall. Claire stared at the photographs as she relaxed her grip on the shotgun.

Most of the framed pictures were of a mother, father and two sons. Some of the photographs featured members of the extended family, old and young.

Claire bit her lip, reaching forward and smearing the dust covered glass on the photograph of a young boy. The child was smiling as he offered a large fish to the camera.

***

Claire was not sure how long she had been sitting on the edge of the bed. The sun was lower in the sky and the shadows were longer on the wall. Dried tears stained her cheeks.

She wiped her cheeks and stood. She cast one more glance at the photograph of the young boy as she left the room. The boy with the fish. A silly picture.

Claire struggled against oncoming tears.

Claire was still sniffling when she entered the empty living room. The door stood wide open as the swath of dwindling sunlight created pockets of shadows in every corner. Claire stopped as she raised the shotgun.

"Carrie?"

No response. Pinpricks of sweat dotted Claire's forehead.

"CARRIE?!"

A clatter sounded to Claire's right as she spun. Her finger tightened against the trigger.

Carrie stood in the kitchen. Stacks of canned food had been removed from the cupboards and now lined the counter next to the sink. Carrie stood next to the sink with an open can of beans in her hand. Despite the shotgun, Carrie was smiling.

Claire lowered the shotgun and sighed, emotion and adrenaline drained from her limbs.

"What are you smiling about?"

Carrie's smile grew wider as she set the can of beans aside and twisted the knob on the faucet.

Water flowed freely into the basin.

Claire began to laugh.

The laugh carried far more weight than was warranted. It felt good all the same.

The fire burned low in the fireplace. Glowing embers cast a warm hue on the dark room. Outside the moon hung high in the clear sky, but the blinds had been drawn. The two women relaxed in relative safety.

Claire lay on the couch, sipping a glass of wine, a luxury that until yesterday she'd assumed was as lost as the world before the Spread. Carrie sat curled in a chair opposite the couch. Two empty plates sat on the coffee table between them.

Carrie watched the fire as it slowly died.

Claire eyed the wine glass in her hands.

"Are you worried about the baby?"

Carrie nodded.

Claire sipped her wine as she looked up at the embers.

"Have you thought about getting rid of it?"

Carrie scribbled on her whiteboard and flipped it. Firelight danced on the board.

Too much death already.

Claire sat up as she stared at Carrie.

"How well did you know the father?"

The corners of Carrie's mouth turned down as she wiped the board and scrawled again.

He seemed kind.

Claire sipped her wine.

"Was he?"

Carrie flipped the board, wrote and flipped it again in the firelight.

No.

Carrie's fingertips reflexively touched the scar on her neck.

Claire wondered about the story behind that scar; decided that there wasn't enough wine in the bottle to fuel that train of thought.

"And you still want to have his baby?"

Carrie inhaled as she wiped the board with the heel of her hand and scrawled. She looked up as a tear seeped from the corner of her eye.

I want to have my *baby.*

Claire leaned back on the couch. All of her arguments seemed suddenly pointless. There was too much pain, comfort, hope and fear in the moment. Sometimes, surviving was enough. Everything else was like a glass of wine. A forgotten luxury.

Claire set her own glass on the table.

"I'm going to bed. You should too. You need your rest."

Carrie spun her whiteboard for the final time that evening. The pen bobbed for a second before she flipped it back into the light of the wavering flames.

You should shower.

Claire's brow furrowed.

"What?"

Carrie looked back over her shoulder at the kitchenette. Claire followed her gaze right to the faucet above the sink. Claire locked eyes with Carrie.

"Holy shit."

The shower was cold and short. Freezing water and months of grime swirled around the drain. As Claire scrubbed exhaustion from her skin, she briefly thought that between the wine and the water, she could die happy if she died in that moment.

Later, she would realize just how right she'd been.

The Spread: Day 253

Morning sunlight flared off the row of bottles. A loud crack split the silence as the first bottle disintegrated. Two more sharp pops echoed amongst the Appalachian peaks, and a second bottle shattered. Uphill beyond the bottle, Carrie raised a heavy revolver. She smiled.

Claire stepped up next to her.

"You're getting better, but…."

Carrie's smile disappeared as she turned to face Claire and cocked her head in a mannerism that Claire had come to learn meant: *And your point?*

"Bullets aren't cheap," Claire said as her hand gently encompassed Carrie's, still holding the revolver.

"These days," Claire smiled. "They're priceless."

Claire's smile disappeared.

"Every shot counts."

Carrie bit her lip. Claire smiled again.

She couldn't help herself. There was a lightness in Carrie that made her want to smile. As dark as the young woman's journey had been, she had held onto something that Claire could not define. Innocence? Hope? It was as though Claire had lost something, something important, and it had been returned to her in the form of Carrie.

Claire shrugged off her thoughts. She tried not to indulge them. She had learned that thinking was like diving into the ocean. The deeper you went, the darker it got.

"Take aim for me."

Carrie brought her arms up into the stance she had been taught, as Claire placed a gentle hand on her elbow.

"Loosen your elbow a little."

Claire released the elbow as she felt it drop slightly. Claire's boot nudged Carrie's shoe.

"Widen your stance."

Carrie slid her foot to the right. Claire gripped Carrie's upper arms.

"Turn your shoulders."

Carrie obliged as Claire stepped away.

"Try it again. Fast as you can."

Carrie squinted as her finger squeezed the trigger. Another loud shot. Another bottle burst. Carrie pumped the trigger two more times. Each time, the gunshot was followed by the sound of shattering glass. Claire stepped forward as Carrie looked past the barrel of her pistol, her expression equal parts disbelief and delight.

Claire took the pistol from Carrie and opened the cylinder. Ejected shells tumbled to the ground. Claire flicked her wrist and the cylinder snapped shut. She looked up at Carrie.

"You've done this before, haven't you?"

Carrie shook her head slowly.

Claire waved a dismissive hand toward the line of broken bottles.

"Not that." Claire raised the revolver. "This. You've fired something like this before."

Carrie's gaze darted to the ground.

"I've watched you all morning. You weren't scared of this when I handed it to you. When it went off. When it jumped in your hand."

Claire handed the pistol back to Carrie as she continued speaking.

"You weren't scared. Most people see guns as dangerous things. Something to be feared."

Claire and Carrie locked eyes, with only the sunlight between them.

"So if you don't fear guns.... There must be something you fear."

Something ugly flashed in Carrie's eyes as she reached up and touched a finger to the scar on her neck.

"Did you miss?"

Carrie shook her head.

"Then you're a natural…or a survivor." Claire cracked yet another smile. "I'm glad you're on my side."

Claire sat on the couch. Firelight flickered across her skin as her fingers traced lines on a map. The steady sound of a knife on a chopping board echoed from within the kitchenette, the unceremonious fate of an unfortunate rabbit.

Claire smiled as she listened. Carrie had proved to be as much a natural in the kitchen as she had been with a gun. As her finger settled on her target, Claire mused that perhaps the Lord did work in mysterious ways.

A familiar tapping issued from the kitchenette. Claire looked up from the map and was greeted by the whiteboard.

What are you doing?

Claire looked back toward the map. "Looking for the nearest hospital."

After a moment, the tapping resumed. Claire looked up again.

Why?

"Because you insist on having that baby. And we can't do that here."

Carrie scowled as her finger tapped the board again.

Why?

"Because home birthing died with the last hippie," Claire said as she folded the map, "And he died with everyone else during the Spread."

Claire stood and crossed the room to the breakfast bar.

Carrie wiped the board with her sleeve as her eyes remained fixed on Claire.

"Just because you and I are immune, it doesn't mean that your baby will be."

The corners of Carrie's eyes were becoming wet. Claire's voice softened.

"Before the *Book of Revelations* became a best seller, I was a nurse. I sat in on a few deliveries. I know how this works."

Carrie looked up at her, eyes wide as a fawn's. Claire's hand closed around Carrie's.

"You have to trust me."

Carrie's fingers guided the marker across the board. She flipped it as Claire read.

We're safe here.

It was Claire's turn to shake her head.

"No. We're not. We saw this place from the road. We're burning a fire to stay warm. That's a bad combination. We have to move on. Soon. Understand?"

Carrie slowly wiped the board clean.

"Carrie?"

The pen hovered above the board as Carrie looked up at Claire.

"We will go to the hospital. You will have this baby."

Claire's hand reached forward and her fingertips touched Carrie's cheeks.

"And he will be beautiful."

Carrie bit her lip as she looked down at the board and wrote. She flipped the board.

She will be beautiful.

Claire's laughter was uncontrollable.

The Spread: Day 258

Claire woke in a tangle of sweat soaked sheets. Her breath caught in her throat. Morning sunlight flared in her eyes. Guilt swelled in her chest.

In the end, she had buried her husband.

She had buried her son.

The graves that came after were the hardest to dig. No matter how she rationalized it, each time the shovel had moved earth, she had been burying the promise of *hope*.

And just like the Howlers, that promise had returned.

Back from the dead.

The Spread: Day 276

Sunlight blazed off of the axe blade as it swung downward and split the log. Claire's hand clenched up on the handle as she raised it again and buried it in the stump. She looked down at the split wood and decided that it would be enough for another few weeks.

Claire bent as she began to collect the wood. Her arms were beginning to fill when a humming sound filled the air. She frowned.

Humming wasn't the right word. Something deeper, further away. Claire's eyes widened.

The wood clattered across the ground as she sprinted toward the cabin. Her boots ground the soft earth as she leaped the porch rail and charged up the steps.

Carrie looked up from the counter as the door burst open and Claire stormed into the cabin, grabbing the binoculars that hung on a peg next to the door. Before Carrie could react, Claire was back outside on the porch.

The truck was more primer than paint, but it had once been blue. It was traveling at a steady pace along the highway. Claire's finger rolled the focus wheel as she attempted to count the occupants. Judging from the size of the cab, it couldn't be more than three people. She continued to track the truck as Carrie stepped through the door behind her.

Carrie tapped Claire's shoulder.

"Not now," Claire said as she watched the truck disappear behind a thick screen of trees. It had showed no signs of slowing.

Carrie's hand clutched Claire's shoulder.

"It's okay," Claire said as she turned. "I don't think they saw—"

Claire was a second too late as she reached for Carrie. The pregnant woman's knees buckled before Claire had a full understanding of the situation. Claire's hands closed around empty space as Carrie fell back into the cabin. She grunted as she hit the floor. Claire dropped to her knees as Carrie's eyes rolled back into her head.

Carrie's breathing was ragged.

Claire leaned forward.

"CARRIE?!"

Claire's hand was wet.

She looked down at her hand. It was splayed on the floor near Carrie's thigh. A pool of fluid was seeping through the pregnant woman's pants. Claire looked from her hand to Carrie.

The younger woman's eyes mirrored the panic in her own.

The sun had almost set. Carrie lay on her side wearing nothing but an oversized T-shirt. A blanket had been pulled up to her chest. Claire stood at the foot of the bed sorting through the remaining towels. The pile at her feet were soaked through with a mixture of fluids, not the least of which was blood.

Claire set the towels aside as she stepped around the bed and placed a hand on Carrie's sweaty forehead.

"Breathe easy. Okay?" Claire said in as level a voice as she could muster. "We can do this. Right?"

Carrie scribbled on her board in between ragged breaths.

Do I have a choice?

Claire looked through the slotted blinds at the disappearing sun. "I don't think we do."

Claire knew the drill from her life before the Spread. She had done a clinical in Maternity. She'd only practiced as a nurse for two years before her son was born. After that, her husband had supported the family. It was a natural transition, Mac was a good provider and Claire was a lousy nurse. In the end, she had done what she could to provide for her family after the Spread, but it wasn't enough.

This time would be different.

Claire ripped open the plastic covering a syringe and grabbed a small bottle of alcohol from the medical bag. She was halfway across the living room when she stopped cold.

It was a soft sound. Familiar. The muffled slamming of a car door.

Or a truck.

Claire dropped the syringe and the alcohol. She darted over to the fireplace and scooped up a bucket of water sitting on the floor. In one swift motion, Claire doused the fire, dropped the bucket and disappeared into the hall.

Claire barreled through the doorway, but Carrie was barely aware of her. She was clutching her belly, her eyes were closed. Sweat ran along her exposed flesh.

Inside Claire a switch flipped. She snapped off the camp lantern and plunged the room into darkness. Carrie groaned.

But Claire was gone.

Claire careened around the corner into the living room as the door began to open. The shadow of a large man fell into the center of the widening swath of moonlight. Claire swept up the shotgun by the fireplace as the door swung inward.

There was no thought. No consideration. Later, Claire would add up the factors. They hadn't knocked. They had waited until dark. He was holding a pistol.

If those facts had been different, it would not have changed her course of action. A cold fact in the world of the dead.

Claire pulled the trigger. The shotgun blast was thunderous in the small space. Orange flames flashed. Claire worked the pump and fired again.

The first blast disintegrated the man's head in a shower of blood and bone. The second blast shredded his chest and propelled him back into his companion. The mangled corpse crumpled onto the porch as the smaller man pitched backward over the rail.

Claire was moving forward. Her boots slipped in pools of blood as she stepped onto the porch and trained the shotgun over the rail. The smaller man was pushing himself to his feet in the moonlight.

The man looked like he had passed boyhood by only a few years. The pistol he held looked too large for his hand and his cocked cap cast an irregular shadow across his youthful, innocent features.

"Wait—" he croaked.

Claire fired, and the man's boyish face was stripped of flesh in the furnace of the shotgun blast. The man's knees buckled. He pitched forward, his split brainpan leaking into the hungry West Virginia soil.

Claire dropped the empty shotgun and pulled a pistol from her waistband. Her attention was now focused on the truck parked outside the cabin. Its primer-covered fenders shone in the moonlight, but the cab remained obscured in shadows.

The steps creaked as she descended the porch, the pistol held steady in front of her.

Claire closed the distance between her and the truck with a practiced efficiency. Occasionally her eyes flicked toward the trees. Dark shadows danced there, empty threats from ages past. The cries of dead coal miners and loggers who had given their lives to an unforgiving land.

Claire focused her attention back on the truck. Sometimes the cries of the dead were closer than you thought.

She reached the truck and rose from her half crouch as she rounded the fender. Claire spun around the passenger's side and leveled the pistol at the cab. Beyond the window, the inside of the truck was empty. Claire sighed. She lowered the pistol as she stepped away from the truck.

Mistake.

Cold steel pressed against Claire's neck. The sound of a hammer being drawn echoed along the ridge. The voice that followed was thick and full of satisfaction.

"What do we have here?"

Claire turned. She stared at the enormous dark figure holding an equally large pistol. Claire searched for the eyes of her executioner. She had hoped that the last thing she would see would be something… human. Some glimmer of what mankind had once been. Some glimmer of something that even she had lost.

Claire saw only shadow. Then something else.

Something moved in the darkness behind the figure.

Claire smiled.

"Are those your last words?"

The large pistol dipped slightly.

"What?"

Claire did not flinch when the gunshot boomed in the night air. Blood splattered her face as the man's pistol plummeted to the ground. The man's shattered face fell forward into the dirt as his lifeless body collapsed.

Claire turned toward the porch.

The revolver tumbled from Carrie's hand as she fell to her knees. Carrie's glistening eyes wavered as they stared into Claire's.

Claire felt her heart rise. That thing that most men had lost, the thing she feared she had lost. It was there in Carrie's eyes. And it was worth fighting for.

The howling began in some far-off valley. Maybe in a trailer park. Maybe in a holler beyond that. Both women heard it and understood with a certainty colder than death.

The gunshots had alerted them.

The Howlers were coming.

The Spread: Day 277

Clouds had begun to roll across the sky toward the retreating sun. The wind picked up speed, causing the trees to sway drunkenly. Carried with the wind was an eerie chorus, queer sounds that echoed both human pain and lamented its loss. The world was slipping into shadows and darkness.

A storm was coming.

The interior of the cabin was as dark as pitch. No light from the outside world permeated its walls. Claire drove the final nail in the plank and stepped back to admire her handiwork in the lamplight.

All of the windows and doors were now boarded shut, but even though the cabin was fortified, it was not soundproofed. The chilling cries of the Howlers seeped through the walls and into her bones.

Claire shivered.

There were a lot of them. Too many.

She set the hammer on the coffee table and picked up the lantern as she turned to check on Carrie.

Something was very wrong with Carrie's pregnancy. There was too much blood. It was too thick. Carrie's shirt was soaked through with sweat, and her body was trembling slightly, uncontrollably.

Claire knelt beside the bed as she stroked a few strands of hair away from Carrie's damp face. The two women looked into one another's eyes.

Carrie's hand flexed as she scrawled on the whiteboard propped on the nightstand.

Something's wrong.

"Nothing's wrong," Claire reassured her. "You're just missing the best part of giving birth. The drugs."

Claire offered a smile that the younger woman ignored.

Baby not right. Carrie panted. *Twisted.*

Claire inhaled. It was breeching.

"I've done this before," Claire lied. "We can fix it."

Carrie's wet hand closed around Claire's. Her eyes were hopeful.

Promise?

"Promise."

Carrie released Claire's hand as she swiped the whiteboard. It clattered to the floor. Carrie wrote on the night stand.

Are they close?

A soft thump sounded from somewhere in the darkness beyond the hallway. It was followed by another.

Claire's eyes grew hard.

"They're here."

There were only a few outside the cabin. Claire heard a handful of whines and cries. It was a hollow, reedy sound. Forlorn when alone, ominous in a chorus.

Claire counted ammunition in preparation for a very ominous evening.

The rain had picked up. It battered the roof as she checked her watch. It was well past sunset. The rest of the Howlers would arrive soon. It would be a long night.

Claire glanced at the fireplace. The cabin was cold and dark. The comfort of fire was for a different world, one that had come full circle. Predators and prey.

Claire loaded the shotgun as she watched the door.

Carrie wailed as she rolled onto her side. Beyond the boards covering the windows of the bedroom, the glass shattered. The sounds of the storm flooded the room. Wind, rain and thunder intertwined into a maelstrom of noise.

Beneath the fury of Mother Nature was a sound that was much more insidious. A sound that was eternally longing. A sound that was hungry.

The howling.

They had arrived at the cabin in force. Too many to count. Legion.

Claire stood in the kitchenette, her arms propped on the breakfast bar, the shotgun in her hands.

It was only a matter of time.

The boards across the door splintered and cracked as it slammed inward. The wind wailed as it whipped the sounds of the dead through the onslaught of pouring rain. The first Howler stepped through the door.

The rain had done the creature no favors. Much of its dead flesh had begun to slough off of its withered and split muscles. Maggots infested its rotting organs, slick with rainwater. The water had dislodged them and they wriggled out of the cavity that had once been its torso.

Its face was worse. Its lower jaw was broken and rotting. Worms writhed where its nose had been and a single eye rolled in a lidless socket. It reeked of decay, and the noise that came from its torn throat sounded like a cry from the belly of Hell.

The shambling thing stepped on its own liver after the organ plopped to the floor. The liver squished and popped beneath the Howler's tattered loafer. The creature did not notice as it turned toward Claire.

In another life, this sight would have sent her reeling into madness. But not in this one. In this life, the vision of living death in front of Claire was not a remarkable specimen.

She shot it in the head.

The Howler's head exploded like a balloon filled with black pus. Ichor and gore fantailed across the walls as the creature dropped to the floor. Claire chambered another round as two more stumbled through the doorway. There were so many more behind them.

Claire fired again and the shotgun blast licked flames as it disintegrated another head. Claire pumped the shotgun and squeezed the trigger. Bits of bone and rot were ripped out of the third Howler's neck. The creatures dropped onto the floor next to the first.

More of the undead shambled through the doorway. Slick with rain and putrefaction, howling with a hunger that knew no satiation, they moved toward the kitchenette. Claire dropped the first shotgun and picked up the second.

Claire fired, chambered and fired again. Two more went to the floor as she rendered their skulls into pulp. She fired the last round and watched the Howler on the porch flip backward into the throng.

She dropped the shotgun and picked up the two pistols lying on the breakfast bar. More Howlers poured through the open door. Claire aimed high and began pulling the triggers. One bullet caught one of the living dead in an empty eye socket and split the back of its skull. Strings cut, it buckled.

The second Howler stumbled over the bodies as a bullet grazed its cheek, tearing away loose, rotting flesh. In an astonishing feat of lifeless agility, the creature kept its balance.

It lurched into the kitchen.

Claire did not hesitate. She leapt and rolled over the breakfast bar, landing on her feet as more Howlers poured into the cabin. Claire spun to face them and took a step toward the hallway.

Her boot slipped as it burst a plump coil of loose entrails. Claire watched the room upend as she fell backwards onto the floor. The air exploded from her lungs as one of the pistols slipped from her hand.

Claire blinked away starbursts. They were replaced by visions of the encroaching dead. Her hand groped for the missing pistol. It closed around something else.

Claire scrambled to her feet and swung the hammer. It collided with the nearest Howler's temple and the living corpse's head imploded. Sweat poured down Claire's neck as she swung the hammer again and buried it in another Howler's forehead. A loud crunch accompanied the blow. The Howler stumbled backwards and the hammer, embedded in its brain, went with it.

Claire spun and fired the pistol as she darted down the hallway.

The Howlers continued to crowd the living room of the cabin.

Carrie was mewling as Claire braced the door to the bedroom. Claire glanced over at the bed as she finished situating the dresser in front of the door. The sheets were saturated with blood. Carrie's eyes had rolled back in her head, and the veins in her neck were threatening to burst through the skin.

Claire stepped away from the door as it shuddered in its frame. She glanced at the shotgun leaning in the corner and did the math.

The door wouldn't hold for too long. The ammunition was limited and even if every shot hit its mark, they would be overrun in a matter of minutes. However, Howlers were mindless herd animals. They were like lemmings. By now, most of them would have moved to the front of the cabin. The window next to the bed faced the rear. With the storm raging outside in the dark, the two women had a chance of slipping away undetected.

It was time to deliver the baby.

Fast.

Claire bent over the end of the bed, her words barely audible over the storm and the unnatural choir in the hallway.

"Carrie, the baby has breeched. I need to reach inside and turn it."

Carrie's response was to arch her back and let out an whine that was far more disturbing than anything the undead could utter. It caused the the flesh on Claire's neck to ripple.

Claire composed herself as the door shuddered again.

"Okay."

She reached forward and peeled the blood soaked sheet away from Carrie's thighs. The sheet slipped from Claire's fingers as she stared, slack-jawed.

Carrie's distended belly looked ready to burst. Dark veins pulsed beneath the taut skin, and her thighs were black with blood that had pooled under the flesh. Claire felt her gorge rise.

Claire took a step back. She knew that they were far beyond a simple breech. Deep in the shadows of her mind, a voice whispered an ugly scenario.

A *miscarriage. Death in the womb.*

Behind Claire, the frame of the door cracked. They were out of time. Claire didn't have a scalpel, nor any real training.

Nor did she have any options.

She pulled a knife from her belt and stepped around the bed. Carrie's belly throbbed as the young woman groaned. She had bitten through her lip, but her panicked eyes remained fixed on Claire.

"I'm going to have to perform a C-section," Claire said as she stared directly at Carrie. "It's going to hurt."

Carrie did her best to nod.

"A lot."

Claire turned and leaned over Carrie's quivering belly. She attempted to steady her hand as she brought the knife down. The howling reached a fever pitch outside the buckling door. The tip of the knife touched the soft flesh beneath Carrie's navel.

Carrie's stomach split open like a rotting fruit. Black ooze, blood, and organs spilled over the edges of the widening tear as Claire screamed and dropped the knife.

Something was moving inside the grisly cavity that was once her belly. Claire turned numb as she watched the infant struggle to free itself from its mother.

It was a perversion. It had died before becoming fully formed. Its bloated flesh was wet with Carrie's blood and bruised beneath. One hand had failed to develop. It had no eyes. Part of its skull was collapsed.

It had teeth.

The infant thing began to chew on the fleshy soup of organs and skin that hung near Carrie's pelvis. The final blessing of Carrie's life was that her mauled torso blocked her view of her newborn child's undead gluttony.

It did not block Claire's view. Inside her, something began to crack.

An anguished and pathetic sound issued from Carrie's ruined throat. Tears streamed down the dying woman's cheeks as her hands clutched the soiled sheets.

The door splintered again. It did not register with Claire. Her hand coiled around the shotgun. Carrie's wide eyes watched as Claire brought the weapon to her shoulder and curled her finger around the trigger. Claire looked down the barrel and fixed her eyes on Carrie's. She expected to see fear, desperation or even relief.

The younger woman's eyes were pools of sorrow. Pools of unimaginable depth.

Claire felt her eyes begin to water. She did not blink.

"I'm sorry."

She pulled the trigger. Fire flashed from the barrel and the child was shredded into ribbons of soft flesh. A geyser of blood, bone and skin—some her child's, some her own—splattered across Carrie's face.

Her eyes did not close.

The tears came for Claire as she felt something. Something important. Inside her, a seam split. It was a tiny tear, but it was there. And that was where all unraveling began...with a tiny tear.

She pumped the shotgun and fired again. Carrie's head evaporated in a shower of blood. In the darkness to come, Claire would console herself with the fact that Carrie could not return.

It would be a small consolation.

The door shattered. The howling sounds filled the cabin as the living dead stumbled and staggered into the room. Their mouths were ravenous as their jagged teeth and broken nails dug into the soft feast of Carrie's corpse. Blood sluiced through their fingers and smeared their quivering lips.

Several of the Howlers wandered over to the open window. Outside, the storm had reached its peak. Wind whistled and thunder sounded above black clouds.

Somewhere beyond that, a broken and empty sound rose above the tempest.

In the dark, something howled.

BLACK FRIDAY

KARIN FULLER

Karin Fuller is a weekly newspaper columnist for the Sunday Gazette-Mail *in Charleston, West Virginia. Her stories have appeared in two horror anthologies (*Dark Tales of Terror *and* The Mothman Files*) and two general anthologies (*Mountain Magic: Spellbinding Tales of Appalachia *and* Stories from the Hearth: Heartwarming Tales of Appalachia*). Her work has also been published in a number of magazines, including* Family Circle *and* Woman's World. *Her fiction has twice won* Writer's Digest *national contests (in 2008 and 2012). She lives in South Charleston with her daughter Celeste and their collection of animals.*

Never dreamed I'd see you out here again, not after last year," Vince said.

He shifted the bags from the bench to the floor and gestured for Miller to sit.

"I still contend it was a clean hit," Miller said. "That Xbox was in my cart."

Vince laughed.

"In your cart, yeah, but still in her hand at the time," he said.

Miller shrugged. "Minor detail."

"You're lucky she didn't whap you with her cane," said Vince.

"What time did you get here?" Miller asked.

"A little before 3 a.m. If the weather hadn't been so nasty, she'd have insisted on earlier, but there was no way I was standing in line for five hours in that mess. Two was enough."

"Seems like a much bigger crowd," said Miller. "Didn't think the deals in the paper were even all that good, but you wouldn't know it from the way people are acting. They're even buying up stuff that isn't on sale."

"I noticed that, too," said Vince. "It's like everyone forgot about the recession, especially Mags. Just look at all this stuff."

"I've already made two runs to the car," said Miller. "Might have to run some of it home if she buys too much more."

"Truth is, if it wasn't such a pain lugging all this around, I'd be out there with her. I'm just—how was it your grandpa used to say?—oh yeah. I'm et up with it. Caught up in the frenzy. Been whipping out my MasterCard like it's a pistol and I'm in the old West."

"I'll watch your bags if you'll come back in a bit and do the same for me," Miller said.

Vince was half standing before Miller had hardly finished speaking the words. He clapped his friend on the back.

"Fifteen minutes," he said. "That's all I need."

"No problem."

"Finally got another sitter," the man in the expensive-looking black suit said, as he tapped the security monitor.

"One down, but one up," said the other man, who was dressed just as nicely.

The mall benches were normally a hot commodity on Black Friday, with most occupied by tired-looking husbands surrounded by bags. But not this year.

"It's working even better than we anticipated. Looks like we might have our answer to the president's prayers."

"That's a mighty big leap you're taking. Remember how much this product was rushed. We don't yet know...."

First Suit held up his hand to stop the words, then put his finger to his lips.

"I won't listen to your negativity. Not today."

Second Suit leaned closer to the monitor, shook his head. "Lady right there just put something back," he said.

"And we got ourselves two more sitters," said the first.

"Time for an increase?"

"Believe so." He turned the valve on the tank. The output changed from whisper to hiss.

Miller was clearly agitated. It had been forty minutes since Vince had left, claiming all he needed was fifteen.

"Should just leave his packages," Miller muttered. Except his own wife had been by and added eight bags to his stack. There was no lugging that, not alone.

He'd never been much of a shopper, had often argued against traveling all the way into town to waste a day at the mall, especially a day during the first week of deer season. But he'd already gotten his buck, and it had been a fine one. Worthy of mounting. And that had left him feeling generous enough to get up at the crack of midnight and drive the nearly two hours it took to arrive at the nearest mall.

Miller looked at his watch again. Another minute had passed. He cursed under his breath, imaging all the deals he was missing out on.

And then, there he was. Vince was jogging toward him, laden down with so many shopping bags he was banging into people left and right.

"I'm so, so sorry," Vince said. "I don't know what came over me. It was like I was—*Har! Har!*—trying to singlehandedly end the recession."

Miller was standing, looking almost frantically from one store to the next.

"Don't forget your Macy's coupon," Vince said. "They were trying to limit one to a customer, but a fight broke out."

"That what the sirens were?" Miller asked.

"No, this just happened. That was something else."

A pair of mall cops raced by, followed moments later by two state police.

Vince gave Miller a light shove. "Get moving. I kept you long enough."

Without another word, Miller headed for Macy's.

"I think you need to back it off a bit," Second Suit said. He tapped two of the monitors with his pen. "Looks like they've got these under control, but it's clearly too much."

First Suit was smiling as he looked from one monitor to the next, to the next.

"Minor altercations," he said. "Same stuff happens every year, without our assistance."

"These aren't lab rats," said Second Suit. "I think we should back it off."

First Suit stared him straight in the eye, then reached for the valve and twisted it hard.

And the hiss turned to a roar.

***

Vince and Miller had carried their bags to the car, filling each beyond reason. Boxes had to be smashed or discarded to get them to fit. But they had. And now the men were back inside. Ready for more.

"This must be how it feels to be a woman," Vince said.

Miller laughed a little too hard.

"Food court?" he asked. "I'm suddenly starved."

"Not sure anything's open, but I'm game," said Vince.

The men stepped on the escalator behind a woman with an almost cartoonishly ample behind. Voluptuous in the Jessica Rabbit sort of way.

"Wouldn't mind having me a bite of that ass," Miller said.

"Do it," said Vince.

"Do what?"

"Take a bite. Just grab hold of her hips and get yourself a mouthful. Sink your teeth right on in."

Miller was surprised when a bit of drool escaped the corner of his mouth. "You're insane," he said.

"You won't, I will," said Vince.

And he did.

The woman screamed.

As did many others. Men and children as well. All throughout the mall. There was screaming and yelling.

And gnashing of teeth.

"Holy crap! Shut it off!" Second Suit yelled.

But he need not have yelled. The tank had been emptied. Test Tank 2719 from Genesis Clinic had hissed its final belch into the mall's ventilation system.

First Suit was dragging his fingers through his hair, pacing the length of the room. Second was looking anxiously from one screen to the next.

"They're…biting each other," he said.

"Consuming," First Suit said, without even needing to turn to look at the screens. If he had, he'd have seen the gore from hundreds of shoppers driven mad by the gas.

It had only been meant to increase their appetite for simple consumer goods. To get people to open their wallets again, to not be so blasted careful about every dollar they spent. Stores were closing. People were losing their jobs. The country needed its people to start spending again.

To start consuming.

Just not each other.

CALLING DEATH

JONATHAN MABERRY

Jonathan Maberry is a New York Times *bestselling author, multiple Bram Stoker Award winner, and Marvel Comics writer. His latest novels are* Assassin's Code, *a vampire-themed techno-thriller from St. Martin's Press and* Flesh & Bone, *the third installment in his multi-award-winning zombie series for teens (now in development for film). His previous novels include* Rot & Ruin, Dust & Decay, Patient Zero, The Wolfman, *and others. He has written extensively about vampires and other monsters of myth and legend in his nonfiction books:* Vampire Universe, They Bite!: Endless Cravings of Supernatural Predators, Wanted Undead or Alive: Vampire Hunters and Other Kick-Ass Enemies of Evil, *and others. He's the editor/co-author of* V Wars, *a vampire-themed anthology from IDW. He was a featured expert on The History Channel special* Zombies: A Living History. *Since 1978 he's sold more than 1200 magazine feature articles, 3000 columns, two plays, greeting cards, song lyrics, and poetry. He teaches the Experimental Writing for Teens class, is the founder of The Writers Coffeehouse, and co-founder of The Liars Club. Jonathan lives in Bucks County, Pennsylvania, with his wife, Sara Jo. Find out more at* www.jonathanmaberry.com.

It weren't the wind," said Granny Adkins.

The young man perched on the edge of the other rocker, head tilted to lift one ear like a startled bird, listening to the sound. He was stick-thin and beaky-nosed, and Granny thought he looked like a heron, the way they looked when they were ready to take sudden flight. "Are you sure?"

"Sure as maybe," said Granny, nodding out to the darkness. "The wind fair howls when it comes 'cross the top of Balder Rise. Howls like the Devil himself."

"Sounds like a howl to me," said the young man. "What else could you call it?"

Granny sucked in a lungful of smoke from her Pall Mall, held it inside for a five count, and then stuck out her lower lip to exhale in a vertical line up past her face. She didn't like to blow smoke on guests, and there was a breeze blowing toward the house. A chime made from old bent forks and chicken bones stirred and tinkled.

She squinted with her one good eye—the blue one, not the one that had gone milky white when a wasp stung her there forty years back—and considered how she wanted to answer the young man.

Before she spoke the sound came again. Low, distant, plaintive.

She left her initial response unspoken for a moment as they sat in the dark and listened.

"There," she said softly, "you hear it?"

"Yes, but it still sounds like a—"

"No, son. That ain't what I meant. Can you hear the sound? The moan?"

"Yes," he said, leaning into the wind, tilting one ear directly into its path.

"Now," said Granny, "can you hear the wind, too?"

"I...." he began, but let his voice trail off. Granny waited, watching his face by starlight, looking for the moment when he did hear it. His head lifted like a bird dog's. "Yes.... I hear it."

They listened to the moan. It was there, but the wind was dying off again, and the sound was fainter, thinner.

"That, um, moan," the young man said tentatively. "It's not the wind. You're right."

She nodded, satisfied.

"It's a separate sound," continued the young man. "I—I think it's being carried on the wind." He looked to her for approval.

She gave him another nod. "That's another thing about living up here in the hills," she said, tying this to their previous conversation. "When you live simple and close to the land, you don't get as blunt as folks in the cities do. You hear things, see things the way they are, not the way you s'pose them to be. You notice that there are more things around you, and that they're there all the time."

The young man nodded, but he was half distracted by the moans, so Granny let him listen for a spell.

His name was Joshua Tharp. A good name. Biblical first name, solid last name. A practical name, which Granny always appreciated because she thought that a name said a lot about a person. She would never have come out onto the porch if he'd had a foreign-sounding name, or a two first-name name, like Simon Thomas. Everyone Granny ever knew with two Christian names was a scoundrel, and half in the Devil's bag already. However, this boy had a good name. There had been Tharps in this country going back more generations than Granny could count, and she knew family lines four decades past the War of Northern Aggression. Her own people had been here since before America was America.

So Joshua Tharp was a decent name, and well worth a little bit of civility. He was a college boy from Pittsburgh who was willing to pay attention and treat older folks with respect. Wasn't pushy, neither, and that went a long way down the road with Granny. When he'd shown up on her doorstep, he took off his hat and said "ma'am'" and told her that he was writing a book about the coal miners in Pennsylvania and North Carolina and was using his own family as the thread that sewed the two states together.

Now they were deep into their third porch-sitting, and the conversation had wandered a crooked mile through late afternoon and on into the full dark of night. Talking about Granny and her kin, and about the Tharps here, and the Tharps that had gone on. Joshua was a Whiskey Holler Tharp, though, but there was no one left around here closer than third cousin with a couple of removes, so everyone told him to go see Granny Adkins.

"Hell, son," said Mr. Sputters at the post office. "Granny's so old, she remembers when God bought these mountains from the devil, and I do believe the Good Lord might have been short-changed on the deal. You want to know about your forebears—and about what happened when the mine caved in—well, you go call on ol' Granny. But mind you bring your full set of manners with you, 'cause she won't have no truck with anyone who gives her half a spoonful of sass."

Granny knew that Sputters said that because the old coot phoned and told her. Wrigley Sputters was a fool, but not a damn fool.

Come calling is exactly what young Joshua did. He came asking about his kin. That was the first day, and even now they'd only put a light coat of paint on that subject. Granny was old, and she was never one to be in a hurry to get to the end of anything, least of all a conversation.

Joshua's people, the true Whiskey Holler Tharps, were a hard working bunch. Worked all their lives in the mines, boy to old man. Honest folk who didn't mind coming home tired and dirty, and weren't too proud to get down on their knees to thank the good Lord for all His blessings.

Shame so many of them died in that cave-in. Lost a lot of good and decent folks that day. Forty-two grown men and seven boys. The Devil was in a rare mood that day, and no mistake. Guess he didn't like them digging so deep.

Granny cut a look at the young man as he sat there studying on the sounds the night brought to him. He was making a real effort to do it right, and that was another good sign. He came from good stock, and it's nice to know that living in a big city hadn't bred the country out of him.

"I can't figure it out," said Joshua, shaking his head. "What is it?"

Granny crushed out her cigarette and lit another one, closing her eyes to keep the flare of the match from stealing away her night vision. She lit the cigarette by touch and habit, shook the match out, and dropped it into an empty coffee tin that had an inch of rain water in it.

She said, "What's it sound like?"

That was a test. If the boy still had too much city in him then there would be impatience on his face or in his voice. But not in Joshua's. He nodded at the question and once more tilted his head to listen.

Granny liked that. And she liked this boy. But after a few moments, Joshua shook his head. "I don't know. It's almost like there are two sounds. The, um, moan, and something else. Like a faint clinking sound."

"Do tell," she said dryly, but with just enough lift to make it a question.

"Like…maybe the wind is blowing through something. A metal fence, or…I don't know. I hear the clink and the moan, but I can't hear either of them really well." He gave a nervous half-laugh. "I've never heard anything like it."

"Never?"

"Well, I…don't spend a lot of time out of doors," he confessed. "I guess I haven't learned how to listen yet. Not properly, anyhow. I know Granddad used to talk about that. About shaking off the city so you could hear properly. But until now I don't think I ever really understood what he was saying."

Another soft moan floated over the trees. Strange and sad it was, and Granny sighed. She watched Joshua staring at the darkness, his face screwed up in concentration.

Granny gestured with her cigarette. "What do you think it might be?"

"Is it…some kind of animal?"

"What kind of animal would make a sound like that, do you suppose?"

They sat for almost two minutes, waiting between silences for the wind to blow. Joshua shook his head.

"Some kind of cat?"

That surprised Granny, and now she listened, trying to hear it through his ears. "It do sound a might like a cat," she conceded, then chuckled. "But not a healthy one. Had a broke-leg bobcat get his leg caught in a bear trap once and hollered for a day and a night."

"So—is that what it is? A wounded bobcat? Is that clinking sound a bear trap?"

Granny exhaled more smoke before she answered. "No, son, that ain't what it is."

"Then…?"

She chuckled. "It'll keep. You interrupted your ownself, son. You was asking me a question before we heard yonder call."

He nodded, but it was clear that he was reluctant to leave the other topic unfinished. Granny felt how false her smile was. The mysteries out in the dark would keep. Might have to keep without the other shoe ever dropping.

"I…." Joshua began, fishing for the thread of where they'd been. "Right…we were talking about the day Granddad left for Pittsburgh. He said it was because there was no work, but he never really talked about that. And when he moved to Pittsburgh he always worked in a foundry. He never wanted to go back to the mines."

"No…I daresay old Hack Tharp would never set foot in a mine again. 'Specially not in these hills, and probably nowhere. Lot of folks around here with the same thought. Those that stayed here gave up mining. I know men who wouldn't lift a pick-axe to go ten feet into a gold mine, not after what happened. Hack was one of 'em."

"Tell me about him. He died when I was ten, so I never had a grown-up conversation with him. Never got to really know him. What was he like?"

Granny smiled, and this time the smile was real. "Hack was a bull of a man, with shoulders from here to there and hands like iron. A good man to know and a handsome man to look at. Hack worked himself up to foreman down in the Hangood Mine. Swung a pick-axe for twenty long years down in the dark before he was promoted, and still sucked coal gas for twenty more as the foreman. The men liked him, no one crossed him, and his word was good on anything he put it to. Can't say as much about a lot of people, and can't say half as much about most."

Joshua nodded encouragingly.

"But Hack up and moved," said Granny. "He was the first, and over the years more'n sixty families have left the holler. Ain't no more than a hundred people left on this whole mountain, and I know of four families that are fixin' to leave before long. Might be that I'll be the last one here come next year, if I'm even here a'tall."

"People started leaving because the mine closed?"

"They started leaving after the mine closed. This place went bad on us that day, and it ain't ever gone to get better."

The moaning wind and the soft metallic clank drifted past the end of her statements almost as if it was a statement itself.

Joshua cleared his throat. "Do you remember when Granddad left? I got the impression it was pretty soon after the disaster."

"It were on the third Sunday after the cave-in. Hack packed up only what would fit into that old rattle-rust Ford pickup of his and drove off. Never came back, never called, never wrote. But...before he left, though, he came to say goodbye to ol' Granny." She sighed. "'Course I wasn't Granny back then. Just a young, unmarried gal who thought the sun rose in the morning 'cause it wanted to see Hack Tharp."

"Pardon me if this is rude, but...were you and Granddad sweethearts?"

Granny blew out some smoke. "There was no official understanding between us, you understand. Every girl in five counties wanted to catch Hack's eye, but for a while there I had some hopes. Maybe Hack did, too, 'cause I was the only one he lingered long enough to say farewell to. And, I blush to say it to a young feller like you, but I was something back then. You wouldn't know it now, lookin' at this big pile o' wrinkles, but I could turn a few heads of my own. Thought for a while that Hack might have been charmed enough to stay 'cause I asked him, but the cave-in plumb took all those thoughts out of his mind. He was set on leaving, and he knew that I never would."

"Even if he'd asked?"

She sighed. "There are some things more important than love, strange as it sounds. At least...I thought so back then. You see...I had a talent for the old ways. With a talent for dowsing and a collection of aunts who were teaching me the way things worked in the world. Herbs and healing and luck charms and suchlike. Some folks call us witches. Even seen it in books. Mr. Sputters at the post office showed me a book oncest called *Appalachian Granny Magic*. And I guess it's fair enough. Witch comes from some older word that means 'wise,' and that's all it is. Women who know such and such about things. My Aunt Tess was a fire witch. She could conjure a spark out of green wood with no matches and a word. My own mammy was the most famous healer in the holler. People'd come from all over with a sickness, or send a car for her to deliver a baby."

"I heard about that. Granddad told me a little. He said you could find water. He called you a dowser. Is that the right word?"

She nodded. "I been known to do that now and again. Mostly I make charms to ward off badness and evil. Half the rabbits in these hills walk with a limp since I started selling they's feet to ward off ill luck. And you can walk for two days and not find a soul who ain't wearing one of my snakeskin bags on their belts. Real toad's eyes in 'em, too, because fake charms don't stop nuthin'." She smiled. "Does that scare you, young Joshua? All this talk about witches?"

"Not as much as that sound does," he said, nodding to the night. "It's really creeping me out."

Granny puffed her cigarette.

"But the witches thing?" Joshua said. "No, I read up on that when I started researching this area for my book." He cleared his throat. "You were telling me about how Granddad came to say goodbye."

"So I was. Well...Hack Tharp stood four-square in my yard, not two paces from where I sit right now. 'Mary Ruth,' he said, 'I'm gone. I can't live here no more, not with all the dead hauntin' me. My brothers, they never had a chance. They was so obsessed with earning that bonus that they went crazy, picking and digging like the Devil was whipping them, and then that whole mountain just up and fell. And it went down fast, too. Killed 'em before they could git with God. I was right outside taking a smoke when the mouth of Hell opened up and swallowed those boys. I haven't had a night's sleep since it happened. And I won't ever sleep a night if I stay here.'"

"Weren't your fault," I told him. But Hack shook his head. 'I ain't saying it is. And I ain't losing sleep 'cause I feel guilty about being on this side of the grave when all my family was taken by death. No—the bosses killed all those men—killed my own brothers, two of my cousins. Killed sure as if they blew the mountain down with dynamite. Killed 'em by digging too deep in a played-out mine. Killed 'em by greed, and that's an evil thing. Greed's one of the bad sins, Mary Ruth, one of them seven deadly sins, and it made my brothers sell their souls to old Scratch himself.'"

"I didn't know Granddad was so religious. He never went to church when I was a kid. Not even on Easter and Christmas."

"I suppose," said Granny, "that he lost the knack. Seen a lot of it after the collapse, just like I seen a lot of folks suddenly hear the preacher's call before the dust even settled. Since then, though...well, ain't no one in this holler don't believe in the Devil anymore, so the unbelievers have started believing about God by default."

"Was there an investigation?" asked Joshua. "Did the authorities ever determine that the mining company was at fault?"

"Investigation?" Granny laughed. "You got a city boy's sense of humor, son. No, there weren't no investigation. And even if someone wanted to investigate there weren't no way to do it."

"Why not? I've read a lot about mining, and a structural engineer could do a walk-through look at the shoring systems, the drill angles, the geologist's assessment of the load bearing walls of the mountain and—"

"No one's ever going to do any of that."

"Why not?"

"'Cause they'd have to cut though a million tons of rock to take that look."

"They could just examine the areas dug out when the bodies were removed."

Granny studied him for a moment. "Your granddad didn't tell you?"

"Tell me what?"

She sighed. "Those dead men are still there, son. The company never dug them out. Nobody ever dug them out. That whole mountain's a tomb for all those good men."

Joshua stood up and stared at the darkness again, looking toward Balder Rise. The wind blew from that direction, carrying with it the soft moan. "God," he said softly.

"Oh, God didn't have nuthin' to do with what happened that day," said Granny. "Your granddad spoke true when he said that it were the evil greed of the mining company that brought the ceiling down. They dug too deep."

"That's something Granddad said a couple of times, and now you've said it twice. What's that mean exactly?"

"The mining company was fair desperate to stay in business, even though most of the coal had already been took from old Balder. They kept pushing and pushing to find another vein. Pushed and pushed the men, too, tempting 'em with promises of bonuses if they found that vein. Understand, boy, miners are always poor. It's really no kind of life. Working down there in the dark, bad air and coal dust, it's like you're digging your own grave."

The moan on the wind came again, louder, more insistent. The black trees seemed to bend under the weight of it.

"The company kept the pressure on. Everybody needed that vein, too, because the company owned everything. They owned the bank, which means they held the mortgage on ever'body's house, and that's the same like holding the mortgage on ever'body's souls." She shook her head. "No, a lot of folks thought the Devil himself was whispering in the ear of ever'body from the executives all the way down to the teenage boys pushing the lunch trolleys. Infecting them good-hearted and God fearing men with their own greed. Spreading sin like a plague. Makin' 'em dig too hard and too deep, with too much greed and hunger."

"Digging too deep, though, you keep saying that. Do you mean that they over-mined the walls or—"

"No, son," she said, "that ain't what Hack meant, and it ain't what I mean."

"Then, what?"

The moan came again, even louder. So loud that Joshua stood up and placed his palms on the rail so he could lean head and shoulders out into the night. Granny saw him shiver.

"You cold?" she asked, though it was a warm night,

"No," he said, without turning. "That sound…."

Granny waited.

"…it sounds almost like a person," Joshua continued. "It sounds like someone's hurt out there."

"Hurt? Is that really what it sounds like to you?"

"Well, it's something like that. I can hear the pain." He shot her a quick look. "Does that sound silly? Am I being a stupid city boy here or—"

"You don't sound stupid at all, son. That's one of the smartest things you said. You know what's happening?" she asked. "The city's falling clean off you."

He studied her.

"It's true," she said. "Your daddy might have been born in the city, and you might have been born and raised there, too, but you still got the country in you. You still got some of the hills in you. You get that from ol' Hack, and I bet he was always country no matter how many years he lived in the city, am I right or am I right?"

"You're right, Granny," said Joshua. "No one would ever have mistaken Granddad for anything except what he was. He…loved these mountains. He talked about how beautiful they are. How they smelled on a spring morning. How the birds would have conversations in the trees. How folks were simple—less complicated—but they weren't stupid. How he wished he could have stayed."

Granny closed her eyes for a moment, remembering Hack. Remembering pain. Remembering the horror of that collapse, and all the things that died that day. Those men, her love, this town.

"Is something wrong?" asked Joshua.

She opened her eyes and rocked back so she could look up at him. "Wrong?"

The moan cut through the air again. Louder still.

"I suppose you could say that nuthin's been right since that mine collapsed," she said, and Granny could hear the pain in her own voice. Almost as dreadful as the pain in that moan. "Close your eyes again and listen to that sound. Don't tell me what it ain't. Listen until you can tell me what it is."

Joshua closed his eyes and leaned once more on the rail, his head raised to lift his ears into the wind.

After a full minute, he said, "It sounds like a person…and that clinking sound…that's definitely something metal."

She waited.

Joshua laughed. "If it was Christmas I'd say it was Old Marley and his chain."

When Granny did not laugh, Joshua opened his eyes and turned to her.

"That's from the—"

"I know what it's from, son. And it ain't all that far from the mark." She sucked in some smoke. "Not a chain, though. Listen and tell me I'm wrong."

He listened.

"No, you're right. It's, um…sharper than that. But the echoes are making it hard to figure it out. Almost sounds like a bunch of little clinks, almost at once. That's why I thought it was a chain, you know, the links clinking as it blew in the wind."

"But it ain't a chain," she said, "and it ain't blowing in the wind. Ain't echoes, either."

There was a stronger gust of wind, and the moan was much louder now.

Joshua pushed off the rail and walked down into the yard. He stood with his hands cupped around his ears to catch every nuance of the sound. Granny chain dropped her cigarette butt into the empty coffee tin and lit another.

The moaning was so loud now that anyone could hear it. So loud that anyone could understand it, and Granny watched for the moment when Joshua understood. She'd seen it so many times. With friends, with her own daughter—who screamed and then ran inside the house to begin packing up her clothes and her babies. She hadn't come back.

Granny had seen a parade of people come through, stopping as Hack had stopped, wanting to say goodbye. Only one of them ever came back. Norm McPhee wandered back to the mountains after spending the last fourteen years in a bottle somewhere in Georgia. He came back to the holler, back to Balder, back to Granny's yard, and he stood there for an hour, his eyes filled with ghosts.

Then Norm had walked into the woods, found himself a quiet log to sit on, drank the rest of his bottle of who-hit-John, took the pistol from his pocket, and blew his brains all over the new blossoms on a dogwood tree.

Granny smoked her cigarette and wondered what Hack Tharp's grandson would do, because she could see his body language changing. He was slowly standing straighter. His hands fell slowly from behind his ears. His eyes were wide, and his mouth formed soundless words as he sought to speak the thoughts that his senses were planting in his head.

He turned to her. Sharp and quick, but his mouth wasn't ready to put voice to the thought that Granny could now see in the young man's eyes.

"I can hear them," he said at last.

Them.

"Yes," she said.

"It's not just one sound, and it's not an animal. There are a lot of them."

"Yes," Granny said again.

Something glistened on Joshua's face. Was it sweat?

"Granddad said that forty-nine people died that day. Mostly men, a few kids."

"Yes," she said once more.

"All of them digging down in the earth," said Joshua, and his voice sounded different. Distant, like he was talking to himself. Distant, like the wind. "All of them, digging like crazy." His eyes glistened. "What did Granddad say? You just told me…that those men were so obsessed with earning that bonus that they went crazy, picking and digging like the Devil was whipping them."

"And then that whole mountain just up and fell," agreed Granny softly.

"It killed them fast. Killed them before they could get with God."

She nodded.

"Like the mouth of Hell opened up and swallowed those boys," Joshua said, his voice thick, his eyes filled with bad, bad pictures. "God."

"I already said it," whispered Granny, "God didn't have nothing' to do with what happened."

The moans were constant now. The voices clear and terrible. The metallic clinks distinct.

Joshua laughed. Too quick and too loud. "Oh…come on! This is ridiculous. Granny, I don't mean any disrespect, but…come on. You can't expect me to believe any of this."

"I didn't ask you to."

That wiped the smile off his face.

"Granddad left because of this sound, didn't he?"

Granny didn't bother to answer that.

The moans answered it.

The clank of metal on rock answered it.

"No," said Joshua. "You want me to believe that they're still there, still down there in the dark, still…digging?"

Granny smoked her cigarette.

"That's insane," he said, anger in his voice now. "They're dead! They've been dead for years. Come on, Granny, it's insane. It's stupid."

"Son," she said, "I ain't told you none of that. I ain't told you nuthin' but to listen to the wind and tell me what you think that is."

The voices on the wind were filled with such anger, such pain.

Such hunger.

The incessant clank of pick-axes against rock were like punches, and Joshua actually yielded a step backward with each ripple of strikes. As if those pick-axes were hitting him. More wetness glistened on his face.

"Granny," he said in a hollow voice, "come on…."

Granny rocked in her rocker and smoked her cigarette.

"All these years?" asked Joshua, and she could hear how fragile his voice was. It had taken three weeks of the sound before Hack had up and left. A lot of folks had played their TV or radio loud and late to try and hide the sound.

One by one people left the mountain. Took some only months, took others years.

Joshua Tharp stood in the yard and winced each time the wind blew.

He won't last the night, she thought. He'll be in his car and heading back to the city before moonrise.

"All these years…digging…."

His eyes were suddenly wild.

"Has…has…the sound been getting louder all these years?"

Granny nodded. "Every night."

"Every night," echoed Joshua. He stood his ground, not knocked back by the ring of the pick-axes this time. Granny thought that either he found his nerve or he lost it entirely.

"I 'spect one of these days they'll dig they'selves out of that hole." She paused. "Out of Hell."

The picks rang in the night.

Again and again.

Then there was a cracking sound. Rock breaking off. Or breaking open.

Joshua and Granny listened.

There were no more sounds, clangs of pick-axes.

There was just the moans.

Louder now. Clearer.

So much clearer.

"God…." whispered Joshua.

"God had nuthin' to do with the collapse," said Granny. "And I expect he's got nuthin' to do with this."

The moans rode the night breeze.

So loud and clear.

TIMES IS TOUGH IN MUSKY HOLLER

JOHN SKIPP & DORI MILLER

Interesting story behind this story. Back in 1988, when John Skipp was editing the very first original post-Romero zombie anthology, Book of the Dead *(with Craig Spector), their good friend Dori Miller brought them a fucked-up little tale that Skipp did not buy, but thought was so conceptually brilliant that it haunted him ever since. When it came time to write for this anthology, 24 years later, Skipp abruptly remembered Dori's deranged scenario, wrote her an email, and asked if he could take a crack at it. The ensuing happy back-and-forth jam resulted in the hideous story that follows.*

John Skipp likes making crazy books and movies, laughing, long walks with his dog, and performing "Synchronized Drowning" events with close family and friends. He publishes a lot, as both writer and editor.

Dori Miller likes creating strange confections, wild herbalism, sound healing, writing streams of consciousness, existing with her Sacred Sphinx and perfecting her Persephone impression between worlds. This is her first published story.

Fear has a nasty odor about it. Especially in bulk, and in close quarters. Panic sweat takes on a harsher tang. Desperate tears have a weight you can taste more than smell.

Wet acid farts don't help much, neither, but they are unquestionably top of the bill. The air is tart and thick with sulfurous fumes that remind me just how close to Hell I am.

Down here in the tunnel, it's all cracking whips and clattering chaingang chains, us woefully whimperin' and groanin' through our metal choke collars as they drive and drag us, the Unlucky Dozen, down the corridor to our deaths.

I am #2 in Row Two. That's who I am, as of right this moment. They're keepin' it simple, God damn them, though my pitiful history's laid bare.

I should have been nicer to Lester. I know. More respectful. Should never have stole those chickens. Should never have rubbed up against that little girl, nor shot her dog and daddy.

I am so fucking scared.

There's a big crowd this morning, from the distant fairground sound of it. The biggest since God brought the hammer down, let Satan take over the show. Everybody's here. At least everyone accounted for, or so Leslianne (#2, Row Three) informed me. And as a hairdresser, she should know. It was her keen ear and yappity mouth that brought her to this sorry fate, beside me.

As we move down the tunnel, Lester M. Barkley's voice booms through the PA system above. *Blaloom, blaloom.* Can't understand a word he says, but the tone is half carny, half evangelic. And the intention is wholly clear.

He is whipping up the survivors—what four hundred or so remain—in a frenzy of community spirit mixed with old-time showmanship. Promising safety. Promising control.

Promising a spectacle they will not soon forget.

I picture the twelve of us, strung up like Christmas bulbs on nooses. From above me, to all sides, I hear cheering and suspect that it will not be as simple as that.

We do not know what is about to befall us.

We just know it is bound to be terrible indeed.

The man before me is tall, and I am sadly foreshortened, so I cannot see the three rows of chairs until we are passing among them. Twelve chairs. Three rows. Four chairs to a row. All equipped with their own chains, vertically straining upward to near-vanishing point.

"Sit the fuck down," says Ezra, my personal tormentor. It was his sister I molested, his dog I shot, his daddy who died, then rose up just enough to claim his eight-year-old daughter as she came to him in tearful lamentation.

I can expect no mercy from Ezra, do not even bother to beg. He straps me in, making sure it hurts.

"Oh me, oh my," he says. "How I love that country pie."

Leslianne is crying now, though I cannot see her. Most of us are. Why I don't, I cannot say. If I could move my neck more than a fraction of an inch to either side, I would bear witness to their sorrow.

Then from above us, the trap doors clatter open.

And we are hoisted aloft.

In weightlessness, the grinding of chains all but drowns out the wild cheering of the crowd. But louder it grows, as up and up we rise in tandem, writhing and screaming. Until brilliant sunlight strikes our faces.

And, blinking, we see what we've come to at last.

My head pops up from the scaffolding floor like a Whack-a-Mole, crunches to a halt as my shoulders strike wood and grind there, making me shriek till the yanking stops.

Then steady I hang. And before me is the back of the head of #1, Row Two.

Just beyond him, at floor level, are the hungry damned, slavering at their leashes. One for each row.

Sliced off at the knees.

So that all they can do is crawl.

To the left and the right, I recognize Jed and Clem Ziph. Two of our strongest and fiercest defenders, until they got bit and joined the other side. In hellish rebirth, they are muscular and fearsome. Jed is Row One. Clem is Row Three.

I cannot yet see which demon awaits me.

I cannot see Lester M. Barkley, but I hear his voice boom from the speakers, the words painfully clear now, echoing throughout the Musky Hollow State Fairgrounds and out into the hills.

"Dead no longer means dead and gone," he says, and the crowd knowingly moans in concordance. "Dead means dead and here. That's the tragic truth to which we all are adjusting, by stages.

"To the extent that we all work together—with great discipline, restraint, and strict adherence to the law—even the most lost among us can still contribute to the grander cause that is our ultimate survival...."

"GO FUCK YOURSELF!" screams #1, Row One.

"As for those who cannot or will not," Lester concludes with a flourish, "we bring you...*live pie!*"

And the leashes unleash, as the crowd goes wild.

There are roughly ten feet between the first row of heads and myself. Jed and Clem close the distance quick. By their arms, they pull forward, the air electric with cheers and screams.

Clem descends on his row's #1, begins to chew through to the skull. I bear witness from behind, see the blood and meat spraying.

Directly before me, blackened hands drape themselves around the back of the head of Row 2, #1. I never learned his name. I never will.

They do not let them move on till the faces are devoured completely.

Clem's the winner, to date.

To the extent that I can turn my head, I see him rottingly claw his way forward to Leslianne, her shrieks so much louder than my own that I can barely hear myself screaming.

Then I see the daddy that I done wrong, crawling directly toward me.

Now fear has a different smell, sun-ripe and rotten. It's the smell of death that has outstayed its welcome, overwhelming me from eight, six, then four feet away.

Sideways, up above, I see the motion picture screen that is projecting our demise for the hollering crowd. Far closer, I sense the digital cameras, here to capture every moment.

Then it all comes down to the jaws before me. The milky eyes. The clamoring hands. Coming closer and closer. Till Death's dank breath assails me.

Breathes into my nostrils.

Rips my nostrils away.

I scream, and he chews off my lips, first the top, then bottom, teeth grinding against mine as my tongue snakes out sluglike and is torn from my throat.

Then the shock, the merciful shock sets in, and I find myself going away.

As I die, something passes between us. An awful understanding, one shred of meat at a time.

It's the Devil, sayin', *Welcome home. They will all join us, most sooner than later. Lester. Ezra. All and sundry. All the world.*

I die, and am reborn in hunger.

Now the world smells just like me.

THE GIRL AND THE GUARDIAN

SIMON McCAFFERY

Simon's story, "Lifeboat," appeared in The Zombie Feed: Volume One *(Apex Publications). His other stories have also appeared in* Book of the Dead 2: Still Dead, Mondo Zombie, *and* Best New Zombie Tales Vols. 1 *and* 3. *Other credits include* Lightyear, PSYCHOS, *and* Best New Werewolf Tales. *He has a novella set to appear from Books of the Dead Press in early 2013.*

This one's for Angela and Alex

In the evening after the sun retreats behind West Virginia's blue Allegheny Mountains, the creature glides through the furnace-lit sky on huge gray wings to perch in this particular hickory tree, battered but unbending amid the more regal red spruce, so it can gaze into this hollow and through the window of the tarpaper cabin where the young human girl plays with her garage-sale dolls until her father returns from town to tuck her into bed.

On many nights this does not occur until fog invades the hollow and the moon is riding high above the scudding rafts of clouds.

Tonight is one of those nights; the air is clear but muggy and a mist has settled into the valley. The cabin is a patchwork of scavenged lumber, sheet metal, the obligatory tarpaper, and other odds and ends. The narrow turnaround is littered with garbage, scrap appliances, and the carcass of a 1974 Pontiac Grand Am that grins crazily from behind a screen of scrub.

The girl is dressed in her nightgown, serving imaginary tea to two dolls and assorted, much-loved stuffed animals. These toys are the girl's only companions. She has no siblings or nearby friends. She is five years old, but there is no money to attend preschool. No boys or girls from the town proper ever visit this secluded corner of the woods. No one comes calling except the occasional sheriff's deputy, game warden, or the stern young woman from social services.

The creature knows all of this just as it knows that the girl's name is LORI and that her father's blood pressure and liver are none too good and that a Mason jar containing four thousand dollars in cash and a paper wrapper of gold eagle coins is buried in the rich soil mixed with traces of bituminous coal, limestone, and shale beneath the decaying chicken coop behind the small pump house. Buried by the girl's dead grandfather, a treasure now long forgotten. And probably for the best, considering the father's appetites.

The creature gazes down, unblinking, ignoring the owls, hawks, and small woodland animals that scurry about their nocturnal business. It possesses no recognizably human context for any of this—intellectual or emotional—just as it does not know why, through millennia, it is periodically drawn from its plane of existence through a thin tear in reality to haunt the foothills of this once-primeval mountain forest. Or why it now sits for hours in the gloom of this lonesome place, wings folded against its broad back, watching the young girl with its red bicycle-reflector eyes. Occasionally it emits a hollow, high-pitched cry that registers at the very limit of the human auditory range, a buzzing insectile sound like standing beneath high-tension power lines. It is not claiming its territory or hoping to startle prey from cover. It is not calling to a mate. It feels none of those earthly urges.

It is not a large sandbill crane or a cryptozoic owl or a gargoyle or an Old Testament angel come to prophesy disaster or rain judgment for the town's sins, which are no more evil and banal than the ugly little acts committed in rural regions of Ohio, Oklahoma, or Maine. *It* simply *is*.

When the creature first began visiting the dilapidated cabin that smelled of wood smoke, the girl was terrified. Of its glowing, maroon eyes, its huge, batlike form, its reedy, whistling call. She would cry out, and her father would stagger into the tiny bedroom lit by a single small lamp and tell her to go to SLEEP, he was EXHAUSTED, that a new day of toil and drudgery was only hours away. The girl named LORI would scrunch her eyes and sob and bury herself beneath her thin pillow and blanket. Eventually the father, WALT, cursing his life and his long-departed wife, affixed a rectangle of cardboard to block the window using silver-gray tape nearly the color of the creature's leathery skin underneath the fine coat of gray hair. How dark and cheerless the interior of the girl's room must have been after that small porthole was blocked.

In time, the girl stopped crying out for her drunken father. She removed the cardboard barrier. Sometimes she even stared up at the creature roosting in the hickory tree before returning to her tea parties and games. Once she held up a little pink hand against the windowpane and waved. She has come to believe that the creature is a guardian angel sent by her mother, CATHERINE, who lives three states away and does not communicate with her ex-family. A guardian to watch over her and pluck her nightly prayers from the crisp air like fireflies as they float heavenward.

Fervent prayers that her father will stop drinking the evil liquid that makes the veins in his neck and forehead stand out like wires when he is angry, and causes his breath, clothing, and even pores to reek like kerosene.

That her long-AWOL mother will return home.

That the kindly grandfather whose merry whiskered face has already faded like an old Polaroid memory snapshot still looks down on her from the hard blue sky.

That MONICA, the young woman from social services who drives the apple-green Volkswagen Bug, will return and bring her a handful of lollipops and stickers like the ones given out at the public health clinic. LORI always coaxes the slim brunette lady to sit for tea with her stuffed animals if WALT is not at home to curse and rudely suggest she drive straight back to her office in Belington.

Following traditional folklore, the girl sometimes catches a thistle seed and blows it into the air. (If it doesn't hit the ground and the breeze carries it from sight, your wish will come true, but only if you don't *tell* anyone the wish.)

The creature registers these childish longings, but they invoke no sympathy. It accepts without question the separate veils of existence it has passed through on more than one occasion during its long life, but human concepts of grief, isolation, or an afterlife are meaningless.

And so it is on this evening that the girl sits playing on her bed (a box and sagging twin mattress resting atop four cobweb-filled cinderblocks) beneath an indigo sky flecked with mica stars, waiting for her father to return from the smoke-filled roadhouse on the edge of the dying mining town. His routine is to come home at twilight from whatever day labor or odd job he has scrounged, feed her supper, and then leave for the tavern. Tonight he is very late. The creature sees the girl yawn, but she serves another round of make-believe tea and cakes.

When he finally approaches from some distance, the creature notes that the father is not traveling in his battered oil-burning pickup. WALT is returning home on foot, his filthy thermal shirt and jeans stained with more than Old Crow whiskey.

And he is not alone.

The creature's senses tap into invisible sources of information that you and I have only speculated exist and so can clearly see and hear them long before they arrive. A dozen or more men and women, and several adolescents. All afoot, some sticking to the narrow dirt road, others fanned out along the culverts and fields. Something is wrong with the cadence of their collective footfalls. Something is *very wrong* with them—their hearts no longer beat in steady autonomic lubb-dubb rhythms, pushing and pulling blood through the veins. They are stiff and cold. Their minds have been emptied except for stuttering misfires of fragmentary memory and sorrow, overshadowed by a single primal urgency.

For the first time, the creature shifts on its perch.

WALT and the other denizens of the honky-tonk eventually appear at the edge of the moonlit woods, snapping twigs underfoot, swaying and staggering, weaving around the stands of trees, rocky outcroppings, and abandoned washing machines, crisscrossing the gullied drive half-choked by weeds.

The dead-but-living things pay no heed to the creature. It watches them from the hickory tree, mute and motionless.

Slowly the crowd coalesces, like honeybees subdued by smoke. They mill at the lip of the ravine, jostling one another with unfocused eyes, jaws working silently, drawn down to the soft yellow square of light like phototropic, well, moths. Then WALT (who looks like he has been dropped from the pinnacle of a hundred-foot spruce like a ball bearing inside a giant, coniferous pachinko machine) leads the shambling charge into the valley toward the shack.

The creature watches, a statue striped in shadow.

The dead-but-still-living things surround the shanty, white hands hammering its thin walls. WALT mounts the leaning porch and breaches the single door, while the others batter at the girl's bedroom window. Glass shatters inward. The creature hears the girl's sharp shrieks.

Sensing the girl's vibrant young lifeforce, the dead-alive things surge forward.

Something alien stirs inside the creature's mind, raw emotion it has never felt and cannot articulate. Something that might be described as EMPATHY shot through with sizzling thermite veins of pyrotechnic OUTRAGE.

Increasingly disturbed, the creature squirms.

It could easily fly away into the humid night, could be standing atop the rusted-steel suspension bridge on the edge of town within a minute. Instead, the creature drops lightly from the thick bough and lands on the carpet of pine needles. It unfolds its seven-foot gray body until it stands fully upright. The wings unfurl to their full span.

Down in the hollow the girl screams and screams.

The creature leaps high into the air, its terrible three-taloned hands open, quite suited to grasp and rend.

In moments it perches atop the canted, jigsaw roof. The creature hesitates, retracting and opening its wings as it feels the surface shift under the new weight. Below it, something snarls and then slams its fists against a cheap pressed-wood door, and the girl screams again.

The creature stalks forward, and the roof collapses with a brittle crack.

It falls through space and flattens the kitchen nook table and mismatched chairs. The jaundiced light, supplied by naked electric bulbs flares and dies, plunging the shack into blackness. Several of the dead-but-living things turn and converge on the creature, arms outstretched and jaws working.

The creature shakes itself loose of moldy pink insulation, shattered beams, and wiring. Its height does not permit it to stand fully upright, but, in the blink of an eye, it decapitates the bartender and blood-slicked exotic dancer, and slashes the mustached Fish and Game deputy nearly in two, from clavicle to crotch.

WALT is forcing his way through the remains of the flimsy bedroom door. Inside, the girl cowers below the pale hydra of arms, grasping hands, and hungry mouths at the window. She shrieks again as her creepshow father claws his way inside.

The creature grips WALT's right leg, wrenching him backward with such force that the damaged femur is dislocated and torn from its socket. WALT's torso slams against the doorframe, and he glares stupidly at the interloper. The last things WALT's dead orbs register are those large, reddish eyes and a sickle-shaped mouth filled with small razor-sharp teeth.

The creature squeezes through the unblocked doorway and into the bedroom it has gazed into on so many nights. It ignores the writhing mass of hands and grunting faces. The girl huddles against a wall in her dirty, threadbare nightgown, her breath hitching in her throat. Her small hands cover her eyes.

The seeking arms and avid faces suddenly withdraw and disappear at the sound of an engine and tires crunching on gravel.

Silence fills the room.

The wind whispers and the spray of glass shards glimmers.

The girl peeks through her fingers, and her green eyes expand with wonder at the sight of the creature up close.

Motionless, it gazes back. The white-hot imperatives it felt roosting in the tree ebb. It tastes the cool copper of WALT and senses that same lifeblood, still stirring and hot in the fragile preadolescent girl. It weighs the strange urgings of appetite and a sudden yearning to fly back to the scarred hickory tree and cloak itself in shadow. CONFLICT is another utterly alien sensation.

The creature stands at the edge of slanted moonlight, a silver-gray archangel, clearly uncertain.

The girl wipes her tear-streaked face and smiles. She slowly rises and steps closer. She stands on her tiptoes and raises her thin arms—

A short time later the creature emerges from the destroyed cabin to find the remaining dead things feasting on MONICA, sprawled halfway out of her Bug. MONICA, who had escaped from her besieged apartment and raced across the rutted, unpaved roads, propelled by a terrible premonition. MONICA, who had spurred and slewed her little car through the haunted woods to rescue LORI, only to be ambushed by WALT's former tavern entourage.

The girl rests in the creature's powerful arms as they glide high above the sluggish bend of river, hulking bridge, and moon-silvered rail lines. The Blue Ridge Mountains to their right are as black as the played-out mines and the tarpaper shack. Down in the narrow streets and back alleys of the town, more dead-but-living figures stroll beneath the ugly, yellow sodium-vapor lamps. Fires burn. The cool night air is lanced with the sporadic pop of gunshots and distant shouts.

A half-ton dually truck rockets through Main Street's sole, blinking red light and demolishes a northbound sedan. The dually's windshield explodes in a storm of crystal safety glass as its driver and passengers fly through the night air like Appalachian redneck Lost Boys.

A wide-eyed, bearded man in a denim jacket and hunting boots stops and stares up at them from the steps of the courthouse. A moment later he is swarmed by several of his former neighbors, and his shotgun discharges uselessly.

The creature soars higher on the thermals and emits a piercing cry that sounds like every person in the world talking simultaneously through a high-speed digital telephone trunk line, played backwards. The girl hugs the creature's side, clutching her favorite doll, her eyes closed tight against the height. Her young heart races but she is no longer afraid. The air grows colder and whips her blonde hair.

Again, the creature emits that otherworldly cry, instinctively modulating the frequencies, and the sky itself seems to shiver.

There is nothing remaining in this world for the girl.

There is nothing for the creature.

The veils part.

ON STAGGER

G. CAMERON FULLER

G. Cameron Fuller has published novels, sudden fiction, literary and genre short stories, and nonfiction feature articles and commentary. His short story, "Figure-Ground: Proof and Circumstance" won the Crime category in the 7th Annual Writer's Digest *Popular Fiction Writing competition. He can be reached through his website at www.gcfuller.com. "On Stagger" was written for his wife, Karin, in honor of their greater collaboration, and his stepdaughter, Celeste, in the hope that her high school years don't require she do anything like Seth had to do. At least not again.*

Seth lowered his head and rubbed the back of his neck, trying to ease the ache. Throughout the cafeteria around him, voices scattered and plastic trays shuffled across plastic folding tables as the students of Massey High went on about the business of lunch. Tuesday, only a few minutes left of lunch period, two down and three more to go. So far, so good.

"Not bothering us today," Kyle said, and Seth wondered if his friend was reading his mind. He raised his head and looked across the table; he blinked but didn't say anything.

"Maybe you should go out for football after all, even though it's kinda too late," Kyle said. "Maybe they'd leave you alone if you did that. You could get Smitty on your side."

Seth just scrunched his face and shook his head, his hands going back down to what remained of his sandwich. Kyle always came up with these complicated, imaginary solutions. And he was always looking for a savior, it seemed like. Like Smitty would ever have anything to do with him anyway.

"What's with your neck?" Kyle took a last spoonful of his peas and carrots, shoveled it in and spoke around it. "You keep rubbing it."

"Stiff," was all Seth said before he took a final bite of the cheese sandwich his mother had made that morning. Sometimes when he looked at Kyle, he wondered why they were even friends. A mismatched pair, Kyle small and wiry, his big head bobbling on a pale frame, Seth hulking and slow, always conscious of being tall and thick. Kyle from up on the hill, with his beauty-pageant mother and a successful father who owned several D'Nunzio's Pizza franchises in two states; Seth was from the edge of town near the river and the railroad tracks, where he lived with his mother and father. He loved his folks, but he knew that they were…different. His dad did all sorts of odd jobs, whatever he could scare up, and his mother, well, as near as he could figure she just tended her garden in the right months and watched TV through the winter. And then there was his grandfather.

The movement in the center of the lunchroom caught his eye, and he looked up to see Them getting up from the jock table. All the jocks and the wanna-bes were standing up at the same time, along with the girls who swarmed around them 24/7. No more than appendages. Couldn't they see they were nothing to Alex and his crew? Seth's eyes locked on Sarah, and he thought she looked in his direction, briefly, fleetingly. She was different. She knew. He could tell.

Kyle saw Seth watching and turned. "Oh, shit."

But They made their way toward the tray window, Alex in front, of course, followed closely by Danny and Jay—a real snake, that guy. Whenever Alex gave him or Kyle a hard time, Danny was always right up with his *fuehrer*, a fireplug with a crew cut, but Jay always hung back, watching, tall but coiled somehow, swaying slightly, a little half-smile on his face. Alex was his constant tormentor, but Seth had Jay pegged as the one with the dead heart. Seth watched Alex and his crew dump their trays with staged casualness and head toward the exit.

As soon as they were through the double doors, Kyle leapt up. "We made it," he said with the same relief Seth had felt earlier, two days down, three days left in the week. "It's over. Let's get out of here."

The harassment was always worst at lunchtime, when Alex had nothing to do and too much time to do it in. Seth rubbed the back of his neck with his right hand as he stood up, lifting his tray with his left. He had seen right over Sarah's shoulder as she glanced at him, he had seen Alex's eyes, head down, flicker toward Seth and Kyle. Seth knew. It wasn't over. It might never be over.

***

Seth and Kyle were not mismatched buddies. They hadn't grown up together, had gone to different grade schools, but they'd met at the school assembly on the first day of middle school where they found themselves sitting next to each other.

They quickly discovered they were both glad to be back at school after a long, solitary summer, and they had both spent their last summer weekend watching the Dr. Who marathon on the SyFy channel. Both boys were small, dwarfed by their peers, technogeeks and proud of it. Their chief difference was that while Kyle's dad could afford all the Xboxes and iPads Kyle wanted, Seth knew how to use mother boards and hard drives and chips to rig what he wanted. They both belonged to all the really cool lists—Kyle by subscription, Seth by hacking. The alliance was formed.

Throughout their three years at Underwood Middle, they began to diverge physically, with Seth slowly becoming the hulk he was by high school, but Kyle basically staying the same size. Seth slowed as he grew, while Kyle remained the hyperkinetic ball of energy he was when they first met. By high school, Kyle's curly hair had become almost like a tassel on his bobbing head, the only other change the progressive thickening of his glasses, but Seth had grown relentlessly taller and thicker, not an ounce of fat, but a large boy who was still an undersized runt in his own mind.

Kyle was jabbering away as they placed their trays on the conveyor belt and headed for the exit. He was still talking as they pushed open the doors, but Seth wasn't listening. He knew what they would find on the sidewalk outside the cafeteria.

And sure enough, there they were, Alex with Sarah and Jay swaying rhythmically between two other girls.

Alex smiled, toothy and feral. "Are you guys following us?"

Kyle started to mumble denials, his words crashing into one another, but Seth just said, "Don't be whack," and made to skirt around the little contingent. Alex stepped in front of Seth and Kyle, but it was Seth he focused on, and the two stood, chest to chest.

"You are following us. Don't you girls have something better to do than come sniffing after us?"

That was Alex's ultimate insult, to call boys he picked on girls. Seth glanced at Sarah to see what she thought about that.

"I'm talking to you, not her." To emphasize his point, he jabbed Seth is the chest with a finger.

Seth batted the finger away. "Fuck off."

"No, you fuck off, you freak. You and your butt boy here."

Seth sighed. He was surprised that he didn't feel in the least frightened. Alex had scared him before, often, but this time he only felt tired. And the back of his neck hurt like hell. He felt like he might be about to get the shit kicked out of him, but he couldn't manage to care. He just wanted it to stop.

"What's your problem, Alex?"

"The only problem I have in this world is you." Alex jabbed Seth's chest for punctuation, and Seth could see Kyle's head swiveling, looking for a teacher. "You and butt boy."

"You think we're gay or something?" Seth glanced at Sarah. Her eyes were wide. "Is that it?"

"Keep your faggot eyes off her, faggot!" Alex's voice rose, louder and higher-pitched. The more excited he got, the more eloquent he became.

"Whatever," Seth said and started to step around his tormentor, but Alex shoved his chest, hard. Seth felt the back of his knees catch against something, and before he could catch himself, he pitched backwards over Danny, who was on his hands and knees behind him. Seth's hand burned along the cement as he tried, but failed, to break his fall. He felt the skin of his palm tearing open and banged his elbow on the cement before crumpling to the walk.

Shit! The last time Alex had knocked him down, Seth had split the skin on both knees and they had taken weeks to heal. He glared up at Alex, who wasn't even looking at him but laughing and puffing out his chest and strutting around like a bantam rooster. The son of a bitch.

Seth scrambled to his feet, his neck suddenly burning white hot. "That's it!"

Alex just smiled and crouched slightly on the balls of his feet, shaking his hands like he was about to go. "You wanna go, faggot? Bring it. Do your best. I won't hurt you. Much."

Seth got his consolation then—Sarah looked positively stricken. With her reaction, he felt like he had won this round.

"Never mind," Seth said. "We'll both get detention."

"Chickenshit!" Alex hissed. "How 'bout tonight then. Out by Red Rock at midnight. Just you and me. Or you can bring your butt boy and Jay'll be ready. We'll kick both your asses."

Seth was about to say never mind again, it wasn't worth it, but then he saw that snake Jay hanging back, staring, swaying, and he was suddenly overwhelmed by a deep cold, a terrible revulsion. His glance flickered over to Sarah and back to Alex. When he spoke, he felt dead calm inside.

"I'll be there by myself. You bring the jaybird. We'll see who leaves."

Alex stepped back a half step, as if startled, but he recovered quickly.

"Okay, then, faggot. Midnight." He started to back away and his followers swept in with him, including Sarah. "Your funeral, butt boy. Tonight you di-i-e-e-e...." He let the word draw out as they walked across the grass expanse toward the front doors of Massey High.

Seth looked at the raw scrape on his palm and felt his elbow. More blood. But it didn't hurt that much. He wasn't quite sure what just happened, but Kyle seemed to be, as he bounced up.

"O-M-G! That was amazing! O-M-G! What'd you just go and do, you fucking crazy man! Insane!" Then he stopped short, looked up at Seth. "You're not really going to go, are you?" And his forehead crinkled as it dawned on him: "I don't have to go, do I?"

The rest of the school day passed very slowly for Seth. It wasn't that he had trouble concentrating on his schoolwork—he got all As without paying attention most of the time anyway—and it wasn't like his mind kept wandering, the way it did when something important was coming, which was a constant distraction. Not like that at all. It was as if his mind had just stopped. If he was conscious of anything, it was the flex of his muscles under his Think Geek t-shirt.

At one point, he glanced up to see the big round white clock with black numbers tick past one.

The few times he did think about his midnight showdown, he found himself wondering why he wasn't worried more about it. Or worried in the least. He had never been a fighter, or even much of an athlete, and he expected that anyone in Alex's crew could whip him up one side and down the other. Alex and Jay would be there, and either of them could knock him all the way to next week, but strangely the prospect of it didn't make him uneasy. When he stretched out his hands, he felt like he was inhabiting them for the first time in his life.

The white clock with black numbers ticked past two.

He rubbed the back of his neck, which had stopped aching sometime after noon and now only felt tingly and cool.

When the final bell rang at 2:50, he stood calmly, empty inside. Whatever happened, it would be over tonight. "Just stand up to bullies," his father had always said, but Seth knew that didn't necessarily work, because he had stood up to his dad many times, and it had never done more than get him a black eyes and a swollen face. Once, his father had broken his arm. His mother said it was an accident, but she always covered for his father. He had always felt like his parents were never straight with him, like there were terrible secrets in Dad's past or Mom's past or their past together, but some things were always closed off. There was something they were hiding from him, from everybody.

At his locker, he stowed everything. He would take nothing home with him tonight. He would go meet Kyle at the Daily Grind and do some surfing, and then about 7:00, he'd go see if he could find his grandfather. His grandfather lived in a small shack at the edge of the State Forest, and Seth went to him whenever he needed advice or comfort. His grandfather lived like a hermit at the edge of the wood, but he always had time for his grandson. He claimed Seth was the only person he really liked.

Whatever happened, it would be over tonight. He would make certain of that.

As he pushed through the glass entrance doors, he saw Sarah standing over by the flag. She saw him come out and had clearly been waiting for him.

"I need to talk to you," she said, her hand on his forearm. Her voice was so melodic and clear that Seth often wondered if she was some kind of angel fallen to earth. He got kind of tongue-tied around her.

"Um. Okay."

"Don't go tonight," she said.

He blushed. "Don't worry. It'll be fine. What's the worst he could do?"

She punched his shoulder. "Asshole. I'm not worried about you. I'm worried about Alex. He's my boyfriend."

Seth wasn't sure how he could have so misread her intentions. "Well, um...."

"I know what I'm talking about, Seth." She looked at him steadily, and he felt like he was going to fall into her blue eyes. "If you go tonight, you'll kill him."

He frowned and began to stammer like Kyle. Before he could get a word out, Sarah had turned and fled, and all he had left was the faint scent of jasmine and patchouli.

"You want to come inside, Azarel?" Seth's grandpa always called him by his middle name, and it warmed him just to hear it. He stood aside, gesturing Seth into his small cabin. Pepaw must have been at least 65 or 70, but he looked and moved like a man in his 40s.

"Sure, Pepaw. Thank you."

Inside, a small fire in the fireplace was the only light. Seth realized that Pepaw must have known company was coming, because he never lit the fire for himself. Ever since Seth was a small child, he'd noticed that Pepaw functioned just fine in even the blackest night. "I prefer moonlight," he had said once when a ten-year-old Seth had finally gotten up the courage to ask.

Pepaw's quarters would have been called an efficiency apartment if they were in a downtown. "That one-fucking-room hovel," was what Seth's father called it. To Seth it had always been a magical place: a small table, a tiny ice box with actual ice in it to keep things cool, a cot to sleep on, a couple of waist-high bookshelves with twenty or thirty volumes stacked in them; herbs hanging upside-down from a thin line stretched over a tub sink. There were always strange things sitting on the table or on the floor: the skull of a small deer or some hawk feathers or a figure Pepaw was whittling. Pepaw's cabin was always warm and dark and safe, the only shiny things being the knives over the huge cutting board on the counter by the sink.

Pepaw called it his "gutting board," which Seth had always thought was cool, although tonight, when he remembered that, he felt a thin shiver snake up his spine.

"You don't seem worried." Pepaw indicated one of the two chairs by the small table.

"What makes you say that? How do you know where I'm going tonight?" Seth had always had the feeling the Pepaw knew things he had no right to know, not that his knowing was rude or out of line, but that it was…impossible. He knew things he couldn't know.

"Hm." Pepaw sat down across the table. "You wanted to talk to me about something."

"I just…." Seth looked down and traced his forefinger around on the worn wood of the table. "I think I have to fight tonight."

"Have to or want to?"

Seth thought about that for a moment. "Maybe both, I guess. There are these guys at school. Jocks. There always worrying at me about… whatever. Usually stupid. They just want to pick fights."

"Ah. I know those boys."

"You do?"

Pepaw laughed. "Not the ones you know. Boys like them. So which one is it? There's usually one who's in charge."

An image of Jay flashed through Seth's head, but he said, "Alex."

"Who are his people?"

"Esteps. Alex Estep. The bane of my existence."

Pepaw laughed. "I can imagine! But there's another one you think is worse."

Again, something he shouldn't know but did. "Yes. Jay."

Pepaw made a rolling motion with his fingers, a get-on-with-it motion.

"Oh. Uh. Sorry. Johnson. Jay's one of the Johnson boys."

Pepaw slapped the wood of the table, and Seth startled.

"Those Johnsons are crazy people. Crazy black." He looked hard at Seth.

"They're white. I mean, Jay is, and so's his brother."

"No." Pepaw laughed again. "Not black like skin, which is brown anyway, but black like no light. Black like dead." He shook his head. "A lot of those Johnsons get it. They're always into trouble. The women are like frightened mice, and the men, hell, they're usually sick from the whores by time they're fourteen or fifteen."

"Jay's my age. He scares me." Seth pinched his collar closed as if feeling a chill on this warm night. "There's something bad wrong about him."

"Hard to tell. Maybe the whores, maybe someone in his own family. All I know's every Johnson I ever saw from around here had caught it by the time they were a teenager."

"Caught what?"

"There's a lot of it down in the valley, near town. That's one of the reasons I stay away. Too many of them around, hunting."

"What are you talking about, Pepaw?"

"The story is it started with one of us. Here in these hills, maybe. Some kind of mutation, acts like a disease. It imitates us, but where we walk, they kind of stumble around."

"I never could tell what you were talking about more'n half the time, Pepaw."

"I'm talking about you, boy. And the difference between you and them. Us and them." Pepaw rapped the wooden tabletop with two knuckles. "What time do you have to meet them?"

"Not until midnight."

"Okay, good. Let's go for a walk. I was going to tell you about this sooner or later, Azarel. Looks like now is the time." Pepaw stood, urged Seth to his feet, and led him out of the door of his small cabin. "The Change is happening to you. It's what happens in our family when boys become men."

"Jeez, Pepaw," Seth said as they strolled up the walkway. "I know all about puberty."

"No, I mean a different kind of change. When we become… grown." He paused and put his hands on Seth's shoulders, looked into his eyes. "There are bad things in the world, Azarel, and they go by lots of names, but for as long as I can remember, most of us have called them Stagger…."

Seth sat on Red Rock for several hours. Red Rock was named for what it was: an enormous red rock the color of blood, but gritty like sandstone, perched on the edge of the steepest mountain in an area of southern West Virginia known for the steepness of its mountains. Red Rock was large enough that it could have held a small baseball field, had there not been the problem that a home run would have gone sailing over the edge and plunging down a thousand feet and more into the valley below.

Seth had come out there many times over the years, but he wasn't one of the party crowd that came out to Red Rock to drink beers. Every few years or so, someone fell off of Red Rock—usually, someone who was part of the beer-drinking crowd—and there 'd been calls for a safety fence to be put up all around, but they'd never come to anything. Mostly because no one seemed to have any idea where to get the funds.

As he was sitting there, he watched the sun set out to the west and the daylight dim. He had the same inner quiet he'd had all day at school—utter silence most of the time—but now and again he wished Sarah was there. With him. And he wondered if she really did know, or if she was just saying that.

A few thoughts of things his grandfather had said floated through—about contagion, about bodily fluids, about the Change and how it started in his family, about the Hunger for living flesh in the Johnsons—but Seth didn't hold onto any of them. Just as Pepaw had said, he couldn't process any of them just yet. He had to be ready. "Don't think. Just do," Pepaw had said.

"Well, well, well," came a voice behind him. Alex, Seth knew without turning. He stood, running his hands down his thighs, and turned slowly. Alex was there, but Seth's eyes locked on Jay. He was something much worse than a snake. Seth watched him swaying slightly.

"Well, well, well," Alex said again, stepping forward. "I'm surprised you didn't chicken out."

"Why don't you just stop bothering me?"

"Your butt boy's not here. Jay'll just hang back." He took two more steps closer. Seth didn't move. He wasn't scared, and after talking to Pepaw, he didn't think he'd ever be scared again.

"We don't have to do this, Alex. No one will know."

"Yes, they will, because I'll tell them. You did everything you could to get out of fighting me, and then I kicked your ass." He shifted his weight to the balls of his feet, raised his fists. His fighting stance would look almost comical if Seth didn't know how much more serious this was than even he knew. "You'll be lucky if I don't throw you off this rock, Steff."

"Now why do you have to—"

Alex jabbed a right, and Seth slapped it down.

"Ah, lucky butt boy," Alex said and jabbed again. Seth moved slightly and the punch whistled past his face. Alex swung a roundhouse left, and Seth smacked it away.

"Now you're pissing me *off*." Alex jabbed and hooked, and Seth slapped the jab and slipped the hook. He was surprised at how much

Alex telegraphed his punches. He wondered why he'd ever let Alex taunt him for so many months. Three more punches, and not one landed.

Seth hadn't even shifted his feet much, turning only to keep Alex in front of him.

Two more jabs. Seth caught the second one, savoring the look of surprise on Alex's face. He yanked Alex's arm down and brought his knee up hard. A loud crack and Alex's face went pale.

"You broke my fucking arm!" He looked like he was going to cry.

"Go away, Alex." Jay's words were flat and harsh. "Now!"

Alex took a couple of faltering steps backwards as Jay moved forward. He hissed something at Alex, who turned and ran into the darkness. Seth heard him crashing through the woods and looked back at Jay.

"You know," Jay said. They faced each other, each of them at an angle, barely ten feet apart.

"My pepaw told me about you people. I didn't think you were real."

A dry laugh from Jay. "Your Pepaw is a blight on the earth."

"And you are a mockery of life."

They roared and clashed together, their arms locked, each of them frozen, straining, their face less than an inch apart. Jay's lips drew back from his teeth, and his lower jaw protruded. Just like Pepaw had said to expect: "That's the hunger of the dead, boy. The hunger for life."

"You think…you can…." Seth stopped trying to talk, putting all his will into his muscles. This would be over in a second.

Suddenly, Seth relaxed and dropped to his knees, turning, throwing Jay off balance, and as he teetered forward, Seth yanked down on Jay's shirt collar, smashing his face into the rock between his legs. Jay howled like a wounded animal, and Seth locked his legs around Jay's neck, twisting his body sharply, suddenly, until *crack*, Jay's neck snapped and his body twitched and his limbs jerked and he went limp.

"That's how you kill Stagger," Seth heard Pepaw say as he stepped from the shadows. Seth hadn't noticed him, so focused was he on that one moment with Jay.

"He's really dead?"

"He was dead already. You just stopped him." Pepaw patted Seth's shoulder. "You did fine."

"What if there's an investigation?"

"When we're done, they'll think he just fell off the cliff and the animals got 'im," Pepaw patted Seth's shoulder and crouched down beside him.

"I have a lot to learn."

"Yes, you do," Pepaw said, crouching down beside Seth. He looked down at Jay's motionless body. "We're not them, you know. They're dead, but don't believe it. That's why people call them zombies. They have a disease, while we're—We are what we are. Let's eat."

LONG DAYS TO COME

K. ALLEN WOOD

K. Allen Wood's fiction has appeared in 52 Stitches, Vol. 2; The Zombie Feed, Vol. 1 (*Apex Publications*); Epitaphs: The Journal of New England Horror Writers; *and* The Gate 2: 13 Tales of Isolation and Despair. *He is also the editor/publisher of* Shock Totem, *a biannual horror fiction magazine. He lives and plots in Massachusetts. For more info, visit his website at* www.kallenwood.com.

It was a quiet Sunday afternoon when the bruised sky spat death from its gullet.

Lindsay called it the Apocalypse, the beginning of the end.

I scoffed at the time, but she was right.

As the day waned, the deluge continued unabated. The battering on our roof was a relentless reminder that life in Orbisonia had gone astray, but we were oblivious. We went from window to window and stared through the oily liquid in rapt fascination, pondering a world stained by the blackened dollops that fell from the sky and clung to everything like molasses.

The sharp edges of our '81 Buick Rustbucket smoothed with the dark slick. The branches of trees hung heavy, dripping.

Behind our home, the Blacklog Creek swelled, crept slowly, steadily, up the hill toward our back deck, gurgling a promise of ruin.

Yes, we watched, dumbfounded and enthralled, because with it all came a sort of curious beauty. We were spellbound—until the grounds of the old Cromwell Church Cemetery beyond our driveway, across the street, began to churn from below. The earth pulsed as if breathing. Centuries-old headstones toppled. The ragweed and timothy-grass roiled in the muck and mud like so many charred bones.

It wasn't until the first bony hand rose from the ground that Lindsay's prophetic declaration of apocalypse rang true. What slowly emerged from that mired wasteland of death was not just the bones of a long-dead and forgotten soul (as if that would have been normal) but a creature, a vile perversion of life, coated and dripping with the same filth that fell from the sky.

Fear—true, indefinable dread—grabbed hold. Lindsay screamed at the sight, her shrill voice attracting the attention of the undead thing.

It moaned, deep and guttural, like wind howling down the Blacklog Valley. It stalked unsteadily toward us.

Lindsay made a vague noise, then fled to the bedroom, slamming the door behind her. I called out, but she remained silent.

Backing away from the window, I resisted the urge to flee as well. Instead, I wrenched the couch away from the wall and shoved it against the front door as a makeshift barrier. The creature was still coming forward, with others behind it, and still more clawing their way from the muddied earth, all shambling their way toward the house. Some were missing parts—bits of skull, lower jaws, hands, arms, ribs; one grotesquerie even clawed and flopped its way along, little more than a torso and upper arm—all of them animated by some ungodly manipulator.

I stood in awe of it all, part of my mind still refusing to believe it was real, as if I were being hypnotized by disbelief, maybe denial.

At some point, primal instinct or fear whispered to me and I realized that the windows would not hold them back for long, that they wouldn't stand idly outside looking in, waving a good, neighborly wave.

Rushing from the living room, I stumbled down the basement stairs, fumbling for the light as I went. The smell of must and earthen decay was unusually strong. In areas where the grout had come loose, the stone wall seeped black sweat. Stacked in a corner, I grabbed seven planks of wood that were meant for a new shed and roughly hauled them back upstairs. I got a hammer and a box of nails from the storage closet off the kitchen.

When I returned to the living room, four of the monsters that had risen from their graves thrashed at the flimsy window screens, tearing holes in the wire mesh. They snarled in unison at the sight of me, despite having no visible means to make sound, let alone see. *As if they should be moving at all,* I thought pointedly. Within the blob-like skin that clung to their reanimated bones, small white worms pulsed and twisted like mosquito larvae in pools of stagnant water. Behind the creatures, dozens more hitched and stumbled down the mud-slick drive, their ghost-white skulls shining beneath the slime-skin like fire in the night.

Without thinking, for fear that *fear* would turn my legs to jelly and my bowels to free-flow, I slid a board in place over the first window, propped it with my knee, and pounded a nail through the top left corner, then the right. With each crack of the hammer, the swarm of dead slammed against the windows with increased furor.

As I put the final nail through the board covering the second living-room window, I heard glass shatter. It wasn't until Lindsay broke her silence and screamed again, louder, more distraught, that I realized it was the bedroom window that had imploded.

I burst through the bedroom door, almost taking it off its hinges, and found Lindsay frantically trying to press herself further into the corner, as if by sheer will she could melt into the wall and find shelter from the unholy monstrosity that was crawling through the window. Hammer in hand, I swung my best Roberto Clemente swing at its skull. It struck wetly, the force severing head from body, and the thing fell from sight. But, immediately, more filled the space it had left behind.

"Lindsay," I shouted, "I need the nails and a board from the living room. Go. Now!"

She whimpered as she crawled on all fours from the bedroom.

The hammer slammed and smashed and crushed, repeatedly bringing death to the dead.

Lindsay returned, and I slidd the board into place, pounded nails as if they were skulls. She helped me secure the bathroom and kitchen windows, though without uttering a word. I pried up a few thick floorboards from the living room and nailed them zig-zag across the door frames.

We holed up in the windowless reading room and sat quietly among the books, many of which described things far more monstrous but not nearly as frightening as those which stalked us beyond our walls.

Outside, the rain continued, relentless.

The TV was out, but the electricity and phone still worked. I called the police to report what I assumed no one would believe, but all I got was a message telling me that the circuit was busy. I gave up after the hundredth or so time. Anna Howland, our next-door neighbor, called late in the afternoon. She and Olin, her frail and sickly husband, were taking refuge in the upstairs bedroom. For now, she said, they were safe, as it appeared that the living dead only had an appetite for us. Anna promised to be our "eyes on the outside," and then abruptly hung up when Olin began coughing loudly.

We would hear from Anna just one more time.

I set down the phone, pulled Lindsay closer. Whatever hell had descended upon the world, we would wait it out, I promised, we'd be okay.

But while our defenses seemed enough to hold back the dead, our old home had flaws, and the poison water (that's what Lindsay called it) exploited them. Mold grew, exploded to life in fuzzy blacks and whites and blue-greens. Within days, coughs and sneezes raked our throats raw, destroyed our lungs with malignant indifference. Blood spatter riddled the walls and floors like evidence of tiny gunfights.

I breathed, and lived, so I coped.

We rationed our food like prudent doomsday survivors, boiled and potted tap water in every container we could find. When the electricity went out a week into the ordeal, we existed by the meager light of candles, until the candles were nothing more than formless clumps of wax.

Though it was midsummer, the world grew cold and then colder. The soft plop of cancerous rain turned to an arrhythmic beating of ice that mercifully, for a time, distracted us from the incessant moaning of the dead.

In the small fireplace we burned our things for warmth, that which was not securing the doors and which had less meaning first. Eventually, our most precious items—the symbols of our life and love—went up in dark sooty smoke that stabbed at our eyes and blackened our walls and ceilings and lungs.

As the life we had once known faded to ash and memories, so did Lindsay.

She wept in harmony with the sky, withdrew further within herself. As the weeks stretched on, she shrugged off my attempts to embrace her, to soothe her fears. Everything will be all right, I said. She didn't respond, didn't hear. Didn't seem to care.

A few days after I found her mindlessly licking a picture of a pizzaburger on a Hidd'n Valley Restaurant to-go menu, our food stores began to dwindle at a rapid pace, and Lindsay no longer muttered of hunger. I knew she was stealing food when I slept, and in response I selfishly squirreled away my own stash, though I told myself (and knew better) that it was for both of us.

Two days later, the food was gone—all but my personal hoard.

Rapidly, Lindsay withdrew even further, deeper into what I imagined was a perfect world of her own design. She embraced a newfound obsessive-compulsive disorder: rummaging through the empty refrigerator and dusty cabinets we'd yet to burn; flipping light switches and pushing buttons; changing TV channels that no longer spoke to her, expecting a miracle that would give her the same hope that I so dearly clung to.

Days and nights merged, bled together into meaningless shades that glowed dimly along the boards covering the windows. I tried to ignore the neverending rain and the heavy pitapat of ice, the groans of the dead and the rat-scratching of their fingers as they tried to find their way into our home, but it was a constant presence. The sky wept endlessly, the dead never rested. And I loathed what all of it meant.

I missed Lindsay, I missed love, but I held onto hope—until Anna's sorrowful wailing woke us in the night, quietly echoing between our bare walls.

It was a death knell, the ringing of the bells. "Olin," I whispered to the darkness. He hadn't been long for this world before the end came down, and I was surprised he'd lasted so long. When Anna's sorrow turned to agony and then ceased altogether, I knew that Olin hadn't remained dead—nor Anna alive—for long.

In the absolute dark, I wept.

What did death mean in light of instant, corrupted rebirth?

Lindsay leaned in close, yanking me from my contemplations—her labored breath cold and rotten on my bearded face, her teeth a staccato chatter in my ear—and insisted I offer to help remove Olin's body, as if she'd put all that we'd witnessed from her mind. When I refused (on the grounds that the dead were not quite dead), she begged me to steal a leg, or an arm, even *"just a couple of goddamn fingers."*

At first I was baffled, but then I knew….

God, I knew.

I no longer recognized her voice; her soulful Pennsylvanian drawl had become a husky, croaking, inhuman thing. The hunger and isolation played her like a twisted marionette on a dark-dark stage.

The following morning, when there was enough light so that I could see her eyes, they were crazed, wanting, dangerous. To my beloved wife, I was just as the body of Olin Howland had been the night before—meat, survival.

When the sun behind the clouds dipped below the horizon, blackening the cracks of faint light along the boarded windows, I could still see her staring in my mind's eye, wicked desire flooding her veins and corrupting her heart....

Two weeks before the clouds and rain cleared and the naked sun shined for the first time in months, shucking the bodies of the dead to the ground once more, I buried Lindsay down in the basement, in seven shallow graves dug out of the frozen earth. All of her. In pieces.

My final memory of Lindsay—eyes wild, mouth contorted in primal rage, swinging the ceramic bedside lamp—festers. As does the gash on my forehead.

The wound will heal...

But my heart, I'm sure, will remain broken for long days to come.

HIDE AND SEEK

TIM WAGGONER

Tim Waggoner's novels include the Nekropolis series of urban fantasies and the Ghost Trackers series, written in collaboration with Jason Hawes and Grant Wilson of the Ghost Hunters *television show. In total, he's published over twenty-five novels and two short story collections, and his articles on writing have appeared in* Writer's Digest *and* Writers' Journal, *among others. His horror novel,* Like Death, *was published through Apex Publications in 2011. He teaches creative writing at Sinclair Community College and in Seton Hill University's Master of Fine Arts in Writing Popular Fiction program. Visit him on the web at www.timwaggoner.com.*

Red stagger-ran down the street, bare feet sliding awkwardly on snow-slick asphalt. Three other Cold Ones followed close behind him, one male and two females, although gender distinctions no longer meant anything to their kind. All were between five and eleven years old, although concepts such as *children* and *age* were meaningless to them now, too. Like animals, they understood only the most basic of notions—hungry and full, move and not-move, safe and danger. This latter concept they understood only too well, for it was the reason for their current flight.

A loud noise sounded behind them, one Red couldn't name, but an instant later he felt one of his Hive—a female who had once been an eight-year-old girl named Courtney—pitch forward and fall to the asphalt, her right shoulder a shredded ruin. She felt no pain, and therefore, neither did Red. Despite her injury, she immediately tried to rise to her feet, but her right arm no longer functioned. It slipped out from under her, and she flopped onto her side. Red sensed the small ones inside her already hard at work, staunching bleeding and repairing damaged muscle, but it had been too long since the Hive had last fed, and Red knew they wouldn't be fast enough. He tried to close off his link to the girl, instinctively sensing there was nothing he could do to help her. But he was too unpracticed at leading his Hive, and such control eluded him. So even though he didn't look back as the Warm Ones approached her, he still saw them through her eyes, and since she did not look away, neither could he.

There were two of them, both male, bodies covered by the puffy-thick not-skin they put on when the white flakes fell from the sky. The eleven-year-old boy Red had once been would have recognized their coverings as fleece-lined hunting jackets, and the objects protecting their heads as caps—one emblazoned with the West Virginia University logo, the other with the words John Deere. The males carried long metal tubes that Red, so-called because of the tattered red T-shirt he wore, knew were bad. They inflicted damage that even the small ones had trouble repairing and were to be avoided at all costs. The hunters had been running, but now they slowed as they approached the wounded girl, lungs heaving, breath misting on the frigid air. One of many telltale signs of a Warm One, for Red's kind had no need to breathe.

The first was short, stocky, his thick black beard sprinkled with snowflakes. A thin white tube stuck out of his mouth, white smoke curling from the glowing tip. "Lucky shot," he muttered.

"Luck's got nothing to do with it. I'm just that good." This one was taller and thinner, his face covered with patchy stubble. The skin beneath his lower lip bulged outward, and he turned his head and spit a stream of brown liquid onto the ground.

"Yeah, right," Blackbeard said. "Shootin' kids ain't that hard."

"They ain't kids no more, you know that. The little fuckers can move fast enough when they want to," Stubble-Face said.

"You ever worry that you're gonna shoot a person by mistake?"

"Hell, no! These things don't move like us, and they don't look like us. And you can spot that blue-tinted skin of theirs a mile off. Now let's get on with it. We still got a couple hours of daylight left, and I want to get some more huntin' in 'fore it gets dark."

Stubble-Face spit another brown stream, raised his shotgun, and stepped toward the girl.

"Not too close," Blackbeard warned.

"I know!" Stubble-Face snapped. "This ain't my first goddamned rodeo."

Red knew the reason for the hunters' caution. When a Cold One ceased functioning, the small ones inside tried to leave the body in an attempt to find a new home within the closest Warm One. The transfer could be accomplished by a simple touch, though a bite was best: a fresh wound made a wide-open pathway for the vegrandi. Red didn't understand that the odds of a successful transfer were low. The Warm Ones whose bodies had resisted the vegrandi during the time of the Change usually resisted them now. Still, in rare cases a successful transfer did occur, and a new Cold One would be born. Red hoped that would be the case this time. The hunters were bigger than him, just like the Teacher. Since she had ceased to function, leadership of the Hive had fallen to him, and he would gladly relinquish it if a stronger King or Queen came along. If a successful transfer occurred, perhaps one of these men would become the Hive's new King, and he could resume his previous position in the Hive as a Seeker. He would like that very much.

So while Red ran down the street, the surviving members of his Hive close behind him, he mentally urged the girl to attack Stubble-Face, and she obeyed. Useless arm hanging limp at her side, she rolled onto her feet, bared her teeth, and prepared to spring.

But before she could attack, Stubble-Face unloaded both barrels into her face, and Red's link with her was cut off. All he could see now was the street in front of him, abandoned homes on either side, most with windows boarded over. Red didn't remember that a good many of these houses had been abandoned before the Change. Arthurstown, West Virginia, had been a coal-mining town ever since its founding in the late 1800s, but the mine had played out before Red had been born. In its own way, that had been as big a change as the day the vegrandi—nanotech devices that had been created to ensure a long, healthy life in humans—for reasons unknown malfunctioned and began transforming their hosts into Cold Ones. Spreading more rapidly than the common cold, the vegrandi, named after *vegrandis*, the Latin word for 'small', had reshaped the world in short order. Most folks didn't survive the Change, but those who did became Cold Ones. A lucky few were spared the Change—again, for reasons unknown—and those survivors became the Warm Ones.

Red felt the urge to stop running and return to recover the girl's body. Since the Teacher had ceased to function, the Hive hadn't eaten regularly, and they were hungry. The small ones inside them needed fuel, and while their preferred raw material was the blood and meat of Warm Ones, when food was scarce, they could subsist on the flesh of their own kind, if necessary. The nourishment derived from ingesting the substance of another Cold One was minimal, but it was better than nothing, and in the world after the Change, "waste not, want not" was more than a mere homily.

There was more to Red's urge than mere practicality, though. The small ones inside him had shut down most of his higher brain functions—as they did for every Cold One—so he didn't remember that the girl, Courtney, had been his sister. But he still felt a stronger connection to her than to the rest of the Hive. He felt a responsibility toward her—to guide her, protect her—that went deeper than merely being her King. He slowed, stopped, turned, and started to head back. So strong was Red's urge that the two remaining members of his Hive also slowed, turned, and began following.

The small ones inside Red screamed a warning. He was King. The Hive's survival depended on him. There was nothing he could do for the girl, and the remainder of the Hive must be protected. Red turned around once more and resumed running at his full speed, awkward and spastic as his movements were. The small ones commanded, and he obeyed, and through his link he urged the other two to run with him. But somewhere inside him, in a place so deep that even the small ones were unaware of it, Red felt a distant, faint echo of something that might have been sorrow.

Red repeated his command for the others to run, pushing his will upon them harder this time, and they increased their speed. The Hive, now down to three in all, ran. Red didn't need to look back to know the Warm Ones followed.

When they were well fed, Cold Ones didn't tire. But when they had gone too long without feeding, as Red's Hive had, the small ones made them conserve energy whenever possible. So even though the two Warm ones still hunted them, Red soon began to look around for a place they could hide. They had left the residential area where the hunters had found them and entered a business district. Family Fixin's Restaurant, JD's Gun and Pawn, Dietz Diesel, B&B Liquor, Derma-Doodlez Tattoo, and more, their windows boarded over or broken out. The streets were cluttered with abandoned vehicles—Ford, Dodge, and

Chevy pickups mostly, their bodies nibbled by rust—many of them smashed into each other or wrapped around light poles. No people, no animals, only a gentle wind and large snowflakes falling from the sky. Little snow had accumulated on the ground here yet, and the small ones told Red that this was good, that the Hive would leave few tracks for the Warm Ones to follow, and those they did leave would soon be covered by the falling snow. A building caught Red's attention, and although he couldn't read the sign above the entrance, couldn't even conceive of such a thing as language anymore, the small ones whispered that this would make a suitable hiding place. FRANKIE'S BODY SHOP, the sign said, above the words a cartoonish image of a grinning, green-skinned, square-headed monster with metal bolts protruding from its neck. The boy Red had once been would have smiled at the irony, but now he paid no attention to the sign as he approached the building.

The body shop's front door had been torn halfway off its hinges some time ago, likely by Cold Ones seeking nourishment in the first days after the Change had swept through Arthurstown. Red pushed the door aside and entered, his two companions following close behind. He looked around and saw a counter with a computer and printer on it, along with a customer waiting area with a coffee table covered by old magazines, uncomfortable-looking chairs, and vending machines for snacks and soda. The small ones said this would make a good hiding place, but Red wasn't sure. He'd been a Seeker before the mantle of leadership had fallen to him, not a Hider. He wished the Teacher were here. She would know—

He glanced to his right and saw another door, this one intact. He walked to it, the other two Cold Ones staying where they were, waiting for their King to issue a command. Red pushed open the door and stepped through. This area was much larger than the outer room, and while little light filtered through the grimy windows, Red had no trouble seeing. The small ones enhanced both hearing and vision, and he could see as clearly as if the garage was illuminated by floodlights. A trio of vehicles—two pickups and a Hummer—were parked in the garage, all in various states of repair. Red and his companions could arm themselves with tools from the workbenches lining the walls and hide behind the vehicles, which would help protect them from the Warm Ones' weapons should the hunters find them.

Red summoned the last two surviving members of his Hive, and the three of them went to the workbenches. The girl selected a hammer, the boy a pair of needle-nose pliers, and Red a large, heavy wrench. He then commanded them to take up positions at the back of the garage, behind where the vehicles were parked. They sat cross-legged with their backs against the wall, listening intently for any sound that the Warm Ones might be approaching. The boy and girl sat at attention, their concentration completely focused on their task, and they would continue to do so until their King commanded otherwise, even if they had to sit there so long they ceased to function. But while Red kept guard too, he was King, and thus free to think of other things—inasmuch as his kind thought at all.

Red missed the Teacher. Not long after he had Changed, he had joined her Hive, one comprised entirely of children from the elementary school where she had taught. Red, whose name had been Kevin before the Change, hadn't been in her class—hadn't lived in her school district, for that matter—but one day while out foraging with his sister, he encountered the Teacher leading her Hive across town, in the process of moving her followers to a safer nest. The small ones inside Kevin had instantly recognized the Teacher as smarter and stronger than any other Cold One he had met, and they urged him to take his sister's hand and approach the Teacher. She looked them over for a few moments, her small ones communicating silently with theirs, and in the end she had accepted them both, and Kevin and Courtney became members of her Hive.

She had been a good Queen and had cared for her children well. Some, like Red, served her as Seekers, charged with spying on the Warm Ones, locating their nests and tracking their movements. Other children became Hiders, tasked with finding as many places as they could for the Hive to conceal themselves from the Warm Ones and from rival Hives. The Hive would periodically move between these nests, in order to confuse any who might hunt them. With the Teacher as their Queen, the Hive had fed well and lost few of its members.

But then the day came when Red made a mistake. Less than a month ago, he'd been out seeking when he ran across a Warm One hunting party. If he'd been capable of surprise, Red would've have felt it then, for night had fallen several hours earlier, and Warm Ones tended to restrict their activity to daylight hours. Although he was hungry, the small ones warned him that not only were there too many Warm Ones for him to handle alone, his duty was to his Hive, not his own belly. And so Red did his best to ignore his hunger as he followed the hunters at a distance. Eventually, they led him to their nest, a two-story house with bars on the windows and sentries posted on the roof. Red made sure to stay out of sight as he slowly circled the Warm Ones' nest in order to get a good look at it from all sides. At this distance, the Teacher would not be able to see what he saw, but once he was within range, her small ones would be able to access the information stored in his memory.

When his reconnaissance was finished, Red headed back toward the Hive's current nest, a shabby second-run movie theater that his parents had taken Courtney and him to, back when they'd been Warm Ones. The Teacher had already accessed his memories before he entered, and planned to send a group of Seekers out in the morning to keep watch on the Warm Ones. Once she knew the Warm Ones' preferred travel routes, she would be able to plan an ambush, and then the Hive could feed.

But somehow the Warm Ones had spotted Red. Perhaps he hadn't been quite as stealthy as he had thought while observing them, or perhaps he had fallen into a trap of their devising, for the Warm Ones sought to exterminate his kind whenever they could. Whichever the case, the Warm Ones followed Red back to the movie theater without his knowledge, and while the Teacher received a warning from her own sentries posted outside, it came too late. The Warm Ones burst into the theater and began firing their weapons. The Hive's strongest instinct was to preserve its Queen, and the children moved to shield the Teacher. But she commanded them to flee, and her will was so strong they had no choice but to obey. Red made it out, as did his sister and a half dozen other children. The rest, including the Teacher, ceased to function.

The moment the Teacher was gone, the survivors' small ones conferred swiftly and silently to choose a new leader: Red. They reactivated some of his higher brain functions and established a link between him and the survivors, and voilà, Red became King.

At first he did well enough. He found a new nest for the Hive in an abandoned McDonalds, and there they remained safe for several days. Their hunger continued to build, though, and when it became strong enough, Red's small ones told him it was time for the new King to provide for his subjects. Red decided to follow in the Teacher's footsteps. While he felt no need for revenge against the Warm Ones who'd decimated his Hive and inadvertently crowned him King, they were the only humans he knew the location of, and so he began to plan. He dispatched Seekers to observe the Warm Ones' comings and goings, and after a few more days, when he felt he had enough information, he commanded the Hive to follow him, and they set out.

Red's plan was a simple one, even for his kind. The Hive waited in an alley for a hunting party to walk by, and when they did, they attacked. It was a slaughter, but not the kind that would fill the Cold Ones' empty bellies. When it was over, one human was wounded, but two of the Hive had ceased to function. In the days to come, Red attempted three more ambushes, all equally disastrous, and the bellies of his surviving Hive members remained empty. So Red gave up planning and returned to what he knew from the days before he had joined the Teacher's Hive. He led his followers out into the city streets, hoping that they would come across a lone Warm One—preferably a weak or old one that didn't carry a metal death tube. They searched all through the night without luck, and—despite knowing better—Red commanded them to continue searching after the sun rose.

Which was how they had been spotted by the two humans that now hunted them.

Red had no idea if the hunters belonged to the same group of Warm Ones who'd killed the Teacher. All humans looked more or less alike to him. But they proved just as deadly. And now here he sat, hiding, hunger gnawing away at his insides, his last two surviving followers sitting next to him. He wasn't intelligent enough to understand the concept of failure, but he nevertheless felt a strange emptiness within that had nothing to do with lack of food. Perhaps he should hope the Warm Ones would discover their hiding place, enter, and cause them to cease functioning. At least then the hunger would end. Or perhaps he should command the boy and girl to remain here while he went outside and searched for the hunters. Once they finished him off, the others would be free to seek a new Hive. He remembered how the Teacher had ordered her children to flee when the hunters broke into the movie theater. That was how a King should take care of his Hive, and it's what he should have done long before now. He had tried so hard to be like the Teacher, but maybe he could be like her in the end, at least a little.

He rose to his feet, but before he could issue a command to his two surviving subjects, he heard the sound of footsteps approaching the body shop's entrance. The boy and girl sprang to their feet, and before he could stop them, they ran toward the front office. Their first instinct was to protect their King, but they were so hungry that the need for fresh meat was equally powerful. Red commanded them to stop, but his will wasn't as strong as the Teacher's, and they ignored him.

He saw through their eyes as they reached the front office. The door opened and Blackbeard entered, a fresh cigarette in his mouth. His eyes widened in surprise as he saw the two Cold Ones coming toward him, and he raised his shotgun and fired. He hit the male, blasting away a good portion of his head. But as he fell lifeless to the floor, the girl launched herself at Blackbeard. She swung her hammer at his left temple, and although Cold Ones weren't known for their grace and coordination, she connected with a solid blow. Blackbeard grunted and staggered backward, the cigarette falling from his mouth. He didn't fall, but he didn't need to. The girl jumped on him, bit down hard on his neck, and tore out a chunk of flesh. Blood gushed from the wound, and Blackbeard cried out in agony. He grabbed hold of the girl and hurled her away from him. Her back struck the front of the counter, and she bounced off and landed on her chest.

Blackbeard dropped his gun and clapped both hands over his wound in an attempt to staunch the blood flow. But the girl had bitten too deep, and there was nothing he could do. He staggered, his gaze became unfocused, and he fell to his knees. His hands dropped to his sides, and his blood flowed freely once again, though it no longer jetted from the wound.

The girl rose to her feet, swallowed the bloody gobbet in her mouth, and started toward Blackbeard. She'd had a taste of his flesh, and she wanted more.

The door burst open again, and Stubble Face entered, gun held at the ready. He took in the scene at a glance and shot the girl in the neck, nearly severing her head from her body. She remained functional long enough for Red to witness her slump to the floor, followed a second later by Blackbeard. Then his link to the girl was cut off, and Red—for the first time since he'd joined the Teacher's Hive—was truly alone.

"Dumbass!" Stubble Face said. "I told you to wait for me!"

Red heard him eject the spent shells from his shotgun and reload.

Then he heard the man walk toward the garage.

Red still had hold of the wrench. If he hurried, he could conceal himself between the vehicles, and if he could avoid being spotted by Stubble Face, he could attack from behind, and—

But why should he? He was smaller than the human, and he was alone. With the Teacher as their Queen and with each other to rely on, the children had been strong. But by himself, he was just a King without a Hive, and a small King at that. A Seeker who had been forced to become a Hider, and he hadn't been a particularly successful one. The small ones within shouted for him to not give up, to do something, anything to ensure their survival. But what could he do? He—

Then the small ones helped him remember something the hunters had said to each other earlier, just before they had killed the girl. Killed his sister.

You ever worry that you're gonna shoot a person by mistake?

Hell, no! These things don't move like us, and they don't look like us. You can spot that blue-tinted skin of theirs a mile off.

The small ones tapped into the last of Red's energy reserves and went to work.

Stubble Face entered the garage, mouth filled with chewing tobacco, shotgun raised and ready to fire. He found Red sitting once more, his back against the wall, trembling. Red opened his mouth, and in a voice raspy from disuse said, "Please...don't...hurt me."

Stubble Face froze. For a long moment he didn't react, but then he slowly lowered his weapon.

"What the fuck? How did you get in here, kid? And how did you manage to keep from gettin' eaten by those goddamned things?"

Red didn't respond. He continued trembling, and a lone tear trickled down his now pink cheek.

Stubble Face's voice softened. "Hey, now. It's okay, little bud. I'll take care of you."

He crouched down before Red, smiled, and laid the shotgun on the floor. An instant later Red smashed the wrench into the side of the man's head. Stubble Face toppled onto his side, tobacco juice running out of his mouth, and Red kept smashing until the hunter's head was nothing but a mass of blood-matted hair, pulped brain, and shattered bone.

Red—the blue tint slowly returning to his skin—stood and dropped the wrench to the concrete floor with a metallic clang.

The small ones had discovered a new way to help him hide. And a new way to help him hunt. He would venture out into the city and search for other children like him. They would form a new Hive, and he would show them what he had learned from the small ones. He would be their King…and he would be their Teacher.

But he had one matter to attend to first.

He got down on all fours next to Stubble Face's corpse, lowered his mouth to the red, wet ruin that had once been the man's head, and began to feed.

SLEEPER

TIM LEBBON

Tim Lebbon is a New York Times*-bestselling writer from South Wales. He's had over twenty novels published to date, as well as dozens of novellas and hundreds of short stories. Recent books include The Secret Journeys of Jack London series (co-authored with Christopher Golden),* Echo City, The Island, The Map of Moments *(with Christopher Golden), and* Bar None. *Future novels include* The Heretic Land *from Orbit UK,* Coldbrook *from Hammer, and the Toxic City trilogy, a young adult trilogy from Pyr in the USA. He has won four British Fantasy Awards, a Bram Stoker Award, and a Scribe Award, and has been a finalist for International Horror Guild, Shirley Jackson, and World Fantasy Awards.*

Fox 2000 recently acquired film rights to The Secret Journeys of Jack London, *and several more of his novels and novellas are currently in development. He is also working on new screenplays, solo and in collaboration.*

Find out more about Tim at his website www.timlebbon.net.

He should have had a gun. *Everyone* in zombie movies or apocalyptic stories had a gun. Maybe a Magnum for optimum brain splatter. Or a rifle. With a scope, so he could sit up above the treeline and pick them off as they came for him. He didn't care which. He just wished....

But Philip was not resourceful and had never been shooting in his life. The best he could manage was the baseball bat he now had slung over his shoulder. It became heavier with every lonely mile. With each step, he thought he'd have to drop it if he really wanted to carry on. But he couldn't bring himself to lose it. He'd smashed his wife's skull with the bat, and all that was left of her was smeared on the head, a drying cake of black blood and auburn hair.

"I need a gun," he said, wretched, crying. The trees didn't hear. Neither did the rocks. If anything *did* hear, it offered no reply.

He walked higher into the hills, and a warbler sang him on.

"Going into the hills will be best," he says. "There are mines. Deep, dark, easily defended. And they keep stores of food and water down there in case of cave-ins."

"You really believe that?" Rose asks. The sneer is in her voice, if not on her face. Even now, with everything they're hearing on the news and seeing on TV, she finds time to put him down.

"Yeah," Philip says. Feeling uncertain now, as always when she questions him, even if he knows for sure what he's saying is true. That's the hold she has on him. She strangles his certainty and obscures his world.

So they go, even though Rose exudes disapproval.

But when they leave their neighborhood and start their drive out of Knoxville, they see sights that silence them both, and she scoots over in the seat so that they can touch each other for comfort. It's never the same on TV.

Then in the beautiful foothills southeast of town, the car runs out of fuel. Philip's fault, because he hadn't checked. So they walk, and an hour later they can look downhill and see the car park at the beginning of a scenic walk. People are running and shooting, a car is on fire, and they see more terrible things.

"Up," he says. "That's the only way. Up to the mines."

He's even starting to convince himself.

Two days after he destroyed what his wife had become, close to the most beautiful landscape of hillside, valley, and lake he had ever seen, Philip witnessed a group of zombies taking down a woman and her child.

He had not slept for almost sixty hours. By day he walked, and at night he climbed a tree and cowered, licking moisture from leaves, listening, waiting for them to come. Terror kept sleep at bay. That, and Rose staring from beneath her blood-caked hair with dead, accusing eyes.

He heard the mother and son screaming from a distance and ran to see, crazy ideas of saving them terrifying him. With every step the fear bit in, and by the time he caught sight of them scrambling down a rocky outcropping he knew there was nothing he could do.

Useless, he thought, but it was Rose's voice, and it was him she was talking about.

So he hid behind a pile of felled trees and watched. The woman was helping her young son climb down the rugged cliff face, perhaps believing that she could escape them that way. She was correct in assuming that the dead could not climb.

They fell instead. The first one tumbled, cracking his head on an outcropping and spinning past six feet from the boy. The second and third missed as well, but the fourth struck the woman's shoulder. She cried out, twisted, and lost her grip on her son.

Philip closed his eyes as the boy fell, but he could not close his ears.

"Nate! Nate! Nate!" the woman screamed, and whatever she saw below her—hidden from Philip's sight by a fold in the land and more piled logs—must have been awful. It took only five seconds before she let go and fell after her boy.

Philip ran in the other direction. He ran further than he ever had before, hardly stopping for two hours, and by the time he slid to the ground beside a stream and took a drink, he thought he was going to die.

They find the family late that first afternoon.

"We need to stay away from them," Philip says. "Something's wrong."

"One of them's hurt," Rose says. "That's what's wrong."

"So let them call an ambulance!"

Rose does not even answer. They've both tried calling the emergency services and heard the same recorded message.

When Philip fell in love with Rose, it was her compassion that drew him to her. She cared too much, he would tell her, but at the same time he found her selflessness and concern for others incredibly admirable and attractive. He loved her love for other people. After their wedding, her lack of empathy for him would have struck him as ironic if it weren't so sad. Rose was intelligent and sometimes even superior, and did not suffer fools gladly. And Philip was first to admit that he was a fool.

I can't help it, he'd tell her. *I just don't see the world the way everyone else does.*

"I'm going down there," she says.

"No, don't be stupid!"

"Philip." Spoken with ire.

"I mean it! Look...." He grabs her arm, gently, and pulls her down beside him. The family is gathered around a truck with two flat tires, and Philip and Rose are well hidden up a small embankment, trees and bushes making them part of the land. "Look, Rose. The tall guy there has a gun. He's holding it ready. That's his family he's standing there protecting. The girl on the ground…may be his daughter." They never had children, but Philip thinks he can understand the protectiveness that man must be feeling. He yearned to feel it himself.

"He's not just going to shoot two people coming out of the woods."

"How do you know?" He struggles to keep his voice down. "We haven't got a fucking clue what's happening, and no one else has, either!"

"No need to swear at me."

"I'm not swearing at you! I'm swearing at *everything*. You saw what was happening in town as we left. The smoke. The fires. Those people. You *heard* the *guns*, Rose! And you saw…." They both saw things. Terrible things that do not need vocalizing again. "The news. What people were saying." He points along the road towards the crippled car. "He'll do anything to protect his family. And that's what *I'm* doing."

Her laugh is almost a spit. A cough of derision. It stings, but does nothing to temper his caution.

"Please—" he says, and Rose shrugs him off and stands.

"Hey! It's okay, we're normal, not like *them*."

The man aims his rifle and freezes into a shooting stance, and Philip can't help watching even as he thinks, *I'm going to see Rose's head blown off, he knows how to shoot, perhaps he's done plenty of shooting today already, and her hair will fan out with the impact and her brains will stain the road*. And deep inside where the most hateful thoughts dwell blooms a tiny spark of relief. With Rose gone, he will only have himself to save.

"I'm a nurse," Rose says. That isn't quite true; she is a care worker, looking after old people in an expensive retirement home in the countryside north of Knoxville. But maybe today it is close enough.

Philip stands slowly and steps out into the road, but he does not advance with his wife. Something is still wrong. The girl lies on the road beside the truck's open rear door, and even from this distance he can see the blood.

"Ask what happened to her," he says, loud enough for Rose alone to hear. She ignores him.

"Got bit!" the man shouts. Perhaps he heard Philip after all. "My little girl got fuckin' bit by that crazy old fuckin' loon from three doors down!" Rose reaches them and kneels, obscuring Philip's view. Those around the prone form move back a little, giving her room.

How long ago? Philip thinks, because he has been reading frantic reports on Twitter. Already a timeline seems to be forming. *More than half an hour? Because that seems to be the longest—*

Someone coughs, and growls. And then a scream. It is such a shocking, chilling cry that Philip closes his eyes and turns away, which means that he only hears the gunshot.

He falls to the ground, dropping the baseball bat he's been carrying since the car ran out of fuel. Presses himself flat to the road. Scoots around so that he can look back towards the truck—

And Rose is rushing back towards him, eyes wide, a bloody smear across her left forearm.

Touched her! Philip thinks, and there are more screams. Close to the car three shapes struggle in the road—the bloody girl and two others. The man with the rifle steps around them, gun raising, lowering, coming up again as he struggles with what to do. The shot must have been accidental, and the bullet had gone nowhere. The next might find wet.

But Philip will not wait to see. He grabs up the bat and reaches for Rose's hand as she runs past him, but she ignores him. Her eyes are frantic. She's terrified, and soon he will ask what she saw.

Soon. Because first they have to escape the screaming and chaos. The bloodied girl is up.

And Rose has blood on *her*. Philip runs after her, watching her movements, listening to her breathing. Waiting for something wrong.

Four days after leaving Knoxville, he found a mine.

It was almost a hundred hours since he'd slept. He'd done his best to avoid anywhere there might be people, or the dead—skirting around small towns, staying off roads, losing himself in the wilds. If he heard voices, he ran in the opposite direction. If he heard other things—once there were soft hooting sounds, and then the shuffle of aimless feet—he ran even faster.

He ate little. A hard, dry sandwich found in an abandoned car. Wild strawberries. He drank from streams, and he'd had diarrhea for almost twenty hours. It seemed that the more he drank, the more thirsty he became.

Hallucinations haunted him. Rose trailed him through the trees, wearing the dress from their wedding five years previously. She had only ever worn it once since, when they'd come home drunk one evening and wanted a dirty fuck. Now it snagged on branches and brambles as she came for him, always walking faster than him, yet never arriving. At least Philip still *knew* they were hallucinations, however awful. Soon, even that would change. Perhaps then would be the time to follow that poor mother from a cliff.

And then the mine.

"There it is," he said quietly. The sound of his voice in the wild silence was already shocking him, but it felt like company. "Down there'll be food and water. And somewhere to hide. But I've got to make sure...."

So he found a rock with a slight overhang, from which he could watch the mine entrance, the workings, the buildings, and car park surrounding it. The trees to the west were made ghostlike with dust that had been blown that way over the years, the guts of the earth brought up and exposed to the elements. He waited there for an hour, two, and saw no movement.

He closed his eyes to sleep, but sleep would not come.

"Maybe down there," he said. "Down in the dark." But he was already starting to wonder whether he could ever descend from the world. There could *anything* down below. There could be....

The time came to move. He staggered down the slope and across the muddy enclosure around the mine entrance, ground churned up by heavy wheels and soaked by the previous night's rain. His boots picked up wet soil, each step heavy. His limbs did not belong to him.

There was a green corrugated structure around the mine shaft itself, and one flap of iron smacked rhythmically against its support.

He thought he heard voices. Paused. Turned this way and that, listening to a gentle breeze passing through telephone wires above him. A soft call, like doves in the distance.

"Rose," he said, looking at the mess on the baseball bat.

Three shapes emerged from out of the darkness.

He tries to convince himself that there's no alternative.

They had run for thirty minutes, desperate to put distance between them and the stricken family. Along trails, across the stark open space of denuded woodland now consisting of stumps, rotting trunks, and a creeping undergrowth that seemed to be doing its best to smother the sad ruin. There was one more gunshot from far behind, and a child's scream, and for a terrible moment Philip thought that Rose might turn and go back. But then he started to wonder.

"Rose?" he asks again. She's sitting on a rock beside a stream. She has one trainer off, foot dangling in the water, but doesn't seem to have the strength to remove the other. She has not spoken for half an hour.

Half an hour, Philip thinks. He holds the bat by his side. She laughed at him when he brought it along. *What are you going to do with that? Fucking idiot.* It was her fear talking, partly. But for years now, he had often seen *fucking idiot* in her eyes when she looked at him.

"Rose?"

Her head is dipping, chin touching her chest. He can't hear her panting anymore.

I should circle around. See her face. See if that's a cut—a bite*—on her arm, or just a smear of blood. It looks like a hand print, but that could be where she grabbed it after she was bitten. Bitten.*

They're saying it's the bites.

Twitter has been alive. Panic has gone electronic. The end of the world, with hashtags.

"Rose?"

She snorts. Coughs. Maybe she's just exhausted. But—

Philip raises the bat and waits for her mocking glance, her dismissive comment, her constant denial of all the good things about him, her emphasizing of the bad. Everything that makes her Rose. Yet none of that comes.

So he swings.

The three people were dead. Two were men, one of them with his throat ripped out, the other wearing bib overalls and with a hole where his left eye should have been. He carried a length of hose that he might have been gripping for four days, since he died.

The third was a young woman. She tilted her head to the side and hooted softly, a strangely mournful sound coming from something so dead. She had no face.

Philip swayed. He had no strength to lift the baseball bat when they came. He had a headache from dehydration and exhaustion, and his limbs seemed far away.

Before the battery on his phone ran out, he'd read reports about how the contagion had spread from somewhere deep in the Appalachian mountains, and that the victims' only aim seemed to be spreading the disease. They were fast, he'd read. They ran.

He could do nothing to defend himself now. And as he waited, he wondered whether it would really make any difference if they bit him or not.

WE TAKE CARE OF OUR OWN

JOHN EVERSON

John Everson is the Bram Stoker Award-winning author of Covenant, *as well as the novels* Sacrifice, The 13th, Siren, *and* The Pumpkin Man, *all in paperback from Dorchester/Leisure Books. His sixth novel,* NightWhere, *an erotic horror descent into dark desire, was released by Samhain in 2012. He has had several short fiction collections issued by independent presses, including* Needles & Sins, Vigilantes of Love, *and* Cage of Bones & Other Deadly Obsessions. *Over the past 20 years, his short stories have appeared in more than 75 magazines and anthologies. For more information on his fiction, art, and music, visit* www.johneverson.com.

Let me just state right from the start that I didn't want to go. I had a comfortable apartment in Chicago and there is nothing like a jog by Lake Michigan at 6 a.m. on a pleasant morning in June to start your day. Moving to the sweltering backwoods was not my idea of a good summer. But not having a paycheck was a worse idea. So I took the assignment, packed my back seat with clothes, a stereo, and some DVDs, and my trunk with as much Goose Island as I could fit, and I drove eight hours to the foot of the hills. According to the boys upstairs at Lietzner's Prime Food Additives, productivity seemed to be suffering at one of our main plants hidden out in the boondocks of Appalachia. It also seemed that the boys thought I could be easily repositioned to investigate this supposed lapse. I was expected to pack up my life, drive across country, and spend my summer away from Wrigley Field to find out why. You might be catching the drift that I wasn't particularly pleased about this situation.

You'd be right.

Their one acknowledgement of the difficulty that such a move might pose to their loyal employee was a rather pathetic gift. They gave me the digital Dictaphone I'm recording this on to help me record my reports while I was walking the factory floor. I could slip it easily in my pocket and spit out whatever intelligence I found for the tiny microphone to catch. Never mind that I'd still need to transcribe my words later if I was going to send them a useful document of my findings. But whatever.

The company had rented me a small house near the food additive factory that I eventually found after several wrong turns down roads that ended in tall stands of gnarled trees and brush and the occasional ramshackle, white-frame house. The rent-a-house I eventually ended up in had five times as much space as my apartment and probably cost half as much, but there was something about it that made me uneasy as I unloaded my car.

It was too quiet there.

The gentle but persistently lulling sound of the rush of cars or busses on the El was missing. After I piled all of the food I'd brought on the white-tiled kitchen table and dumped the clothes on the unsheeted bed to put away later, I sat down on the rented couch (nondescript brown, but surprisingly comfy) and stared at the sliding glass doors that led out of the family room to the wilds of the back yard.

The house creaked and the faint wind whispered.

From somewhere far away…or maybe closer than I thought…I heard something scream in pain. A nighthawk's dinner?

The hairs on the back of my neck stood on end. I wasn't afraid of street noise, but this backwoods shit creeped me out. It took me a long time to get to sleep that night in my large bed in my large room in the middle of a very large freakin' nowhere.

My first thought at a report to Chicago: This factory has poor productivity because it is staffed by morons.

I made this determination without spending more than five minutes on the first morning tour. I was met at the door by Jameson Tal, a big man with a flannel shirt and a strong need for a lifetime supply of Listerine.

"I'm sorry they made you come all this way," he explained when he met me at the aluminum screen door that opened on the parking lot. "Things have been a little slow here, but we've had some folks out sick. Now that Mel and Tracey Lou are back, you should see the same kinds of numbers you're used to."

I nodded and tried to smile at his unease. No plant manager ever wanted headquarters sending someone in to look them over. But I wasn't going away. The company had paid my rent for the next 90 days.

I smiled and nodded and held out my hand. "I'm sure it's all good," I said, "but they gave me a summer vacation to hang out with you. So…I'm going to get to know Mel and Tracey Lou and everyone else before I go home. I'm sure I'll be out of your hair before you know it, with a great report."

Actually, I wasn't sure of anything of the kind. I was pretty sure this was going to be one of the longest, most torturous summers of my life. And whether I thought the slugs working the floor were performing up to par or not, I *was* telling Jameson the truth about one thing: I wasn't going home for awhile.

The plant was one of those places that made you feel gray and hopeless as soon as you set foot inside. The kind of place where life wasn't what you lived, it was how you died. Slowly, and painfully. This wasn't the sort of place where people yelled out the lines to The Who's "Teenage Wasteland" with glee as it played over the stereo. This was the place where they laid down and died silently, with their fingers ground in the machines that they fed for eight hours a day. The machines that had no regard for their humanity.

Tal introduced me to the aforementioned Mel and Tracey Lou, and I was less than impressed. They stared at me with empty eyes and barely answered questions when I posed them. The humanistic side of me suggested that they were just scared. Cowed into silence.

The cruel part of me shrugged them off and said they were dumb.

Neither was the case.

I didn't know that then.

And so I asked Mel out for a beer after work. I wanted to know what was going on. What better strategy than to get a man drinking if you want to get to the truth?

Mel didn't offer the truth I wanted.

I took him to the local bar, bought far more rounds than appetizers and got from him that the reason Lietzner's was producing less was because…there was less to produce.

This was not the answer I was looking for.

But I didn't give up. I had the whole summer to burn, whether I liked it or not.

I didn't like it. But I wondered about Mel.

He came to work with bruises on his face. And a silence in his shoulders. He didn't talk easily. I knew in the base of my spine that something was up, whether it related to the plant or not. But I couldn't get it out of him.

"You look pretty beat," I said at one point, thinking that the double entendre was definitely intended, and hoping he would answer.

"Nah," he answered. "Just a bad day."

I didn't believe that, not for a minute. But how do you pry?

I watched him. And I watched the others. For the next few days. The factory worked, as a factory does. People pulled switches and pushed packets from the conveyer to small trollies that took them to other places to be packaged and sold. There was not a problem with the system. If there was a problem, there was a problem with the people.

All I could see was that the people worked slowly. Like machines themselves.

Hands moved left. Bodies shifted in tandem. Legs stepped left…hands pulled product back from the belt and, after a quick addition, placed them back on the belt. Alarms sounded, stopping the line. And then readjustments happened and the conveyers creaked into motion again.

I couldn't see anything going on here that was any more or less productive than any other plant I'd been to. People were bored and they performed like dull automatons. That was factory life, right? I knew what it was like. I'd worked on a line when I was younger. You got into the rhythm, checked your brain out, and prayed for the 5 p.m. bell.

The place smelled like every food you've ever caught a whiff of… only, magnify it by a hundred. It wasn't a pleasant, fruity smell then…it was an overpowering, chewable stench. I hated the days that they made the flavoring for beef stew.

"How is your wife?" I asked Mel at one point. We were sitting in a bar a few blocks from the plant after work.

I hadn't counted on the fist that connected with my jaw as his response.

When I picked myself up off the floor I searched his eyes for a reason. But all I saw was fear.

"Leave her out of this," he said. His voice shook.

"Out of what?" I asked.

"You're here to shut down the plant," he said. "Don't ask how she is. You're going to kill her."

I was still shaking the sting of his knuckles off my jaw, so I just shook my head faster.

"I'm not here to do anything of the kind," I promised. "I'm here to get the plant working back at the level it used to, but I'm definitely not here to kill anybody doing it!"

He didn't look convinced. One of his dark eyebrows slanted down to meet his scowl.

"If this plant closes, she *will* die," he said again.

"You need the health insurance?" I asked, trying to sound comforting.

Instead of the reaction I expected, he laughed. "Insurance," he nodded. "I gotta go."

That was when things got weird.

I'd walked through the plant—but just down the middle aisle on the first couple days. After that, I stuck to watching the floor from the offices overhead, and talking with the managers.

But I knew something was wrong when I decided to walk the floor during a regular shift and talk to the workers as they were running their machines. That threatened to interrupt production, but I thought it might be worthwhile. Mostly, they just ignored me. But sometimes, they acted as if I'd set them over the edge.

They screamed. They lunged at me. I shrunk back, but there was really no need. I hadn't seen the chains that held them to their machines until then.

Chains!

Holy crap. This wasn't just a factory. It was a hidden fortress of white slavery. Part of me said to march immediately to Jameson and demand an explanation. But the other part said to talk to the workers while I had the chance. Once I confronted the boss, I wasn't sure I'd be allowed back on the floor again. On second thought, I realized that if I confronted him, I wasn't sure he'd let me out of the factory alive. They may still keep slaves here in Appalachia, but they sure didn't let on to the outside world.

Note to Headquarters: Perhaps a gun would have been more useful than a Dictaphone?

I stepped closer to a woman in a denim shirt and pants. She fed the machine slowly, methodically.

"Excuse me, ma'am," I began.

She didn't answer. Her hand moved slowly, forward and back, forward and back. It was almost hypnotic.

"Excuse me," I said again.

Nothing.

I reached out and touched her on the shoulder.

And then I got a reaction. Almost an explosion.

The woman's head jerked around and she lunged at me, mouth wide open, eyes bugging out of her face in rage, bloodshot and yellow. She screamed something unintelligible, and I leapt back. Seconds after her arms left the levers of her station, an alarm rang out and a red light began flashing overhead.

I had barely begun to take all of this in and react when two strong hands grabbed my shoulders and pulled me away from the crazed woman.

Jameson.

"What the hell are you doing?" he yelled. "You can't interrupt the line. You of all people should know that!"

He dragged me down the aisle of workers (none of them even glanced at us) and up the stairs to the management offices.

I waited while he gave me a tongue-lashing filled with vitriol so heavily accented I could barely understand him. And then quietly, I asked my question:

"Why are you holding these people prisoner?"

I'm not sure what reaction I expected from him, but it wasn't laughter.

That's what I got. A big belly laugh. His eyes rolled back and he shook his head at me as if I was the rube, not him.

"Why are we holding them *prisoner*?" he asked, still stifling laughter. "Because they are prisoners. There's a group of people down there who are working off their debt to society. We partnered with the state prison to get some cheap labor. We pay them minimum wage, and they work the line every day. But we can't afford to have them go running off and we can't stand behind each one. So they're in leg irons while they do their shifts. They're not always terribly happy people, as you found."

It definitely wasn't the answer I was expecting, and that must have showed. His dark brown eyes lit suddenly with humor, and he raised an eyebrow as he said, "What did you expect, that we still keep *slaves* here in the South?"

I got out of his office quickly, before I let my Barney Fife out with an "Uh, yep."

I didn't care what Jameson said, there was something going on there that wasn't right. And I intended to find out exactly what it was from Mel. But so far, he hadn't been exactly talkative. I needed to know a little bit more about him.

Maybe I'd watched a little too much *Maverick* when I was a kid, or maybe I was just bored. But when Mel left the plant that night at the 5 p.m. siren, I followed.

He drove a rusting Ford pickup through a maze of backroads through the small gray town outside of the factory, and then through forest and swamp. I followed as far back as I could while still keeping the back of his truck in sight—I focused on the numbers at the end of his license plate: 252.

I drove past the driveway he went down and eventually pulled my car into the ditch on the side of the road. Then I walked back to where I'd watched him pull off. I stood on the edge of the driveway, a long, curved gravel road through a stand of overgrown trees.

I could see a hint of the mountains through the breaks in the trees, and the interruption of a white-frame house down at the end of the gravel drive near where the red lights of the Ford flickered and died.

I waited a few minutes to be sure he'd gone into the house, and then, cautiously, began walking down the gravel path. The air was heavy with the end of a summer day; I had to give this place that—it was hot and humid, but the air tasted unlike anything we ever breathed in Chicago. It smelled rich with the scents of life. Organic, heady…clean.

Right now, I could smell the heavy scent of some kind of flowering tree. I didn't know what it was, but the perfume was thick, and not completely sweet. There was a cloying aftertaste of rot somehow, deep within the smell.

Death within the sweetness. So much like life itself—death always growing in the heart of the light.

I breathed it in, and exhaled. And then stole towards the house as dusk slipped through the trees.

The house looked beaten and old…kind of like Mel himself, I thought. I was walking along the side when I heard the screen door of the front of the house crash shut.

My heart stuck in my throat, and I flattened myself to the siding. I could hear the creak of a car door, and then the slam as it shut again. Slowly, I pushed myself to step forward, until I was at the corner of the house, and could peer around.

Mel was walking up the three steps of the front porch, carrying a bag of something.

The screen door slammed again, and he was gone.

I slipped around the corner, daring myself to creep along the front of the house. If he came out at this point, I was dead. Nowhere to run.

But the front door remained silent. I moved closer to the picture window that looked out over the wooden porch. The ledge was lower than my waist, so I carefully knelt down, and tried to stare inside without being seen.

Mel lived in the aftermath of a tornado.

Inside, I could see a couch and old tube television. And in the next room I could see a kitchen table, some half-open dark brown cabinets, and a refrigerator that, from the rounded edges on its door, may have been as old as me.

And then I saw Mel, dashing into the kitchen from some other room in the house. He threw a white package on the counter, and then pulled open a drawer. I watched him slice open the package, and then rip open whatever was inside.

From somewhere deep within the house, I heard a sound.

It reminded me of a heavy door closing. And a sigh. And a tortured scream.

All in one.

Mel turned away from me and vanished down a hallway into the depths of the house. I crept across the porch and moved in the same direction.

The next window I came to looked into a bedroom.

A woman (I assumed Mel's wife) was there, standing near the bed.

I watched as he held her, his arms tight around her waist. She moved against him, jaggedly, and I saw his hands slide up and down her back, grabbing her in passion, pulling her close to him.

Part of me wanted to pull away.... This wasn't something I should be seeing. But the voyeur in me bade me to stay.

I was almost getting turned on when they turned to the side, and I could see her in profile. And that's when I saw the black leather strap tied across her cheek and mouth.

As they turned, I saw that her hands were not completely free either. They were bound in white cloth. Almost as if he'd tied a dish towel around them.

I watched, as he hugged and pulled her close and they twirled around the room. And I began to realize that his hug was as much of a struggle as it was an embrace.

When they reached a certain angle, I could see her eyes.

They were not lit with love.

She looked hungry.

That's when I saw that her hands were not pawing his back in amorousness…she was clawing at him in violence. If her hands weren't wrapped in cloth, she'd have shredded his back in short order.

"I know, I know," I could hear him say through the window. "I brought it. Don't worry."

He pulled back from her, and picked up a white paper package from the dresser behind them. He pulled a red piece of bloody meat from the paper, and his wife's gaze followed it. She lunged forward, and then I could see the chains holding her taut to the bed.

Mel reached around the back of her neck and released the gag. It fell to the floor as her body surged forward. And then he held the meat up over her mouth and she leapt up for it, like a dog. She groaned and pulled against her chains, and when he released the meat, she swiped it into her mouth with her "mittened" claws in a heartbeat.

I'm not sure what I thought at that moment. I couldn't do anything but watch as Mel reached behind him and fed her strip after strip of raw meat. When it was gone, he went back to the kitchen, and returned with more.

I watched as Mel fed his wife until she appeared sated. After a while, she stopped grabbing for the meat, and turned to lie down upon the bed. I could see clearly then the chains that held her ankles and waist.

And I could see the love in Mel's eyes as he inched forward, and slowly, tentatively, reached out his hand to stroke her hair as she slipped into a meat coma.

She was hunger, and he was her slave.

I understood now why his face was sometimes bruised, and marked.

Something was really wrong with Mel's wife.

The weird thing for me was, this was the second time I'd seen a woman in chains today. Somehow it had all gone from strange to stranger.

I slipped away from the window, and back down the gravel driveway. I didn't want to face Mel right now to ask any questions. I wasn't sure what to ask, exactly. "Why does your wife like raw meat so much" didn't seem to be the right entrée. And "why do you keep your wife chained up like a dog" wasn't the best leading question either.

That night, I lay in my bed and kept seeing Mel's wife lunging for the bloody steaks in his hand. I didn't think she cared a whole lot whether she latched onto the meat he held or the meat he *was*. She was hungry. That was all.

Nearby, I heard a too-familiar hum. It closed in, the sound of its hunger growing louder, nearer.

I slapped at it with one firm, fatal smack.

The mosquito died on my arm. Hunger incarnate. Hunger overcome.

I couldn't help but think that Mel needed to do something similar. Though I didn't expect he'd be open to the idea.

I continued to delve into the plant's production and personnel records. And it didn't take too long to see a trend.

Something had happened in January. The first week of the year, the rate of factory sick days suddenly doubled. You could shrug that off, at first, to recovery from over-exuberant New Year's Eve celebrations. We saw the same problems in Chicago, but it was a minimal event. A few days of heightened absenteeism, and then things dropped back to normal.

Here, however…they'd increased.

By February, an eighth of the workforce was absent on any given day, and the trips to the company infirmary had skyrocketed. Six months later, that hadn't changed. And when I looked at the company doctor's appointment records, I saw that he was solidly booked every day of the past month.

I decided a visit to the doctor was in order. Impromptu. I didn't want to wait until July to get in. I set off down the stairs and across the main floor of the plant and down a hallway that led alongside the shipping dock. The company physician's office was all the way in the back of the factory.

The sign on the outside of the glass door said Fagan McLeod, MD. I stood outside for a moment, peering in, and as I did so, the door to my left that led out to the parking lot wrenched open.

A white-faced, gaunt man shambled inside, pushed along by a disheveled woman. Black strips of hair clung to her face, which was beaded in sweat. I saw why instantly. She was having difficulty herding the man forward. She had his arms chained and prodded him with something in the back, but he kept trying to turn on her, and from deep within his chest, moans of anger trembled. They were contained, however, by the rubber gag around his mouth.

"Kin ya git the door," the woman begged of me.

I did. And once they were inside, I followed them.

The waiting room was small, and two other couples were seated along the longest wall. In each case, one of the two was gagged and restrained. Their "keepers" struggled to keep them in place, and I quickly understood why the walls were completely bare of decoration, save for numerous dents and cracks.

This was a holding pen, not a waiting room.

"Can I help you?" a woman called. She poked her head out of a small receptionist's office. I stepped up and introduced myself.

"I'm from the home office," I explained. "I need to speak to Dr. McLeod for a moment."

She led me through a white door and into an examining room and gestured for me to have a seat.

"He's with a patient right now," she said. But I'll make sure he stops in before his next appointment."

He didn't keep me waiting long. A brief knock on the door, and a broad-shouldered man in a white lab coat entered the room. His silver hair curled in a thick wave across his forehead, and his mouth was nearly obscured by a salt and pepper beard and mustache. Behind his glasses beamed two strong, if slightly sunken, blue eyes. He looked like a retired lumberjack wearing a doctor's garb.

"How kin I help ya?" he asked. He didn't sit, choosing instead to lean against the closed door.

"Your schedule has gotten pretty full these days," I noted.

He nodded. "We take care of our own."

"What's wrong with your own?" I pressed.

"Lots of things," he said. His expression didn't change. "Meningitis, the flu, headcolds, congenital problems…I treat them all."

"You didn't mention anything that would require chains and ball gags," I pointed out.

He nodded. "We do have some psychiatric cases as well," he admitted.

"And you see them all on Tuesday, or what?"

The doctor shrugged. "I have patients to see," he said, putting his hand on the doorknob.

"What's going on around here really, doctor?" I demanded. "What's wrong with the people in your waiting room really? Is there some kind of epidemic?"

"Everything's fine," he said. "As long as they come in for their shots every week, everyone stays healthy."

He opened the door and held his hand out, motioning for me to leave.

"Go back to your production reports," he said. "We're taking care of the workers and their families down here. You go take care of the numbers and spreadsheets up there."

With that, he disappeared around the corner and into a treatment room.

I started to walk towards the exit, and then thought better of it. Instead, I followed the doctor. I ducked into the room next to the one he'd entered, and quietly closed the door. Then I pressed my ear up to the wall. I could just barely hear him speaking in the next room.

"…the raw meat has been workin', then?"

Muffled response. A woman's voice. I wondered if it was the woman I'd opened the door for earlier.

"We'll keep on with this dosage," McLeod said. "As long as you can handle him? Otherwise, I can give a heavier sedative to use?"

Muffled response.

"No bites?" McLeod asked. "Good. Keep it safe, and you can keep him home. Now hold his arm for me if you can, and we'll give him his dose."

A sudden crash and McLeod yelled. "Hold him!"

Something pounded against the wall, as if someone had just beat a fist or a bat against it. Then more thumping sounds, and a woman's voice, screaming, "No!"

I hung against the wall, frozen. What was going on next door? Should I break my cover and help? But then it quieted, and I heard McLeod say one word. "Good."

A minute later, he laughed and said, "He is a big one. Better get him out on the line now."

I heard the door next door open, and then the doctor added one more caution. "Watch yourself, Elly. We don't want to lose you, too."

I waited until the noises next door had been quiet for a few minutes, and then I poked my head out of the door. Seeing no one, I walked back down the hall towards the reception area. The waiting room looked much the same as when I left it: three couples sat there, with one partner of each pair bound and gagged.

"Meningitis, the flu, and head colds, my ass," I said to myself.

When Mel got home from work that night, I was waiting for him on his front porch.

"Evening," I said with a smile. I didn't stand up.

"What are you doing here?" He stood halfway down the sidewalk, clearly uneasy with my presence. His eyes shifted back and forth, peering over my shoulders to take in the house. Wondering if I'd somehow been inside? Or looked inside?

"What's wrong with her?" I asked.

"She's fine," he said. "She just needs medicine."

"And meat," I added.

"What do you know about it?" He stepped closer, angry.

"Why is your face bruised?" I asked. I kept my voice quiet. "Are you having problems controlling her?"

"Mind your own business," he growled. "Get off my property."

"I'm not leaving until I know what's going on here," I said.

"Get outta here, or I'm gonna take out a couple a' yer teeth," he warned.

"You want to keep your job?" I asked sweetly. "You want to keep your health insurance? She needs those injections every week, just like the others, doesn't she?"

His eyes widened.

"Yeah, I've seen McLeod's waiting room," I said.

Something in his shoulders slumped at that moment. He stepped onto the stairs and brushed past me to step onto the porch.

"You want a drink?" he asked.

"Sure," I said. "I been waiting here for a long time. Been waiting for an answer for a long time."

"You're not going to like it," he warned.

I nodded. "I pretty much expect that."

He led me into the house and to the kitchen. "First things first," he said. Then he pulled a white paper package out of the refrigerator and unwrapped it. I followed him down the hall and to the room where she was chained. I watched him tenderly kiss her forehead and cheeks as she beat her bound fists against his back. Then I watched him loosen the ball gag and feed her strip after strip of raw meat until she could take no more. Sated, she didn't struggle as he refastened her gag and laid her down upon the bed.

Back in the kitchen, he pulled out two tumblers and poured two fingers of bourbon into each. He emptied his in one gulp, then refilled.

I sipped mine slowly, waiting for the story.

"It all started at the company New Year's Eve party," he began.

"I've always said they should stop spending budget on that," I said. "Nothing good ever comes of them."

Mel nodded. "Yeah. Well, certainly not this year."

"What happened?"

"One of the girls from the shipping department, Plutina Wade, found a new experimental flavor from Dr. McLeod's laboratory and decided to use it in moonshine shots."

"Wait a minute," I interrupted. "McLeod is the company doctor, isn't he?"

Mel nodded. "Sure, he is. But first and foremost, he's in charge of developing new flavors. He had been working on a new one called Huckleberry Pie, mixing some local berries with some other compounds. And Plutina thought that'd make for a great moonshine mixer. And she was right. She and a little group got snockered on the stuff before the clock struck midnight on New Year's Eve. And then when they called for everyone to claim a place beneath the mistletoe, she picked out Fin Kinnane and led him under the red berries of one of the plants that they'd tied to the rafters.

"He gave her a kiss…apparently a pretty good one, probably cuz he saw she didn't look like she could barely stand up straight anymore. Problem was, when the kiss was over, Fin didn't have no tongue anymore.

"He still managed to make a lot of noise, though. But he wasn't the only one. Seemed that everyone at Plutina's table had somehow gotten a bad hunger for their dates that night. There was a lot of blood beneath the mistletoe. And a lot of people got themselves bit trying to bring Plutina's party down. In the end, we got 'em all into the company infirmary and locked up 'til the doc could figured out what was going on."

My eyes must have looked pretty large at this point, because Mel gave me a thin-lipped laugh. "Yeah. Sounds ridiculous, doesn't it?"

"What was in the flavoring?" I asked.

Mel shrugged. "Only Doc knows. All I know is he was experimenting with some kind of wild berry. It wasn't ready for anyone to taste it yet. But once they did, it changed them, and he couldn't come up with a cure. He's been trying for months now."

"What does he inject them with every week?"

"That's just a vitamin shot with a time-delayed tranquilizer. Gives 'em nutrients to keep up their bodies while putting 'em into the quiet zone for three or four days, usually."

"And in the meantime, you chain them up and have them run the assembly line?" I said, my voice rising with incredulity.

Mel looked at me like I was a lunatic.

"What kind of people do you think we are?" he asked. "Those are prisoners from the jail. When we had too many workers out, we started the work program with the prison. Gives them a way to work off their sentence and fills in the places where we've lost workers. You came here wondering why productivity was down? Well, mainly because for a couple months there, we had a couple dozen spots open on the line while Doc was trying to find the cure."

"Doesn't seem like he's been too successful."

A step creaked behind me. "He's working on it."

I felt a pinch in my arm, and just as I turned to see Doctor McLeod's face grinning over my shoulder, he pulled the needle out of my arm. I could see that the syringe was empty.

"What did you…." I began.

I didn't finish. I slept.

When I woke up, there were chains on my ankles. I noticed them when I pulled myself off the cold floor on my elbows, and heard the clink-clink-clink of the metal drag across the floor when my legs shifted.

"What the hell?" I mumbled. The world still seemed blurry and warped.

A door closed behind me, and I shifted to see who it was.

The tall jeans and heavy boots of Jameson Tal stepped across the white tiles towards me.

"Ya shoulda stuck to your sales reports and quotas and whatnot," he drawled. "Thing is, you stuck yer head where it don't belong."

Jameson sunk to a crouch, and shook his head at me. "People don't like that, ya know."

"I was sent here to find out why productivity was down," I said. "You could have just told me that you had twenty or thirty people out with some local epidemic."

"And you woulda had us replace them instead of take care of them."

"Not if you'd told the company that it was an illness related to our products."

Jameson grinned and shook his head. "You think we want a parade of you people down here, putting us all under the microscope?" Jameson shook his head. "We take care of our own."

"You can't hold me prisoner here forever," I said. "And if you let some of the folks from the lab in Chicago or Michigan come down here, they might be able to help Dr. McLeod isolate and cure whatever this thing that he's unleashed."

Jameson smiled and shook his head. "I'll be honest with ya," he said. "I'm not so sure everybody wants this thing cured. I know Jed Boucher says he's never had this much fun with his sister before. I've seen the cat scratches on his face, and I gotta believe him there. In any case, you're not bringing the roof down on us. You're going to send some positive interim reports over the next month or two, while we get the prisoner program workers fully trained. They don't cost nothing extra, so payroll don't know the difference. And pretty soon the line will be running as good as it ever was. Chicago will be happy and wonder why they sent ya. The bean counters won't ask no more questions."

"I'm not sending any such report," I said. Bravado sounds great, but it's almost always a foolish exercise.

Jameson nodded. "No, I suppose technically that's true. *You* won't send those reports, but I will. With your name at the bottom. Nobody's going to miss you back there, and when you stop sending your updates, and they finally get around to asking where you are…I'll just tell 'em that I thought you went home two, three weeks ago…."

My stomach clenched. Was he really suggesting….

"Just remember," Jameson said. "I didn't want to do this. You brought it on yerself."

Just then, the doctor stepped into the room and motioned for Jameson. "I called for an assembly this afternoon," he said. "Everyone's excited."

"Zombies can't live on steaks alone, eh?" Jameson said.

Dr. McLeod shook his head. "No," he agreed. "They need man."

With that, they both left the room. That's when I pulled out my dictation recorder and decided to record my last report. I *did* discover why productivity was down, even if nobody will ever find out. I had to document it, even if this recorder will simply get smashed and thrown away.

Click

The door just opened. The doctor held it for Mel, who led his wife in on a chain. A line of others are now following him through the door.

"I'm sorry, man," Mel said. "But she's hungry. She needs you."

He's releasing the gag from her mouth, and her teeth look stained. Hungry.

The sound of chains dropped to the floor.

She's moving towards me.

"Don't fight it," Mel warned. "It'll go faster then."

I don't want to die. I've moved as far back into the room as I can, but the chains won't let me move anymore. Mel's wife and somebody's husband and a dozen other shambling creatures have entered the room. Their gags are off. My own personal deathrace is on.

I never wanted to come here.

"Ow! Shit, motherfucking bitch…."

"We take care of our own," Jameson Tal called from far away. "And soon you'll be one of us."

Their hands are all over me. Their teeth…. *Shit!*

I'm going to turn this off now. My legs are bleeding, and I can't kick much more. You don't need to hear my screams.

I'm the one "taking care of their own" now.

And they are hungry.

MIRANDA JO'S GIRL

STEVE RASNIC TEM

Steve Rasnic Tem's latest novel is Deadfall Hotel *(Solaris Books). In August of 2012, New Pulp Press will be publishing a collection of the best of his noir and crime fiction,* Ugly Behavior. *And in 2013 ChiZine is bringing out* Celestial Inventories, *a major collection of his more recent strange fiction.*

The car in the Willisville Store parking lot—"lot" meaning a wide patch of rough gravel by the road—was a new one, from Japan. It was smaller than what Betty liked, but she figured the fellow in the driver's seat was getting good gas mileage. No small thing, the way they robbed you at the pump. Betty's store had two pumps, and she hated how much she charged, but she just provided what folks needed—she didn't always set the price. She couldn't help how much things cost people—she just hoped it wasn't more than they could afford.

A lot of the local people just walked to the store and only drove to get to their jobs down in Big Stone or Wise. Obviously this blond-headed fellow wasn't local, and when he got out of the car his colorful tie confirmed it. At least he wasn't wearing a suit. But he was carrying a clipboard, and in Betty's experience men carrying clipboards were usually bad news.

She worried it over as he walked toward the store. Willisville wasn't actually a town anymore. If it weren't for the store providing a few convenient necessities to the locals it would just be a ghost town like Ender's Ivy or Castle's Wood or Drunkard Bottom. Just a weedy spot on the mountain where something used to be. Betty wasn't ready to be a ghost, not just yet. But all it would take was some fellow from the county seat at Wise carrying a shiny metal clipboard.

Not that a young man like this could be charmed by an old gal, but Betty smiled when she gave the fellow a biscuit, another cup of coffee, and a little jar of homemade apple butter as they sat at the small table usually reserved for visiting with friends. "Pretty car you got there," she said, trying to catch him with her eyes. "Bet you get good gas mileage." Her daddy used to say a plain-looking woman like herself had no business flirting with people, but she always had. She guessed it just came natural to her.

He nodded back kind of perfunctory, started thumbing through those clipboard pages like he was going to ignore her pitiful little charms, then spared a second glance for the biscuit, and she knew she'd hooked him. He put down the clipboard, picked up the biscuit, and started spreading on the butter.

"Ma'am," he raised the biscuit to his mouth. "Do you know a Miranda Jo Wheeler? Her, and her daughter Charlene?" He slowly pushed the doughy bread, smeared a greasy cinnamon color, into his mouth like that would give her time to consider her answer.

"Mister, I've known all the Wheelers. Known them all my life. Had Miranda Jo in my Sunday school class when she was just a slip of a thing. But Charlene, she's—" Betty stopped then, poking around her head for the words.

The clipboard man dabbed at his mouth, the biscuit gone. A man could choke to death, eating so quick like that.

"Troubled? Hard to discipline?" he supplied. "Constantly running away—it's all in here." He tapped the paper. "But Ms. Wheeler's ex-husband Randall is the custodial parent. You knew that, didn't you? Whatever reason the girl gave for running away, she'll need to go back to him. Unless—" He leaned closer. "She is truly missing, and something has happened to the child. Or maybe—" He stopped, looked down at his papers without really looking at them. "She has accused him of abuse."

Betty felt befuddled, not sure how the conversation had gotten where it did. "That would be *terrible*," was the first thing she thought of to say.

"Terrible things happen to children, ma'am." He didn't finish with "in these hills," but Betty was pretty sure that was what he thought. "So you've seen her, then?"

Betty didn't want to lie to this clipboard man. She didn't like lying, nor was she good at it.

"Mister," she said. "Did you know that when Charlene left this mountain, her mama said she was sure she'd never see her little girl alive again? That's a terrible thing for a mother to feel. Randall— He's a rough character—everybody around *here* knows that. Miranda doesn't have much money, and she was never very bright, but she tried to do right by that girl. They should have never taken Charlene away. A child *belongs* with its momma."

"Well, ma'am, I'm not the judge. It wasn't my decision. I'm just here to determine the child's whereabouts and check on her welfare. Once I turn in my report, the higher-ups will finally determine how to proceed."

If Betty had been her father, she would have told him that God was the only "higher up" capable of final determination. But she wasn't her father. She was more like her mother, who had her own ways of doing things, and more interested in helping people than judging them.

"I'm not blaming you, Sir," she said. "It's a hard business. I'm sure we all want what's best for the child."

"Well, apparently *someone* has fallen down on the job, ma'am. Because I've had a phone call from a Mrs. Presley—"

"Mrs. Presley? The school teacher?"

"She identified herself as a local grade school teacher, yes. She called to tell us she was driving home from a movie in Big Stone Gap Wednesday night when she saw Charlene walking in the middle of the foggy road *by herself*. She states here." He went thumbing through pages again. "The child's clothes were torn and stained, and there appeared to be blood on her face. Mrs. Presley avoided hitting the child by inches, she says, almost running off the road. When she went back for the child there was no sign of her." He looked at Betty, grim-faced.

Betty thought to say that that was terrible—so much in this world was terrible—it was a word that said what she felt about many, many things. But she figured you could only use the word "terrible" so often in the same conversation before you lost credibility.

"Was she sure it was Charlene?" she asked instead. And maybe just asking that question was perilously close to a lie, because *of course* she was sure. Alma Presley had taught Charlene math for practically all of grade school.

"Sure enough that she has agreed to make a sworn statement. Now, ma'am, I really just have one question for you. Have you seen this child alive?"

"No, I have not," Betty replied without hesitation.

Betty closed the store early. She didn't like to do it—people in their small community depended on her when they had some immediate need. Of course, the fact was people on the mountain had all kinds of needs, and if a need was years, even decades old, could you still call it "immediate"?

If Betty had been another person in a better life she would have gone home to her family, spent time with her special someone, hugged her own children and breathed in the sweet perfume of their hair. Worried about her own for a while, instead of someone else's.

But she had this life, not some other, so instead of going home to an empty house she pushed her old pickup at a stately creep over to another part of the mountain, into a remote hollow where the fog settled into the rippled ground like clots of milk, and the rough slabs of dark wood cabins gleamed like damp stone. Here the people watched you from empty windows and shadowed porches, but didn't wave like they did in the more sociable parts of the county. Most of these folks never left the sorry protection of their falling-down shacks. Most couldn't, and sat still and quiet like moldering pieces of furniture.

The Wheeler house sat by itself below the grade of the road, looking like it had sunk, or been pushed off the edge. Betty eased herself down the path, thinking that if she broke her hip now, and here, she might never open the store again. The bare dirt yard was unsettlingly quiet, without the usual scatter of half-starved chickens and even worse-off cats.

When Miranda came to the door half-dressed and stinking of whisky, Betty wasn't at all surprised, except at how disappointed she was still able to feel. Miranda looked at her blearily.

"Mizz Betty," she slurred.

Betty pushed past her, looking warily into doorways and behind furniture. She registered the piece of bloody fur by one chair leg, the little bit of throw-up under the TV stand. The screen flickered and rolled, showing people with their cut-off heads nodding below their feet. "Miranda, I told you to watch her, to keep her close."

"She's a handful. You don't know—"

"Of course, I know. I told you the way it would be, remember? Remember how we talked about the price you'd have to pay? Something like this, there's always a cost."

Miranda laughed then. It was high-pitched and fading, like someone falling off a cliff. "I said I'd do anything," she said. "*Anything*."

"So has she left? Miranda, when was the last time you *saw* her?

Because other people, *they've* seen her, I can tell you that."

"She's there, in the back. I heard her come in a bit ago."

Betty went a little cold hearing that, but she tried to make that chill over into something hard that would allow her to do what was necessary. "How does she look?"

"I ain't checked on her yet."

"Oh, Miranda. They need—Well, they're like any other child—"

Miranda howled at that, a laugh so ugly Betty couldn't be in the same room with it. So she let it drive her toward the back of the house.

The rooms stank of filth and blood, but not Charlene's own blood. Charlene was long past bleeding. Betty found her lying on some faded potato sacks and a spread of old newspapers like you would leave out for a new puppy. Her eyes were white and big as hen's eggs, her mouth like a split in the rough bark of her face. She tilted her head up, but Betty couldn't tell if the child actually saw her. She made a sound, which might have been a hungry sound, and the tongue came out like a worm peeking out of an infected wound. Betty would have left then, if the child hadn't reached out that dirty little hand with the soft, puffy fingers.

Betty's mother used to say the best thing you could do for a child was talk to it. It didn't matter if you were trying to teach the child or comfort it through some sickness or just keep it occupied so it would stay out of trouble. "Words is magic," her mother would say. "You'll see soon enough, when you have some of your own."

Of course, Betty never had any of her own, and seeing what some of these folk went through, what with the sicknesses and the delinquency and all the things in the world that could take a cherished child away from you, she was just as glad, for the most part. And how could she know she'd be any good at it anyway? How could anybody, until it happened, until you raised your child, or until you killed it?

When Miranda Jo had called her that night, crying and carrying on and so worked up she sounded more like some animal in distress than a normal human being, and asked her to come out to the road and bring her truck, that's exactly what she did, because Betty always tried to do what people asked of her. It wasn't any of her business if they could afford the cost or not—They had to decide that.

It was hard to say if Charlene had run away from Randall and been hit by something—something with someone driving it who didn't care enough or was too scared to stop—or if Randall had just driven along and pushed the girl out—certainly he was capable of that kind of meanness. At the time it didn't matter to Miranda Jo—she just wanted her baby girl back. Maybe if Betty hadn't agreed to do what she did with the knowledge her mother had taught her, Miranda Jo would have cared who did what. But that bridge had been crossed, and the bridge had fallen into the water.

Betty hadn't been able to bring herself to hold the child, or touch her more than absolutely necessary. She had Miranda Jo rub in the salve she made out of certain herbs and certain weeds and mayonnaise and licorice—you'd think they were preparing to roast a pig if you didn't know otherwise. Betty had just said the words, a lot of words, all the words her mother had taught her to make an arsenal against death.

And then she had set that cocoon down the girl's throat, that cocoon for a moth no one had ever had a name for, that cocoon you had to harvest in moonlight and under the weather of despair.

But now that the deed was done and the child had asked in her way, Betty sat down with her to do what she asked, holding the girl as the mother came into the room to watch. She sat down with the stench of her, down with the death of her, and it wasn't much different than with any afflicted child, she guessed, any child that made you uncomfortable with its differences, with its spasms and jerks and mysterious behaviors. All you could do was hold it, and use your words on it, speaking of the wooden children of the world, the stone children, the empty and the cold, and hoping that someday out of the darkness it would find its way back.

BEING IN THE SHADOW

MAURICE BROADDUS

Maurice Broaddus has written dozens of short stories, essays, novellas, and articles. His dark fiction has been published in numerous magazines, anthologies, and web sites, most recently including Cemetery Dance, Apex Magazine, Black Static, *and* Weird Tales Magazine. *He is the co-editor of the Dark Faith anthology series (Apex Books) and the author of The Knights of Breton Court trilogy (Angry Robot Books). In his spare time, he sits on the board of Second Story, a nonprofit organization whose mission it is to encourage creative writing among elementary school students. Visit his site at* www.MauriceBroaddus.com.

Everyone gets trapped in a story. It happens. Each year that ticks by, the body breaks down a little bit more and your reputation—all of your accumulated tales—looms ever larger and runs ahead of you. I know the story that's been written about me. The tales whispered about me around water coolers; conversations stop as soon as I enter the break room. Detective Derrious Marsden, a cop on the fast track, groomed by the brass to go places.... Then, poof, golden-boy status revoked and a star on the rise falls. All I could do was sit here in this uncomfortable seat, stare out the window, and let the scenery of the Appalachian hills distract me.

Every cop had at least one of those cases that haunted them. Darrell Winthrop was my ghost, and I didn't care how far into the hills I had to chase him. Even if I had to trade what favors remained to secure special permission to go into the quarantined zone or suffer my special escort.

Special Agent Rodney Zelenova hummed to himself, eyes hidden by sunglasses. His head tilted back in the seat with the contented expression of a dog catching the passing breeze out the driver's side window. His crumpled, off-the-rack suit hung awkward and loose on him, like the skin of a fat man who'd lost a lot of weight. A grease stain on his tie made him smell like rancid meat and onions.

"This your first shuffler hunt?" Zelenova asked. He was a talker, too. Didn't know how to enjoy a good silence.

"Yeah. Baltimore PD has me on special assignment."

"Ah. You pissed someone off, eh?"

"Something like that." I was a solid enough cop, true po-lice by some measures, but with an air of stink on me. Not the "plant a drop piece on some junkie to close a murder" or the "vouchered cash from a drug bust turned up light" kind of stink. This was worse. It followed me from department to department and partner to partner, not that I had many of those these days. But it was a lingering stench. Now, if I was a famous athlete and had screwed up, all I'd have to do was win a few championships and all would be forgiven. Me, though, nothing I could say or do would ever be seen in a fair light. I'd just pay and pay and pay. There was no balancing those scales of trust, and once a person realized that about themselves, it was hard to come up with reasons to get up each morning. Luckily, I had Darrell. "It's like we've crossed over into another world."

"A parallel universe of poor white trash and shufflers. It's hard enough to keep them rounded up, much less contained."

"No one left behind, my ass. It's like a third-world nation up here."

"Works for some, I guess," Zelenova said with a hint of sadness to his voice.

"Who the hell would this work for?"

"The hill folk? Shoot, from New York to Alabama over to Kentucky. Theirs is a long reach. They migrate about looking for work, for all the good it does them."

"What do you mean?"

"They're the professional poor. It's all they know how to do or be." There it was again. That sadness now tinged with shame. He shared their story and resented it. Weren't too many Zelenovas in the hills, which meant his mother got out and married up. But some part of him still called this place home.

"You got them all figured out." I drummed my fingers along the window edge.

"Some stories ain't that hard to read. Take your Darrell Anthony Winthrop, for example. I could tell you all about him from his jacket. The way he's dressed….the neighborhood he's from. . ."

"He had it coming?"

"I'm not saying that. Just that I know his story," Zelenova said.

"You know him?" I pressed him to see if he'd give up a connection between them.

"I know his type. The story all ends the same way."

"You're a profiling lawsuit waiting to happen," I said.

"It's just us here. True po-lice. 'Less one of us ain't who he says he is."

"You got something to say?" I shifted in my seat to face him. My fingers stopped drumming along the window. My gaze met his sunglasses-hidden eyes.

"Just that I hear things." His sneer confirmed he'd read my sheet and checked the rumor mill in doing his due diligence.

"Everyone's got a story to tell."

"Some of 'em are even true." Zelenova faced the road again, probably unaware of how his accent crept into his voice when he got a little heated.

I returned to staring at the passing greens and browns that passed for scenery. "Where's our first stop?"

"Lester's. You'll love it. A real down-home joint."

I closed my eyes, pretending to sleep, hoping that would discourage any more opining from Zelenova. He fiddled with the radio dial finally settling on some country station with a weak signal. Despite the crackle of static, he turned it up. I could almost picture the malicious glee of his smirk.

I thought of my regrets and the moments I wished I could have back that ended up defining me. The one-nighter with the cop groupie I didn't know or even like. Nor did I have a need to slake. Such things ended up being the final nail in my marriage. I concentrated on what it would be like to catch up to Darrell.

The government cordoned off the area around the Quarantined Zone, wanting more of a buffer zone. Some folks couldn't bear to leave the place they grew up in and knew and the officials were content to let them stay. No one would miss the occasional local poached by a shuffler. There wasn't much difference between them and a shuffler anyway.

Zelenova parked the car a good distance away "as not to unduly spook the locals." Long-dead leaves crunched underfoot as we made our way up the path to Lester's. A neon-red sign bled against the early evening sky. An open bay window allowed peals of conversation and music to blare into the surrounding woods. The overhead fluorescent lights burned noisily. A mounted bass hung on a wall of faux wood paneling next to a wood-framed painting of men fishing on a lake. The twin sentries of a pay phone and an electronic poker machine stood by the front door. A cigarette machine guarded the rear by the restroom. The bar ran the length of the building, topped with half-filled black ashtrays and piles of plastic cups. We pushed through the milling crowd—a sea of hopelessness, fringed blue jean jackets, and Trans Am t-shirts—until we reached Jolene Winthrop.

A cigarette clung to her lower lip like a fish that had resigned itself to the hook. The ghost of blue mascara smeared around her too-small eyes sunken within hollow circles buried in her face. Her nostrils were in perpetual flare. A small mole dotted a cut on her chapped lips that curled to a sneer at our approach. She was thin, like she'd lost a lot of weight recently, her blue jean jacket now a few sizes too large for her.

"What do you want?" The lines around her mouth hardened as she spoke with the hint of a Southern accent. "You don't belong up here."

"Can't say I've had much luck belonging anywhere," I said.

"You look like you been rode hard and put up wet, Jolene," Zelenova said.

"I already asked what you want, Rodney." She cut her eyes and polished off whatever filled her plastic cup. Plopping it back on the bar, she sucked her teeth for good measure.

"We looking for your boy," I said. "Darrell."

"He was the only one I had left."

"He has two brothers."

"Had." She curled her lips, bringing the cigarette to bear without her hands touching it.

"What happened?" I asked.

"Shuffle got 'em."

"We just want to ask Darrell a few questions. We think he has some information that could help us in an investigation."

"You come up here, talkin' like a house a-fire, interrupting my night out because Darrell's done got into some mischief? You dumber than a stack o' toes." Jolene took another drag from her cigarette. She knew how the game worked. Her and her people had obviously seen their share of dirt.

"*Dumber than a stack o' toes.* I'm gonna have to remember that one."

Zelenova's voice lilted for emphasis. "We tried the easy way, but play time's over. Your boy, young squire Winthrop, is a person of interest in a police shooting. I need you to hear me on this: He shot at police. The police. We don't take too kindly to that."

"Oh, Lord," Jolene said with a sudden soberness.

"Yeah, yeah. Jesus, Mary, and Joseph, now it's a party." Zelenova stepped closer to her, letting his girth speak for him. He knew how to use his size. And his eyes. With a quick cut of them, he backed down several good ol' boys from interrupting our friendly chat.

"Ain't no need to blaspheme."

"All I'm saying is that my colleagues back in Baltimore, as we speak, are tearing up every stash house, clearing every corner, and overturning every rock he might have slithered under looking for him." I held my hands up and took a step back to give her room to breathe. "Even if we don't find him, his friends in the city won't be real pleased with him, as their business is being disrupted on account of him."

"Now me, I'm o' a different mind," Zelenova said. "I think when some folks get in trouble, in over their heads, they go home. Back to where they feel safe. Where they are known for exactly who they are and are loved and protected anyway. You know any place like that, Jolene?"

"All we want is to be left alone," Jolene said.

"Afraid we can't do that, ma'am," I said.

"They ain't hurt nobody. I seen to that."

"Where is he, Jolene?"

"He up in Shadow Holler."

She flipped us off as we left.

"How badly do you want this mook?" Zelenova asked.

"Bad." I played with my set of handcuffs, spinning the rotating arm through the cuffs, each click of it ratcheting through like a shot in the night.

"Going up to Shadow Holler bad?"

"Yeah."

"You know being in the Shadow means he as good as dead anyway."

"'Good as' ain't good enough," I said.

"Alright, alright. I get it. It's personal. But if we do this, I have to ask, can I depend on you?"

There it was. The Question. The sum of my life's story boiled down to one question.

My partner (I can't even bring myself to think her name) and I had a drug warrant out on Darrell Winthrop, though we actually wanted him as a suspect in a murder. Cornerboy stuff we could have left to Narco, but we had a body and case and couldn't afford to pass up one for the win column. He'd been keeping his head down but we'd been tipped that he was staying in a motel out in Pigtown.

We prepared to take the motel room. Crouched into position, I glanced over at my partner as she got on the other side, weapon drawn and aimed low. She prepared to give the nod, as she would take the door. Life or death determined in a few seconds, she loved that moment. The rush of plunging into the unknown, heart hammering, adrenaline pumping so hard her tongue tasted like a battery. Suddenly, all I could picture was a shotgun blast caving in her chest as she knocked on the door. Or her head exploding in a shower of brain and blood as she was shot from the window.

"Police!" my partner shouted, pounding the door with her fist. She smiled, a quick flash of a knowing smirk. She held up three fingers.

Three. Two. One.

The door frame splintered with the first kick and we stepped into the room.

"Police!" she shouted again.

My eyes darted about, scanning the room. The shadows danced about, cloying and looming at the same time. The sparse furniture took on monstrous shapes in the dark.

"Clear!" she yelled from around the corner.

I went through the motions. My weapon swept the room, but I hadn't moved more than a couple feet in. I felt the presence long before I heard the furtive sound from the closet. The door cracked open. Darrell Winthrop had an elongated face with his front two teeth so much larger than the rest of his teeth it was like they shoved the rest of them to the back of his mouth. Long brown hair trailed from the back of his camo baseball cap. Like a teenager trying to will, in vain, a mustache in place to impress the ladies, his mustache didn't quite grow in right. He peered right into my eyes. He must've seen something in them. He pressed his fingers to his lips telling me to "Sh." My gun dropped toward the floor, impotent in my hands. Rounding the corner, he skulked toward my partner. I flinched at the first shot…then closed my eyes at the next two.

Silence sucked all of the oxygen out of the room. Just when I couldn't take it any longer, my partner called my name. I followed the sound of her voice. When I turned the corner, Darrell slumped against the wall with two slugs in him and my partner clutching her arm to stanch the bleeding. She kicked Darrell's gun out of reach, then met my eyes. Disgust filled her face and I knew that was the last time she would look at me at all. In that moment, trapped in her gaze, I felt it all slipping away. The ground that was my life shifted under me. My identity, everything I thought I was, ripped from me, leaving me a walking husk going through the motions of life.

Shuffling.

Shadow Holler had a single road that wound through its hills with enough space for one car at a time to travel it. The trail dappled with deeper pockets of shadow; a thick canopy of trees prevented most light from penetrating through to the ground. The hills reclaimed any attempts at intrusion. Though the nearest store was a car ride away, rusted-out grocery carts made bridges in the creek that threaded the hills. Ancient boilers piled up between abandoned mobile homes. Whatever the deteriorated metal drums once held had long since seeped into the earth. Rumor had it that their contents were the cause of the rise of the shufflers.

A litter of cars, like an outdoor graveyard of the best Detroit had to offer through the decades, greeted us until we stumbled across a 1953 Chevy pickup truck. Its split windshield reminded me of outdated spectacles. Its original surf-green paint job long faded, rust now devoured it like a cancer. A spare tire mounted on the side, was bound in place like much of the side rails, by bailing wire. The body, completely trashed out, was held together by caulking and string. It was parked in front of a dilapidated mobile home, old tires strewn about the yard, the house a faded pink with white trim and smashed windows.

"This place is a John Mellencamp song," Zelenova said.

"Over there." I pointed to a clearing that allowed for a better view of the area. The sound of the car prowling the area was sure to draw their attention. I certainly wanted it to. My heart jack-hammered in my throat. I could taste the bitter shock of copper on the back of my tongue.

"That him?"

"Yeah."

"Remember, he's no different than 'is momma. You can't talk t' him like he's people."

"I got this." I unbuckled my seat belt, but Zelenova's hand on my arm stopped me.

"You can't. Not without back up. I'm not going to be part of your suicide plan."

"You willing to go through a door with me?"

He paused and gave me all the answer I needed. "We should wait for back up."

"You can wait." I stepped out my door. I started toward the trail, but knew that Zelenova wrestled with whether to let me go down this path by myself (for which he could never forgive himself) or join me (the man who wouldn't go through a door and almost got his partner killed) in near-certain death. No one wandered into the Shadow alone, especially at night, if they had any interest in seeing home again. I couldn't leave him like that. I couldn't leave him so twisted up by which ever choice he made that he'd end up just like me. I doubled back to his side of the car and caught him as he was unbuckling his seat belt to follow me.

"Remember, you couldn't stop me." I drew my gun on him. "Handcuff yourself to the steering wheel, then give me your keys."

"You don't have t' do this."

"My story is my story. I ain't got no need to add to it, but I only got one shot at a good ending."

Zelenova called to my back as I left him. Who knows, maybe he flipped me off.

Gravel crunched under my feet. It was scary how vast and dark the night was. All of my life, I was always running, like hunting dogs were on my trail. Trying to escape something and wanting to be caught all at the same time. Life hurtling by unlived and unappreciated by me yet building towards something. I thought about how easy it was for a man to lose touch with himself, trapped in a cage of moments. Moments wasted. Moments lost. Moments regretted.

I felt his presence behind me long before I heard him. I turned to face him, but months as a shuffler hadn't been too kind to Darrell. He still had the same long face and huge front teeth that gave him the appearance of a rat. A plaid shirt draped over a faded Metallica t-shirt and torn blue jeans as he shambled towards me. The main difference was three fingers missing from his left hand. Blood dried around the wounds and flies swirled around the stumps.

"Darrell Winthrop? You're under arrest for the attempted murder of a police officer." With a skittish stutter step, I stayed out of his reach while I circled around him. The Chevy impeded his forward movement. With a lazy gnash of his teeth, he lolled his head toward me, as if his heart wasn't in his attempts to sate his hunger. Maybe his own vestigial guilt pressed on what remained of his soul. I pulled his hand around to handcuff him. His hands felt like meat that had been left in the sun. I slammed him onto the hood of the truck while I read him his rights, and then slammed him again for driving me do this. When the echo of his weight against the metal faded, I heard the rest of them.

Shadows bobbed in the dim moonlight, hungry silhouettes against the deeper shadows. The first two shufflers ambled into view; my guess was that they were Darrell's brothers. The first had a black fishing cap canted on his head, glasses with broken lenses, and a thick mustache on top of a week's worth of stubble on his face. With a grungy thermal top under a blue jean shirt, his Adam's apple bobbed along his thin neck in anticipation. I was tempted to run, but I stood there, allowing more shufflers to cut me off from the sight of Zelenova's vehicle, getting used to the idea until I was no longer frightened. The second meandered out of a pigeon coop in back. His green plaid shirt, frayed around the cuffs and elbows, half tucked into faded blue jeans, peeking out from beneath his black leather jacket zipped up along its right side. His long black hair, shaped like a bowl, was grungy and matted. A goatee framed his mouth, which opened and closed as if working a huge wad of invisible chew. They had to be Darrell's brothers. Family always took you in no matter what you'd done. I recognized the deep longing their distant stares didn't quite mask. I knew the desperate, insatiable hunger, what it meant to be consumed by a single thought.

Once you got past being lost in a morass of self-pitying bull, it wasn't so scary once you came face-to-face with it all. Not when you were tired, weak, and worn with an exhaustion that ran to your bones. You got to a place where there was no more fear, no more anger, no more bitterness, no more worry. No more you.

A blank page on which to write a new story.

ALMOST HEAVEN

MICHAEL PAUL GONZALEZ

Michael Paul Gonzalez grew up in Wyoming and went to grad school in Southern Illinois, so open spaces and country folk are near and dear to him. He currently resides in Los Angeles, a town full of zombies of every shape and size. He is the founder and editor of Thundadome.com, and can sometimes be found at MichaelPaulGonzalez.com.

The first time the bus engine hiccupped and backfired, Rosa didn't wonder about a tow or roadside maintenance. She was more troubled by the song on the radio. One of those new pop songs by some disposable diva. Those songs always took a little longer to make it onto the radio stations out in the sticks. And here, eighty miles past Harper's Ferry, was definitely the sticks. Mainstream always traveled slow this way, if at all. Pop songs. Fashion trends. Cures for Necrotic Cannibalistic Hematoma.

Rosa looked up at the sun visor above her captain's chair, two small pictures of her children beaming down at her. The only two reasons she kept driving these shitty routes. More time away from the kids, but more money to support them. She knew they were safe back in Baltimore, back behind the double walls of medicine and military protection. Here, even as the bus labored its way back to sixty-five miles per hour, all she could think about was a painfully slow couple of hours on the side of the road. Creeping fog and cold air and every tree branch that shook in the wind a skeletal reminder of impending doom.

This particular group of senior citizens called themselves Nourishing the Roots. They were all on a destination tour to the African American Heritage Family-Tree Museum in Ansted. Tracing their past, finding their ancestry. That was the first stop, and then there'd be some further exploration to the south, finding connections to the Underground Railroad and Buffalo Soldiers, the trading blocks, the lynching trees. All of these old folks trying to delay death by meeting the ones who went before them.

The bus lurched again, a hard knock from the floor that almost sounded like the drive train breaking loose and slamming into the undercarriage. That was all she wrote. Rosa wrestled the steering wheel hard to the right, tried to guide the mammoth vessel as far out of traffic as she could. It was foggy out—of *course* it was foggy out—and the last thing she'd need was to get slammed from behind by an eighteen-wheeler coming down the hill.

There were lights in the distance, just a half mile down the road, a pale yellow haze in the thickening mist. Half a mile, give or take. Leave the senior citizens here on the bus or lead a parade into town? Was that a town? Those lights could run on a timer, could just be a warning light for the peak of a hill, telling traffic to slow down.

Most of the passengers were asleep, hearing aids out, meds kicked in, dead to the world. There were a few whispering murmurs starting in the back. Rosa had the PA mic in her hand, finger hovering over the button, then thought better of it. If the walkers were coming, these people would die in their sleep and know nothing of it. Waking them up for no reason at all would prove far more painful to her psyche, as the complaints would come nonstop for the rest of the trip.

Rosa slid her finger off the PA address button and quietly walked down the aisle to the back of the bus, whispering reassurances to the few people drowsing awake that there was just a slight engine problem, she'd check it out and be right back.

Outside, the air was cool, the mist thick enough to settle through clothes in a few strides. Rosa looked both ways up the road, but it was no use. Night had settled in, and the fog took care of what little visibility there would have been. She shook her head and went back to the bus, pulling her cellphone out as she went.

The silence of no signal only amplified the pounding in her head. Rosa clicked her phone shut and leaned against the door. It was cold out, but that was better than on the bus, where it was too quiet, too full of the wandering cerebral pulses of all of those dozing ancients. She'd be stuck in her captain's chair, staring at the pictures of her kids on the visor. No, that would make things intolerable.

Headlights were approaching in the distance. Rosa moved towards the center of her lane, waving her hand in front of her cellphone to act as a kind of warning light, get their attention. She hoped it shone brightly enough in the fog. Whatever was coming was moving slow, crawling through the pea soup at a snail's pace. The lights were far enough apart that it looked like it might be another truck or bus, but there was no engine noise. The headlight on the right also appeared to be loose, wobbling a little up and down out of sync with the other.

She checked over her shoulder to see if the other lane was clear and moved into it, continuing to signal, hoping the vehicle would stop. It didn't slow down (slowing down would pretty much be stopping), but instead it moaned. There was a consistent low sussurring sound, like fingernails scratching glass, and the growing sound of gravel crunching underfoot. Rosa checked over her shoulder and saw five more lights approaching, two from off the shoulder and three spaced evenly across the road.

She scrambled back for the bus, easing the door shut behind her as if a rude awakening was still the worst thing her passengers would face tonight.

Walkers. Eight of them that she could see, which meant there were probably more out there in the tall grass. They were trudging towards the bus. She could hear them, even through the glass, that hissing, the sound of air moving through lungs that no longer needed oxygen. Dry leather throats that acted more like the reed in a woodwind instrument, producing odd, muted tones as the diaphragm pushed air in and out. Scientists had classified this noise as droning, since the effect was similar to bagpipes. All of this mundane trivia Rosa had picked up on TV during the worst of the crisis, that's all she could think about now. Not the passengers, not her kids, just stupid facts that weren't increasing her odds of survival in the least—

A slap at the glass as the first one arrived. He was fairly big, baggy overalls hanging from his exposed collarbones with a trucker's cap slightly askew on his head (thank god she couldn't make out his face). Rosa bit back a scream, watching the pale grey palm press against the window and slide down. A second time, then a third. And then.... He stepped back. They all did. The walkers were surrounding the truck in a semicircle from behind, and this big one doffed his hat, held it gingerly over his stomach.

"Mlaaaaaaaaazzzzz...." he hissed. He folded the brim of his hat a little tighter, a slight puff of dander and dead skin escaping into the night. A few bits of scalp and hair were lodged into the rim. He turned his head violently to the side and coughed, reaching into the front pocket on his bib and producing a squirming rodent. This he bit into like a fresh apple, leaning his head back as he sucked the life out of the thing. He cleared his throat, a horrible wet sound. "Maaa'am," he began again. "Sorry you had to see that. Throat's parched, and blood's the only thing that helps. Watched you roll by, sounds like you blew somethin' atoppa the hill."

His face did something then, jerked in several directions at once, producing a seam that stretched taut across his right cheek until the leathery skin popped open under the strain. Was he. . . smiling?

"Ya prolly heard things 'bout our kind. Ain't no reason to be scared, though. We'd just as soon you pass on through 'fore the gov'mint come in lookin' for ya and hunt us down, burn us, like'n they did everywhere else. We dead, but we still people. We got rights."

Rosa hadn't moved, couldn't move until she felt the cracking in her hands. A thin little pop, then a hard crunch followed by a blinding shot of pain. She thought for a moment that she'd balled her fist so tight the fingernails had gone through to the other side. She held her palm up, a bloody mess, shards of her broken cellphone still lodged there. She whipped her hand behind her back, hiding it under her coat.

"We mostly don't have no taste fer people no more. I getcha a wrap fer that hand if ya want."

Rosa's jaw shook loose, worked once, then twice, forming the shape of the word "help" but never quite pushing it out.

"Jes' come up to Rooster's up the road there. He ain't strong like he was on account o' the muscle bein' gone, but he still knows engines. Ya jus' roll his toolkit down, maybe crank a wrench or somethin' less'n his arm snap off."

Rosa nodded dumbly as the walkers shuffled closer to the bus. It was a numbers game. If they wanted to eat her alive, tear her apart and feast on her brains, well, it was just as likely to happen here on the bus as it would be up the road there. She pulled the photo of her kids down from the visor.

"I'm all they've got. You understand me?"

The zombie motioned over to another spindly corpse nearby, this one almost all gristle and bone. She had a few shanks of long hair still clinging to her scalp and was holding half of a very tiny skeleton.

"I got a girl o' my own."

The skinny zombie girl nodded her head.

"She has uh…had…nice hair and uh…I'm sure back in the day, she was—"

"That ain't my girl. The lil'un there, that's her. Forever four and a half. Say hi Manda June!"

The half skeleton twisted grotesquely at the waist and raised a tiny hand, curling the fingers in a feeble little half-wave before burying its face in the woman's chest.

"She gets a little shy still," he said.

Rosa was out of the bus now, the photo of her kids still extended before her like a crucifix to ward off demons. The walkers didn't shift at all, just stood there as the wind hissed through rotting cloth and bone.

"I'm Big Don. Pleasure, ma'am," he extended a hand to her, a bit of his fingertip crumbling off.

"I'm Rosa. This is my girl, Beth, and my son, Chris. I just want to get back to them—" and then the tears came. Big Don fumbled in his pockets for a kerchief, and when he couldn't find one, he tore a bit of shirt off of a nearby shuffler.

Rosa choked a bit at that, the idea of cleaning snot off of her face with a dead man's shirt. She swallowed hard and began putting one foot in front of the other, commanding herself not to run. She thought about locking up the bus to keep the passengers safe, but if the zombies wanted in, they'd already be in. Fifteen minutes up the road and back, she was confident they'd all remain asleep that long.

The trip was a daze. She felt as if one minute she was there in front of the bus, and the next she was back, lightly sweating from rolling the heavy tool case down the road. Big Don was quite the conversationalist, telling her about life after the plague, how they were happy to stay hidden in the hills. The fog was thick enough that she couldn't see any houses or streets. There was just whiteness, then Rooster's Garage, then more whiteness, and finally the bus.

The door was open when she got back. Rosa was on the bus in three steps, hustling down the aisle for a quick headcount. They were four people short; everyone else was still asleep. She bounded back to the front of the bus, ready for war, when she saw her missing fares next to the bus. Two of them were locked in an intense cribbage game with the locals, and the others had struck up conversations with the dead.

Rooster was already under the bus on his mechanic's spider, a healthy amount of banging and cursing (or what would have been cursing had his throat not been shredded) indicating that the solution was near at hand.

"I don't... I mean, thank you," Rosa said.

"Don't say nothin' to nobody 'bout us, that's thanks enough. We ain't here for all you know."

Rooster wheeled out from under the bus, then crawled next to the engine compartment. He pointed at a few bystanding zombies, getting them to hold tools, apply pressure in a few spots as he worked his wrenching magic. After a few minutes, he staggered back to Don and hissed in his ear for a minute or two.

"Rooster says you just broke a belt. He's got somethin' jerry-rigged for ya, says long as you keep it under twenty you should be able to roll it down the hill. Gotta stop at the first town and wait 'til morning; this thing can't come back from the dead but once tonight." He laughed.

Rosa smiled despite herself. She opened the doors to the bus and called out to her passengers. "Okay folks, let's get back on board now. Long night ahead of us. Long day, too."

She saw the old-timers out there, always happy to talk to strangers, shaking hands, saying goodbye, shuffling back to the bus.

"Don...thank you. You're a life saver. Is there.... I mean, is there anyone left for you back in...living? Anyone I can pass a message to for you?"

"You live a nice long life, put in a word to Jesus later on, tell 'im come get us so's we can stop walkin' in circles here."

Rosa nodded and cranked the door closed. The engine rumbled, rocking the bus a couple of times, then sputtered into an unhealthy growl that meant they'd be moving again soon. She eased off the brakes and crawled forward, waving to the crowd as they gathered momentum, keeping it under twenty just like Rooster said. She saw a few of her passengers stirring and breathed a sigh of relief that she'd somehow managed to pull this off.

Except...one seat was empty near the back. She didn't want to cause a panic, couldn't stop without risking the bus dying for good. She raised her hand to where her PA mic was clipped to her visor, next to that photo of her kids, her beautiful, wonderful kids that she would hug into oblivion when she saw them next. That picture was in her pocket now, a lucky charm. There was a slip of paper up there, a note scrawled in a crude brown ink written in the shakiest of hands:

"Thanks for dinner. Have a nice trip."

TWILIGHT AT THE ZOMBIE GAME PRESERVE

S. CLAYTON RHODES

S. Clayton Rhodes makes his home in Marietta, Ohio, with his wife, two daughters, and four cats (none of which are man-eating, to the best of his knowledge). His work can be found in such periodicals and anthologies as Startling Stories, New Blood, Appalachian Winter Hauntings, Dark Tales of Terror, Legends of the Mountain State 4, Necrotic Tissue, The Blackness Within, Shock Totem, *and* The Mothman Files, *as well as others. He is currently working on many projects, including two novels. For more information about his work, please visit his website at* sclaytonrhodes.com.

Blake Kendal didn't know if he could go through with it. Killing Jay, that was.

But then it wouldn't be murder, really. Blake would let the zombies do the dirty work. He'd merely set the stage.

And the stage—no, the perfect stage—was the Zombie Game Preserve.

It was year six after the Apocalypse, after the dead had first begun rising. The earlier plague days had been suffered out of necessity until the governmental forces and all the local efforts got a grip on things. But the deaders proved slow and stupid, so it wasn't as hard as everyone anticipated.

Though they had done enough damage, nowadays they were in limited numbers. Still, the living found uses for the remaining zombies, augmenting the depleted work force, setting them to menial jobs no one else wanted. Sure, they had to be chained, muzzled and fed raw meat occasionally, but on the plus side, they worked cheap. Occasionally toss one a few chickens, and it was good for a week.

Another use they were put to was recreational. Similar game preserves like this one in Canaan were set up throughout the continental U.S. You paid your money and pitted yourself against the ravenous dead.

And lord, how Blake loved to hunt at the preserve with Jay. Or he used to, until he learned what Jay had been up to behind his back.

An oldster wearing a quilted vest and a hunting cap headed towards them, on his way to the parking lot. From a gunnysack, he removed a gray, mummified head. For safety purposes, seniors were required to hunt earlier in the day, when the zombies were most sluggish.

The duffer lifted his prize by its natty hair.

"Got me a good un'," he said, smiling with pride. The thing's dead eyes stared ahead fixedly. "Well, good luck to you both."

Blake smiled in return, then, nearing the first gate, he turned to Jay. "You up for this?"

"You'd better know it, buddy." Jay shouldered his pack of gear while cradling his Ithaca in the crook of his other arm. Shotguns were the best all-purpose weapons. Rifles were fine if you had time to line up a shot. Too often, though, you didn't have that sort of luxury. Scoring something in one of the sweet spots—the head or the heart—was your best bet, so odds of an instant kill were increased significantly with a shotgun.

"Gentlemen," the attendant just inside the second line of razor-topped wire said, "care to check your weapons?"

Blake and Jay had both oiled and cleaned their shotguns and handguns that afternoon. Still, they checked their ammo and chambered rounds. Blake tightened the laces of his Timberlands, while Jay did a little jog in place to get his circulation moving.

As the final gate motor rumbled, Blake's heart trip-hammered. It always did whenever he entered the preserve. After all, this wasn't the same sort of hunting they did in the old days.

The sun was low in the clouds now, reminding him of red wax melting over wool. Blake and Jay had just three hours to bag two each—the legal limit—and return to the gates. Only Jay wouldn't be coming back if things went as planned.

They trudged through high grass, ever watchful of trees, where deaders typically hid, waiting until the cool of night overtook the land.

Blake considered how he was going to do this. All he needed was a momentary lapse in Jay's concentration, but that wouldn't be easy to do out here, where a man didn't dare let his guard down. Thinking a little conversation might distract him, Blake asked after Jay's family, asked how little Jill and Bobby were doing in school.

Jay said the kids were doing fine; Bobby was even the star player on the T-ball team Jay coached, though he admitted he could be a bit biased.

He seemed the perfect family man. You'd never think he was capable of balling his best friend's wife.

And Cindy hadn't been the one to tell Blake, either. No, he had found out all on his own. One day he'd simply left work early with a blinding migraine and had headed home only to see Jay's white pickup gleaming on the street in front of the house. Blake's initial thought was Jay had stopped over to see him and have a cold one. Except there was no way he could've known Blake was going to have a migraine and knock off early.

The truth hit him like a sledge to the stomach. Beneath some sheltering elms two blocks away, Blake waited for fifteen minutes. Twenty-five. When half an hour came and went, Jay finally left. It was everything Blake could do to keep from running him down in the street then and there before he made it to his pickup. But ultimately he decided murder was something to be carefully planned. And relished.

"—Blake?"

"What's that?"

"I asked if something was eating you. Damn, brother, you looked like you were a million miles away."

Blake flashed him his best Don't-worry-I-wasn't-plotting-your-demise grin, and said, "Sorry. Guess I was off in my head somewhere."

"You want to watch that," Jay said. "A man's mind starts to wander here, the next thing he knows some gray Charlie is taking a chunk out of his ass."

Blake laughed. "That's a good point."

"You'd better it. So what's making your forehead crinkle thataway? You have some trouble you'd like to share with your ole buddy Jay?"

Sure, thought Blake. *Why not? We share everything else, including Cindy.* But he said, "Nothing, really. Well, okay. I do have a birthday coming up. I suppose this one's hitting me a little harder than most."

The lie came out so easily it caught even Blake by surprise. Also surprising was how natural it had sounded.

"Oh, that's right," said Jay. "You'll be rounding out the big four-oh, won't you? Ah, don't worry. It's just another number."

"Easy for you to say. You won't be there for another five."

That's good, he thought. *Just keep it going like this and he'll never suspect a thing.*

They came across a creek fed by a natural spring up the mountain and paused to drink and fill their canteens and have a power bar. There was little chance of the deaders fouling the water, since they never bothered with drinking. They got enough liquid from the raw meat the keepers tossed over the fence each night.

Black watched Jay soak a bandana and swab his neck with it. But, dammit, he never laid down his gun.

It was going on seven, and as they hiked on the crickets grew louder, and the shadows thickened like clotting ink.

Then everything went still. The crickets and cicadas stopped their singing—a sure sign something was up. As expected, a zombie lumbered forward, crunching leaves beneath its plodding feet. It clung to a tree limb while attempting to get its bearings. Finally, its gaze lit on Jay and Blake, then it lurched forward.

It was sixty feet away. Too far yet to pick him off.

Jay grinned, bringing up his Ithaca, anyway, getting ready for the moment when the deader's clumsy gait brought it close enough. No matter how many times the deaders had seen the effects of guns on their undead brothers, they never seemed to learn. In that regard they were dumber than any animal.

"He's an ugly one, isn't he?" Jay said, sidelong.

He was, indeed. White, matted hair clung to the peeling skull just above a sloping brow. Death had caused the lips to recede until they no longer covered the ivory-like pegs of teeth.

When the zombie closed in, Jay braced himself for the shot.

It was all the opening Blake needed. Only a second away from squeezing the trigger, Jay went down, struck by the butt of Blake's shotgun. The butt hit him first in the shoulder blade, then Blake brought the barrel down—just above Jay's right ear—for good measure.

Jay lay inert on the ground.

The deader hadn't made it to them yet. Blake had timed it perfectly. Now he brought the business end of the shotgun up when the thing was eight feet away and emptied both barrels into its putrid kisser, erasing half the zombie's face.

So far so good, Blake thought as the zombie crumpled in an untidy heap beside Jay.

He dragged Jay to an oak and propped him up against the rough bark. Then he tied his hands around the back with a length of bailing twine he'd brought along.

The idea was to make this look like an unfortunate accident. "A whole group of them hit us at once," he'd tell the park rangers. "They came out of nowhere. We never had a chance!"

Once they had Jay chewed up, Blake would put a bunch of them down to further validate his story. He'd cut the twine from around Jay's hands, then would make for the main gate where he would tell his tale of woe.

It would work. It would have to.

He ripped open the front of Jay's shirt, sending buttons flying. Using his machete, he cut diagonal hash marks into Jay's flesh. With the smell of fresh blood in the air, the zombies would swarm in like piranhas. He also made some noise, firing a couple of shots into the air with his pistol and beating on his canteen. Anything he could think of to stir the zombies.

"Come and get it, you undead sonsuvbitches," he said.

Sure enough, a couple of deaders answered the call. They materialized from the darkening woods. Then the two became four. The four became six.

Jay came to at that point. He blinked, shook his head trying to clear it. Confusedly, he tried to move his arms and found he couldn't.

"What the—" he started.

Then he heard the zombies approaching. They made low, inarticulate sounds in the backs of their rotting throats.

"Blake?" he said, his eyes full of unspoken pleading.

The message he seemed to think but didn't say was: "What gives here?"

And Blake's answer to this silent question: "You slept with my wife, Jay. You slept with Cindy, and now I'm gonna get my pound of flesh. Or the zombies are, rather." He gave a nervous sort of laugh. "Sorry, but that's the shape of it."

Jay strained at the cord binding his hands. His eyes squeezed tight in a mix of anger, fear and frustration. "Blake, you poor, dumb bastard. We were planning your birthday party!"

Blake felt a cool chill as realization set in. Jay wasn't shitting him, wasn't saying it to save his skin. He could see it in his eyes: this was the truth.

God, what have I done? he thought. He loved Jay like a brother. Why hadn't he confronted him and heard him out first? He owed him that much. This had been the coward's way.

Blake glanced down at his shotgun. No, that wouldn't do; there was too great a chance of catching Jay in the shot pattern. Instead, he pulled out his Colt .22. It had a ten-shot capacity but lacked the shotgun's stopping power, other than with headshots. Meaning he'd have to make each round count. Three deaders closed in on Jay, making those maddening, hungry sounds. Blake'd go for those first, then move in closer and start with the ones further once the path was clear.

He nailed the first between the eyes, with the Colt thundering in his ears. The second one took a wild swipe at him. Blake felt the whoosh of air, smelled the stink of rancid flesh.

Meanwhile, Jay thrashed against the tree trunk, fighting with the bailing twine.

Blake tried for another headshot, but the deader moved at the last second. It was effective enough, though. The bullet grazed its skull, stunning it. That gave Blake time to finish it off. The racket they were making worried him, though. It was sure to draw in more deaders.

The next closest zombie was quicker than the others. It sidestepped one shot, and then with arms raised, it rushed Blake. His next shot was also high and wide, splintering chunks of pine tree but doing nothing to the deader, and before he could fire again, the thing slapped the Colt from his hand.

It didn't matter. Blake simultaneously backed up and gripped his machete, drawing it with practiced ease. One chop was all it took to sever the zombie's head. It dropped to the ground while the still animate body kicked it like a soccer ball. It might have been comical under other circumstances.

"Cut me loose!" Jay demanded.

Blake went around to the other side of the oak, hacking the bailing twine in two, then passing the machete to Jay when he was free.

"Where's my Ithica?"

"I—I tossed it into the brush, okay?"

"Great! Oughta use this on you." Jay white-knuckled the machete grip.

"Use it on the deaders for now," Blake said, drawing his shotgun from its boot strapped to his back, "and you might live long enough to get your wish."

Five deaders loomed in the foliage. Blake blasted the one in front while Jay searched the grass for the fallen Colt.

"Any luck?" Blake pumped the shotgun.

"No."

"Forget it, then. We'll make a run for it back to the gate."

When they turned around, though, they saw they were cut off.

"Looks like we may have overstayed our welcome," Jay noted. He cleaved a female's skull so hard he had to rock the machete to get it loose when she dropped. Two more rushed in, their gray arms flailing.

Blake emptied both barrels on the largest of the lot. It took it in the chest, but didn't go down.

While he took another shot, Jay checked their back.

"Jesus." He gritted his teeth. "Our company is almost here."

"Don't give in just yet," Blake said. "I'm betting none of these deadheads ever played pro football."

Jay nodded, knowing exactly what Blake meant. They would plow through the line like a couple of quarterbacks in the pre-apocalypse days, when there was still such a thing as the Super Bowl. There were maybe fifteen deaders, seven at the front and the rest beyond.

"Stay low and we might get lucky," Blake said.

"Famous last words."

On the count of three, they charged through. Blake shoved two at once and drove a wedge between them. Jay did much the same, and then they ran like hell.

Blake breathed a sigh of relief. They were a couple of miles from the gate, yet, but as long as they stuck to the main trail they should be fine.

Blake was wrong in his thinking, though. As they topped a knoll, they could see as many deaders waiting on the far side as they'd left behind. They'd made too much noise and lingered far too long—never a good idea—and it seemed like every zombie in the whole preserve had come to investigate the commotion.

"Any more bright ideas?" Jay wondered.

"Fresh out. I guess the only thing to do would be go around their flank."

Only the deaders stretched across the main trail.

"We'll have to cut through the woods."

Together they darted into the trees, ducking low-hanging branches, occasionally hurtling logs. They made good progress. Blake estimated it was only another mile to the gate.

Their luck didn't hold, though. Jay took a misstep—either tripping on a root or hitting a slick patch of mud—and fell crashing forward.

"Can you walk?" Blake asked. That, of course, being the billion dollar question.

Jay tried to stand, then had to stifle a cry as his ankle twisted at an unnatural angle.

"Just go on," he said, wincing. "No reason for both of us to die."

"That's crazy talk. Now c'mon, we're in the home stretch."

Without waiting for a response, Blake lifted Jay's arm and put it around his neck, then gripped him around the waist. Jay could put weight on his foot, but by the way he grimaced Blake knew it must hurt like hell.

What had he been thinking, trying to set Jay up? If they made it out alive, he wouldn't blame him if he never spoke to him again.

Then came the very sound Blake dreaded: a rustling in the brush, coupled with low moaning.

"Jesus, no," he breathed. "Not now."

Five figures emerged from the thicket, loping and gnashing their teeth, which shone so clearly in the gloom.

Jay let go of Blake, pulling the machete from his belt, while favoring his one foot.

Blake readied his Mossberg, fumbling fresh shells into its breach. He was able to take out two and maim a third. Another went down before Jay's machete, despite his handicap. That left one, plus the other squirming harmlessly on the ground, half its neck blown away.

But there were more. So many more. Stragglers from the main trail, others from the woods. And all of them kept making those groanings fueled by their insane, fathomless hunger.

Jay gave a good account of himself, given the circumstances, but he couldn't hold out forever. He was soon outnumbered and thrown to the ground.

The last thing Blake heard from him over the wet, slurping sounds was the straggled word: "Run!"

And run he did. He blasted a deader full in the stomach, knocking it off its feet and clearing the way. Then he sprinted onto the main trail. How far to the gate now? he wondered. Surely not a mile. Maybe three quarters?

Blake lost track of how long he'd run, but finally he could make out the red flags flapping atop the gate. It was a welcome sight. Besides that, one of the preserve rangers was on the trail ahead. He'd most likely heard the excessive shooting and understood there had been trouble.

Panting heavily, Black approached and told the ranger to draw his gun. He glanced over his shoulder and saw a handful of deaders, closing quickly.

The ranger stepped forward. At first Blake thought it was to console him—which was silly, seeing as how there was so little time—but then he realized the truth. The ranger was one of them.

Before Blake could pull his Mossberg, the deader wearing the Smoky Bear cap gripped him by the forearm. Normally, he could have easily beat down a single zombie, but this one was particularly strong. Blake was also spent. They grappled a moment, but then Blake felt a tug from behind. The other deaders had caught up, and while he was distracted the ranger-zombie took the opportunity to bite off his index finger, which made a sound like green wood snapping.

Blake bellowed.

Another chunk was taken out of his shoulder from behind.

He staggered forward, arms windmilling.

He felt flesh ripped from his chest but refused to look. Instead, in his last few moments, his focus remained on the main gate, thinking, So close. Soooooo close....

Nine days later:

"There's one, Dad." The boy pointed at the deader staggering out of the forest. "And look, he's only got four fingers on one hand."

"Disemboweled, too, it seems," the older man said.

"Ain't he an ugly one?" the boy said. "You want first shot?"

"No, Tim. You spotted it. This one's yours." He ruffled the boy's hair while they waited for the zombie to get closer. There was nothing they both enjoyed so much as their father-and-son getaways at the Zombie Game Preserve.

HELL'S HOLLOW

MICHAEL WEST

Michael West is the critically-acclaimed author of The Wide Game, Cinema of Shadows, Spook House, Skull Full of Kisses, *and The Legacy of the Gods series. He lives and works in the Indianapolis area with his wife, their two children, their bird, Rodan, their turtle, Gamera, and their dog, King Seesar.*

A life-long fan of all things zombie, one of West's most prized possessions is a movie poster for George Romero's classic Dawn of the Dead, *signed by the cast and crew. It hangs above his desk for inspiration.*

Something bad was about to happen in Hell's Hollow. Sheriff Gleason felt it in his bones. He couldn't sleep, and when he finally crawled out of his bed, he found the street already choked with people, most of them strangers. The population of his little mining community had tripled overnight.

The sight of the town sheriff strutting down the sidewalk froze passersby in their tracks and killed their conversations, as if they were all keeping a secret from him, as if they were throwing some surprise party in his honor. Gleason hated surprises. He offered them a polite nod, a tip of his wide-brimmed hat toward the ladies, but he kept his hand on the butt of his revolver and his eyes alert.

A little skift of snow still clung to mountain tops, and a thick haze filled in the valleys, muting the early morning sun, but the trees and wildflowers made it obvious that spring was now in session. "How come a place that's so beautiful got a name like 'Hell's Hollow?' " That's what people asked as they passed through (nobody ever settled in the Hollow that didn't have business with the mine or the men who worked like moles down there in the dark coal). Well, the story goes that some wagons were passing by on their way out West when a man staggered up the old dirt road that leads down into the hollow, the road the town is still built around to this day. He'd been beaten to within an inch of his life and was bleeding like a stuck pig. When the people in those wagons asked him where he'd been, he told them simply, "Hell," and that's been the hollow's name ever since.

Gleason made his way through the crowds to the Boone Saloon. Lee Boone owned the place, tried to tell everyone that Daniel was his cousin. Some bought it, some didn't. Gleason landed firmly in the "didn't" column, but he never let on. The food and drinks were too damn good.

The place was packed, and so loud that a man couldn't hear himself think, much less listen to what anyone else had to say, but that changed as soon as Gleason stepped in. All eyes turned toward the door, and a silence rippled through the crowd like wind through tall grass. The piano music went on for a minute or two after the conversations died—old Henry probably thought the patrons had finally shut up to hear him play for once. But then he, too, saw Gleason, and his smile faltered along with his fingers.

Gleason's eyes moved across the sea of faces, his hand still on his holster. He saw no immediate threat, however, so he made his way to the bar.

At least Lee Boone was still smiling.

"Mornin', Sheriff," Boone told him, his voice full of cheer.

"Mornin'."

"Your usual?"

Gleason nodded, keeping his eyes on the patrons. A few whispered to each other, but most sat speechless, still staring at him. "Quite a crowd," he said to Boone.

"Yes, sir."

"Some big to-do I don't know about?"

"Don't really know, Sheriff. But who am I to turn away payin' customers?"

Boone brought a plate loaded with biscuits and sausage gravy. He set it down on the bar in front of Gleason and started to turn away, but the sheriff reached out and grabbed hold of his wrist, pulled him closer. "What the hell is goin' on here, Lee?"

Gleason felt a tug on his pants leg. He looked down and saw a boy in overalls, no taller than his bar stool. The boy stared up at him with great curiosity.

"Sheriff," the boy said, "are you really a dead man?"

Before Gleason could answer, the boy's father rushed over. "Sorry,

Sheriff. He don't mean nothin' by that, just repeatin' what he's heard."

"Who'd he hear it from?" Gleason asked, frowning. He turned back to Lee Boone, tightened his grip on the man's wrist.

Boone glared at the boy's father, then looked the sheriff dead in the eye. "Somebody's gunnin' for you."

"Who?" Gleason pressed.

"You wouldn't believe me if I told you."

"Goddammit, who?"

"Tolbert Johnson."

"Johnson?" Gleason's eyes narrowed, and he struggled to calm himself. "I'm not in the mood for jokes, Boone!"

"It's no joke, Sheriff. Johnson came around last night, sayin' he was gonna find you and pay you back for sendin' those revenue boys out to his place."

"Boone, Tolbert Johnson's *dead*. Been dead and buried six feet down for a year now. I shot him myself."

The barkeep gave a slow nod. "You're tellin' the God's honest truth, Sheriff, but so am I. Johnson's dead, no denyin' that, but somehow he's up walkin' around again, and he's still gunnin' for you."

Gleason loosened his grip on Boone's wrist, and the man looked anxious to step away.

When President Rutherford B. Hayes took his seat up in that Oval Office, one of the first things he did was to start a crusade against moonshiners. He sent revenue agents climbing up and down every mountain in Appalachia looking for stills. Sure, when caught, most moonshiners just went to court, paid their taxes and their fines, and then went right back home, went right back to their stills and their shine, but not Tolbert Johnson. No. He gunned down the half a dozen agents that paid him a visit, then came into town looking for more trouble. And trouble was just what he got.

A fly buzzed by the sheriff's ear, and he waved it away. It landed in the gravy that topped his biscuits and rubbed its legs expectantly.

"I put a bullet right through his chest," Gleason said aloud to no one in particular. "He bled out in the street."

Boone nodded. "I know, Sheriff. I was there."

"Dead is dead. There ain't no comin' back from that."

Boone lifted his eyes to the door and frowned. "Try tellin' that to him."

"Gleason!"

The sheriff froze. His hand tightened on the butt of his revolver. His finger found the trigger.

That voice…it can't be!

But Gleason knew it was. He turned slowly, trying to steel his mind for the sight that awaited it, but there was no way to prepare for the impossible. What he saw standing in that doorway chilled him to his bones.

Boone was right. Tolbert Johnson was dead, there was no denying it. His face was now a bearded skull, the remaining flesh dry and splotched with black, like burnt parchment. His left eye was a vacant socket that reminded Gleason of the gaping entrance to the mine; the sheriff imagined things digging in there, busy maggots and beetles carrying out nuggets of brain matter instead of coal. Tattered clothes hung from emaciated arms and legs, and bullet holes pierced its shirt, like tiny windows to a shattered ribcage. And yet, somehow, the thing stood, the thing *spoke*.

"You sent them, didn't ya? They came askin' for folks runnin' shine, and you sent them right to my door, didn't ya?"

The same words, Gleason realized, the same anger, as if the raid had happened yesterday instead of over a year ago. Johnson knew the sheriff would be here having his breakfast, and just like the last time they'd met, he came ready for a fight.

Gleason's stunned eyes fell to the tarnished, rusty revolver the thing held in its boney hand. Would it have bullets? Would it even work after a year in the ground? He looked around at the crowd and decided not to take any chances.

"Johnson." The sheriff held up his gloved left hand, keeping his shooting hand ready to draw. "You've got nothin' against these people here. Let's take this outside."

The thing nodded. "Fine by me."

It backed out of the saloon and out of Gleason's sight.

"Whatcha gonna do, Sheriff?" Boone asked.

"Hell if I know, Lee. I haven't killed a lot of men in my time, and none of 'em twice." He drew a deep breath and made steps for the door. "Keep these people in here out of harm's way."

Boone nodded. "God be with you, Sheriff."

Gleason put his hand on the door, his mind moving a mile a minute. He'd put Tolbert Johnson down once. No reason to think he couldn't do it again.

'Cept Tolbert Johnson was a man. Flesh and blood from the mind o' God. This thing…this is some kinda witchcraft. This is the work o' the devil's hand. Who knows if a bullet can stop it? Who knows if it can be stopped at all?

"Gleason," the thing called, "don't make me come back in there after you!"

The sheriff pushed the door open and shuffled out into the street. Crowds lined the walkways on either side. In front of him, Johnson's corpse stood holding its rusty revolver; its single eye tracked Gleason's every move.

"I didn't wanna shoot them revenue boys," it yelled out. "But I had no choice. I gotta feed my kin."

Gleason eyed the rows of spectators. Some hoisted their children up on their shoulders to get a better look at the upcoming festivities. This is why they'd gathered. This was the show they'd all been waiting to see. Had there been this many a year ago, when he took the life from this man? Had it been such great sport to them then?

"Put down your gun, Johnson. We don't have to do this, not again. Go back to your grave where you belong!"

Confusion flashed in the dead thing's eye like lightning, there and then gone again. It grinned at him; its withered lips cracking and tearing like tissue paper. "Only one of us is goin' to their grave, Sheriff, and it ain't me. Now, draw!"

"Have it your way."

Gleason drew his revolver, his hand a blur. He fired. The bullet streaked down the dirt road, tearing a hole through the dead thing's tattered shirt and whatever remained of its chest beneath.

Johnson's eye widened. The corpse reached up, covered its wound with a boney hand. It teetered there a moment, then fired off a shot of its own before falling.

Gleason felt a sting in his chest and knew the thing's bullet had found its mark. He coughed and staggered up the street with his gun still drawn, waiting for the corpse to move again, waiting for it to try to stand. It did neither.

Johnson was dead again, hopefully for good this time.

The sheriff's strength left him. He dropped to his knees in the dirt next to Johnson's body, staring down at the remains, at the holes burned through its raggedy shirt. It had only taken one shot, just like the year before. A bullet through the chest, and Johnson had dropped like a marionette with its strings cut. But there were more than two holes there.

Many more.

Gleason reached out and laid his gloved hand on Johnson's bullet-riddled chest.

"R—rest now," the sheriff said, then slumped over and joined him in slumber.

The crowds clapped and cheered.

Inside the Boone Saloon, the boy in overalls looked up at his father. "They killed each other."

Boone laughed and smiled at him. "Yes sir-ee, Bob. Always do. Just like clockwork. Same as the real deal back in 1881."

The little boy's eyes widened and he looked back out at the street, watching the volunteers pick up the bodies. "Where are they going?"

"They'll go back to sleep in their graves for another year. We bury them up right. Father Carole gives 'em Last Rites and everything." Boone chuckled. "Though, I don't know how 'last' it really is."

The boy's father patted his son's head and looked up at Boone. "Sorry my boy almost spoiled things."

"Don't worry about it. No harm done. I think we covered it up pretty well, don't you? Besides, I don't know how much they pay attention to the details. Hell, the sheriff still thinks I'm my grandfather every time. But we always have folks park their cars in the lot outside of town, just in case." Boone smiled back at the boy. "We wouldn't want the zombies gettin' spooked, now would we?"

The boy shook his head and his father asked, "So why does the sheriff remember the first shoot out?"

Boone shrugged. "He didn't used to. Who knows. Maybe he's like one of those lab rats you see in the newsreels. After doin' the same thing for so long, they tend to catch on eventually."

The man looked satisfied with that.

"So...." Boone rubbed his hands together. "You folks want to go ahead and buy your tickets for next year?"

"Not right now." The man picked his son up. "Maybe before we leave. Right now, I want to get my boy one of those big caramel apples and head over to that Showdown Hoedown they keep advertising."

"Well, make sure to tell all your friends what a good time you've had," Boone urged them. "Hell's Hollow: always one *hell* of a good time!"

BROTHER HOLLIS GIVES HIS FINAL SERMON FROM A RICKETY MAKE-SHIFT PULPIT IN THE REMAINS OF A SMOKEHOUSE THAT NOW SERVES AS HIS CHURCH

GARY A. BRAUNBECK

Gary A. Braunbeck is a six-time winner of the Bram Stoker Award. His highly acclaimed Cedar Hill Cycle includes the novels In Silent Graves, Coffin County, *and the forthcoming* A Cracked and Broken Path. *His book on writing horror,* To Each Their Darkness *(Apex Publications), was a Bram Stoker Award winner in 2010. Please visit him online at www.garybraunbeck.com or at www.facebook.com/gary.braunbeck.*

Used to be I thought holding services in here was a blasphemy. What good, God-fearing Christian, what man worth his place in Heaven, what human being whose head ain't full of mush or sour-mash could even *think* that the Good Lord would be fine with hearing people sing His praises from inside a place where the carcasses of slaughtered animals were strung up by their hind quarters to flavor and age so they'd be tasty? Didn't seem right, somehow—even if the church'd burned down when folks started going crazy on account of them thinking the Final Days was here at last. I could've kept having services on the grounds on account of them being *sacred* grounds. But I knew that we'd need walls to keep ourselves at least *feeling* safe, even if we knew it was just pissing in the wind and praying for rain. So we moved into this here smokehouse. Where butchered animals are strung up to soak in flavor. All things considered, it seems sadly appropriate to me that I'm speaking to you this last time from in here, from a place where food comes to get itself yummied up. Besides, the Good Lord said that " '...wherever two or more of you are gathered in My name…' "

Ah, well, *hell*. Don't really make any difference now, does it? And I know that we've all done the best we can to keep our souls tried and true, to keep our faith strong when it seems like every hour there's less and less remains for us to have faith *in*. 'Cause that's what human beings do, isn't it? Find themselves some kernel of hope to hold close, 'cause if you got no hope, you got no reason to keep going. Even if you start lying to yourself, tell yourself that this has to end somehow, all you've gotta do is hang in there, stay safe, keep to near the river or on higher ground because water and climbing, they're not so good at that, and maybe for a while that works out for you…then you start…you start getting lonesome, 'cause here you are all safe on higher ground, and you got enough canned goods to last you, but the *quiet*, it starts getting pretty darn loud, and maybe you start talking to yourself just to hear a voice, but since it's you talking to yourself there ain't no surprises in the conversation on account you already know what you're going to say.

So then you turn to your Bible, the same one passed down in your family from as far back as your great-great-gramma, the one in whose pages you've always found comfort, you've always found beauty in its language, its poetry, the one you've read so many times that the corners of the pages are stained with oil from your fingertips so that it even *smells* like you, same way it smells of your great-great gramma's oils, and your mother's, and everybody else whose hands have held it. You start reading it aloud to yourself 'cause if there's nothing out there in what's left of the world for you have faith in, there's always the words of the Good Book, you can depend on them. They're the same beautiful words that were there last time you read them, they'll be there when you read it now, and they'll be there next time. Except when you start reading them out loud—and maybe it's because you're tired, or because you're lonesome, but mostly because you're so scared you haven't been able to sleep for more than fifteen minutes at a stretch, whatever the reason—you don't find the comfort in them you once did. The pages just look dirty and torn and yellow. The words are the same, the Gospels, they ain't changed any, the platitudes, they're still as poetic as ever, but when you hear them being read in your own voice they sound… hollow. And then you get caught up in trying to make them sound out loud the way they used to sound in your head when you was reading them all quiet. Then you start thinking more about how your voice *sounds* reading them than on the words themselves, and you're tired, and alone, and scared...and then something in your brain wakes up and turns on the lantern and you realize that the words, the Gospels and platitudes and the visions of John and...and all the rest of it...you realize that things don't quite add up like they're supposed to. You stop and ask yourself—for instance—how did anyone back then *know* what Christ said when he was praying to God in Gethsemane before the Romans came to take him away? You remember that our Lord and Savior, he was *alone* there, nobody else around...so how is it that the Bible quotes him? Weren't nobody else there. You realize that this Gethsemane business, it ain't the only place in the Bible where things, they don't quite add up. And on account of you noticing these things, you start asking yourself questions that would best be left unasked, then it all starts getting mixed up and you don't know what you're saying, or what you're reading, or if your belief is real or just something you accepted, same way you accepted them stories from the children's books your mama used to read to you when the world was still new and all things were possible.

The question that kept bothering me was, how did we all just *assume* right off the bat that all of you was evil? You didn't ask to crawl out of the earth under which you were buried to walk among us again. You didn't ask for this new nature that makes you...do things to the living. We assumed you was evil because what you were doing was so vile to us. Does a cancer cell think that what it does is evil? Cancer cells, they got no way of knowing, they just do what they was brought into existence to do. It's terrible, what they do, eating away at a body bit by bit from the inside, all the pain...*all* the pain...but right and wrong, they don't exist for cancer cells, so how can we say that each of the cells is evil? How can we force them to take the blame for the one thing, the *only* thing, they were created to do?

I look out at all of you, your dirty clothes and your gray skin and holes left by the worms in your flesh and I can't help but think about something I heard an old Indian gal say once when I was a boy. She said that every living thing has a soul. I asked her if blades of grass had souls, and she said yes. I asked her if animals had souls, and she said yes. She said any living thing that moves and touches and can be touched in return, it had a soul. So I look out at all of you, my *un*-dead brothers and sisters, and see that you are moving, and touching, and that you can be touched, and that means that you have souls, all of you. And what you do, I don't think you see it as being evil. I'm not so sure I see it that way anymore, either. In order for something to be evil, it has to have strayed from the path of righteousness. It has to have made the decision on purpose. It has to have *chosen* that way. You didn't. You asked for none of this, so who were we to judge what you do as evil, and then brand you the same way simply because you're only doing what your nature now compels you to do? I want to say I'm sorry for that. I'm sorry that we started to hunt you down and shoot you like we did. But you won out in the end, didn't you? Turns out there was a whole lot more of you than there was of us. You just shuffled around doing what your nature makes you do and waited for us to start turning on each other. Or die out. Still, I'm sad about what we done, and I hope you can find it in your hearts to forgive…that is, if you know what forgiveness is.

You may be dead, but you're still alive, and that means you've all got souls, and that means that, after you was put in the ground, your souls did not abandon you, and they did not abandon you because maybe there isn't no place for them to go. And that breaks my heart something fierce, because if your souls had nowhere to go, then that means there wasn't no one there to welcome them. And I can't think past that because it scares me worse than anything you've done to others or might do to me.

I'm pretty sure that I'm the only one left. Why you've let me live is something I don't understand. I don't even know if I can say I'm grateful for it. But I want to thank you just the same, here in the house of Our Lord where the slaughtered pigs still hang in all their plump, smoky tastiness. I want to thank you because, you see, when I come down from that higher ground where none of you ever climb, I came down here to sacrifice myself to you. I came down here because I was giving up. I had no faith left. And my faith, my undead brothers and sister, my faith has been tested something fierce in my too-long life. I have held the hands of consumptive children as they rattled out their last breath. I have seen loneliness in the eyes of the elderly that was so overwhelming I questioned the point of letting them go on, living out the last of their days under the weight of that sadness. I have said prayers over the bodies of young men and girls who've taken the knife or the razor or their papa's shotgun to bring an end to their own suffering, however great or small it might have been. I have tried to comfort starving families, soothe the grief of mothers whose babies never drew their first breath. I thought that death held no mystery for me, and no fear because of that. I was ready to go.

And then you started watching me—not coming after me, but watching me. Following me. Listening to me preach the Word. And for that I am grateful, because, you see, I'm not lonesome any more. I have you. You are my new church. You are my new family. You have given me back my faith, my undead brothers and sisters. I have faith in *you*. Only you, and nothing else. You do not come here to worship, you come here to *be* worshipped.

Here I am, dear brothers and sister, on my knees in supplication, worshipping you. There is no end to my life, no beginning to my death. With you, I know now that death is life. And I am grateful. I love you. You are all there is. And I am so dearly sorry for having thought you evil. Please, come. Rise and come to me, place your hands on my head and whisper to me my absolution so that I might better be your humble servant.

Come forward, I beg of you. Come forward and lay your hands on me.

Come forward. Bless me, brothers and sister, for I have sinned against thee….

AFTERWORD

REBEKAH MCKENDRY

My parents' house in Winchester, Virginia, dwells in the Blue Ridge section of the Appalachian mountains. I spent endless summers with my cousins and kin in Grundy, Virginia. And even after I left home, I spent six years at Virginia Tech in Blacksburg, Virginia. Come to think of it, the first twenty-three years of my life were spent traveling up and down Appalachia. These mountains are my home and, at times, my horror. No matter how well I know the mountains, no matter how well I can identify every animal cry, plant, or waterdog (which I have since learned are called salamanders by the rest of the country), the Appalachian mountains still hold an air of mystery. They still are both my beautiful homeland that sung me to sleep for decades, and my nightmare that kept me awake while my mind imagined all the terrors lurking in the woods just beyond my window.

The mysterious nature of these mountains is in no way isolated in me, but echoed in every one of the stories in this book. The characters in this book personify the mountains themselves—isolated, but far from weak. The people of the Appalachian mountains are strong-willed and breathe their culture with every ounce of mountain air. Granny Mustard from Elizabeth Massie's story is tough as nails and ready for any struggle life throws as her, including looters and a brew that brings the dead back to life. In Ben Vincent's "Sitting up with the Dead," a man watches a zombie hoard lay waste to all his friends and family, battling an unstoppable zombie force. A great deal of knowledge, identity, and ultimately culture is born from the struggles these characters face both in the Appalachian setting and in the decaying zombie menace.

Just as the Appalachian land itself is rich with a unique culture and history, the people of Appalachia have developed their own oral tradition. While at college, I always worked summers as a storyteller at Mountain Lake Resort (the place where *Dirty Dancing* was filmed). Nestled high on top of a winding, mountain road in Pembroke, Virginia, Mountain Lake Resort was the first place I came to realize the rich story -telling heritage that the Appalachians bestow upon residents. The resort brought in people from all over the country, but most were "city folk" from out of state who were hoping to have an "outdoorsy" adventure. Mixed in with the trout fishing, hayrides, and sightseeing hikes through the mountain wilderness were campfire tales. Twice a week, the guests would gather around an outdoor fire pit while I regaled them with some of the most frightening ghost stories I had ever heard…all scary as hell…all set in Appalachia.

The funny thing was I never had to sit down and research stories to tell. I knew them all by heart. Stories are found everywhere in Appalachia. For me, telling these Appalachian campfire stories to frightened resort guests was just like retelling old family tales. Not surprisingly, almost all of the stories were about the dead returning from the grave to take revenge on the living. My aunt used to tell me about a Civil War Rebel who would ride his coffin through the mountains at night screaming a vicious Rebel yell at any who crossed his path. My uncle, whose wit could slice you in two, told me stories of misbehaving children and the ill-fated results of their messing around in a mountain graveyard. Grandpa used to sing horror-filled Appalachian folksongs like "Pretty Polly" and "O Death" while we harvested potatoes or fished. Even the Algers down the holler would try to scare me with tales of coal miners trapped underneath my house coming to terrorize me in the night by tapping on the glass of my bedroom windows. The coalminers never showed up at my bedroom windows, but it probably would have been a much cooler story if they had. I'm guessing the Alger boys may have tried tapping on the glass at some point though to see if I was sufficiently terrorized.

Looking back at the history of Appalachia, it comes as no surprise that the culture and oral history has such a strong horror vein. Life was hard and always required a fight. Death was everywhere, be it from famine, poverty, dangers of bootlegging, family clan battles over property or feuds, the Civil War, or even logging and coal mining accidents. Worldwide, cultures that experience prevalent death and tragedy create their own interpretations of it. The living dead often become a way of not only understanding death, but acting symbolically for the people of the culture.

As we have seen in this book, zombies can personify culture, a belief system, a moral, a passion, or most often, a fear. Just as the people of the Appalachian mountains all came from mixed backgrounds and religions but united as one culture in these remote mountains, the zombies in these stories are fast, slow, funny, rage-filled, or even mournful, but all possess the ability to be hell on two rotting legs. It is this clash of cultures, clash of clans, and clash of folklore that made the Appalachian mountains so rich in heritage and mythos. And it is the clash between what we define as living and dead that makes these stories so terrifying. Ultimately, zombies are us. Zombies start as humans, and they end exactly where we will all end with one small difference. They are our worst nightmare.

The stories in this book not only terrify, but tell us something about ourselves through both zombies and the Appalachian setting. In Gary Braunbeck's story, we learn of how both zombies and Appalachian dwellers are often dealt a hand in life that is not ideal, one they did not ask for. As Brother Hollis says in the story, just because one may seem dead, does not mean the soul has died too, and, like the people of Appalachia, zombies will keep rising, and their souls will keep thriving. If there is one main similarity between my Appalachian brethren and zombies, it's that they are both fighters. But Appalachia would never let a little thing like the living dead stand in its way.

Rebekah McKendry is the Director of Marketing for Fangoria Entertainment and additionally is a college professor teaching classes focused on film history and horror films. She has Bachelor's Degrees in Film and English, an MA in Media Education, an MFA in Film, and she is currently completing her PhD in Media Arts focused on horror and exploitation cinema.

ABOUT THE EDITORS

Eugene Johnson has been a storyteller since childhood when he would make up his own comic books and stories. In college he started working in the film industry, working with the Huntington Film Commission and on the films *We Are Marshall, Burning Annie, Unbroken* (with Tony Todd), as well as a handful of independent films. In 2009, he was executive producer of the short film *Leftovers,* a zombie movie that screened at Scream Fest in Los Angeles and at Dragon*Con in Atlanta. His story "Bitten" was featured in *The Zombie Feed, Volume One,* an anthology edited by the Bram Stoker-nominated editor Jason Sizemore. He was also editor of The Zombie Feed website. Eugene currently lives with his family in West Virginia. For more information, visit www.eugene-johnson.com.

Jason Sizemore is a two-time Hugo Award nominee and one-time Stoker Award nominee for his work as an editor. Born and raised in the hills of southeast Kentucky, he currently lives in Lexington, KY, where he runs and operates Apex Publications. For more information, you can visit his personal site at www.jason-sizemore.com.

ABOUT THE ARTIST

Cortney Skinner's artwork appears in books, magazines, comics, and in films. He has illustrated a wide range of subjects including science fiction, fantasy, horror, history, aviation, and children's books.

Beginning his career in the traditional art techniques of pencil, pen, and paint, he added pixels to his palette at the beginning of the digital age. Working in a variety of media and styles ranging from realistic oils to pen and ink illustrations, Skinner also sculpts all manner of people, creatures, and esoteric objects. His conceptual designs and artwork have appeared in films, and his landscapes, still lifes, and portraits are found in private collections.

Nestled comfortably in the Blue Ridge Mountains of Virginia, Skinner shares a creative life and abode with writer Elizabeth Massie.

ONE WAY OUT!

Like classic CYOA books of yesteryear, author Ray Wallace presents a situation and immediately thrusts the reader into making life or death decisions.

Many zombies.
Many deaths.
And only one way out.
Can you survive?

ESCAPE FROM ZOMBIE CITY

A Choose Your Own Adventure Zombie Novel by Ray Wallace

You are one of the last survivors in a city overrun by the walking dead. The news reports say it's the result of a government experiment gone wrong, and advise citizens to remain indoors to wait for aid. But you're not getting any safer, and you'd be wise to get out of town while you can.

It's going to take more than guts and a gun to get you out alive. Maybe you'll find the one way out.

ISBN: 978-1-937009-01-4 ~ ApexBookCompany.com

9348365R00125

Printed in Great Britain
by Amazon.co.uk, Ltd.,
Marston Gate.